Cathi Unsworth began her journalistic career at nineteen on the music paper *Sounds*. Later headhunted by *Melody Maker*, she worked there as a freelance feature writer and reviewer for several years before joining *Bizarre* magazine. She now works as a freelance editor and lives in West London.

The Not Knowing

Cathi Unsworth

A complete catalogue record for this book can
be obtained from the British Library on request

First published in the UK in 2005 by Serpent's Tail,
4 Blackstock Mews, London N4 2BT

website: www.serpentstail.com

Designed and typeset at Neuadd Bwll, Llanwrtyd Wells

Printed by Mackays of Chatham, plc

10 9 8 7 6 5 4 3 2 1

For Derek Raymond, who opened the door, and
Ken Bruen, who turned on the lights.

Acknowledgements

My most grateful thanks to everyone who helped me in the writing of this book, without whom I may never have found my way back to the up elevator: Phil and Brenda Unsworth, Matthew and Yvette Unsworth, Florence Halfon, Joe McNally, Mari Mansfield, Pete Woodhead, Caroline Montgomery, Martyn Waites, John Williams, Pete Ayrton, Ann Scanlon, Richard Newson, Damon Wise, Richard and Helen Cox, Hugh Burbeck, Ken and Rachel Hollings, James B. L. Hollands, Roger K. Burton, Raphael Abraham, Paul Chai, Damjana and Predrag Finci, Michael Dillon, Mark Pilkington, Tommy Udo, Ted Thornhill, Mark Blacklock, Geoff Brown, Fiona Jerome, Claudia Woodward, Lynn Taylor, Lydia Lunch, David Peace and the music of Barry Adamson and Gallon Drunk.

And to Michael Meekin, with love.

You strip off everything that is needed to live in the light – you won't need it any more – then, in a strange transported state, you write your way down cold stairs until you reach a door which you open and walk through; it closes behind you. This is an interior door in you that divides the visible from the invisible, the light from the darkness; you are now on the dark side of existence. Later you might or might not find that door open again and part of you might pass through it. But you will never open it and walk back through it like you did going in. I say nothing about the reader, but as the writer, you will never, from now on, be definitely on one side of that door or the other, because now that you have found what you came for you have been changed, whether that was what you wanted or not.

— Derek Raymond, *The Hidden Files*

The moon was in the gutter…

Reflected in the sky.

Casting its sickly light through a thin smudge of cloud over the dark end of the street. Tonight's revellers, even the most woozy and determined of them, even the drifters with no doorway to call their home, had long since left this part of town. All that remained on the twisting curve of Agar Grove was detritus: discarded fast-food wrappers, crumpled cigarette packets, waste paper fluttering and skittering across the lonely road, hustled along by the wind.

And something else.

Around the corner, footsteps came, a brisk pace, workmanlike. Accompanied by a low whistle, a repetitive little refrain, workmanlike too, but devoid of anything you could actually call a tune. The tall, hunched figure in the black Crombie coat wasn't really aware he was making this noise; his mind was far away, on other things. He was aware of the plastic bags he'd wound around his hands to keep any last vestiges of blood away from the inside pockets of his coat. It had happened in a bit of a rush, and maybe he was being excessively cautious, but it had seemed a reasonable thing to do at the time. What was it they had said? The Freshest Food Daily? Fresher Than The Rest? Fresh Cut Today? A Porky Prime Cut?

A nervous giggle escaped like a sneeze. His mind was going off track again.

No, it was good, this part of the city. Railway arches and the empty stretch of the Grand Union Canal, the disused York Way tube station and the squat gin palaces all boarded up and empty. An industrial estate to his right and beyond, the vast iron gasworks, bleak against the sulphurous sky, the abandoned crescent of railway houses no one ever got round to redeveloping, the great gothic spires of St Pancras like a monstrous fairy-tale castle, and the lines of track that rumbled out trains to the North.

Behind him was Camden: party town, a place to be easily anonymous among the easily inebriated of all ages. He appreciated Camden. For all its bright lights and distractions, overflowing pubs full of rackety loud bands, its market and its colony of winos and tramps, it had its secret places. Lock-ups used by the market traders, railway arches used as rehearsal spaces and makeshift speakeasies, boarded-up places that were easy to break into: once you nosed around a bit you could find them. Underneath, the rattling locomotives constantly hauling commuters here and there, out of the orange glow of the street lights.

But on the other side, the side he had to navigate now, was King's Cross. He hated King's Cross. It was Sodom. Hell on Earth. A portal had opened here, spewing out the sick and depraved, the whores and pimps and junkie scum, clawing and clamouring their way out into the filth-clogged streets, shivering and sweating their way around the gaudy strip opposite the station and the carcinogenic ventricles of roads that surrounded it. He could smell its foetid stink as he walked down the long, lonely, slow-motion stretch of York Way.

No longer calmed by the nearness of water, images raced in fast-forward through his mind. He didn't know it, but his whistling got faster, his feet slapping harder on the pavement.

Red gouts of blood.

A bloody fountain.

Flesh falling, yielding to the sharp smile of steel, carving a smile in white flesh. Flesh flapping open, so easily, quivering, soft as butter, all yellow and red inside.

Screams contained by swathes of tape: a gurgling, rattling cacophony.

Reminding him of pigs dying.

And the beautiful arc of silvery steel.

Now sleeping at the bottom of the Grand Union Canal.

A lot of secrets buried there, under a sickly yellow moon.

The noise of his feet was drowned out by the passing traffic, his round-shouldered, skinny frame momentarily illuminated by sweeping headlights. Just another anonymous drifter, alone in the London night, winding his way along the edge of the main road, the lonely streets of 4am. Down, down and down towards Sodom, blurring into the red, green, yellow lights, the confusion of automobiles and human traffic, disappearing in the crowd.

2

Monday, March 13, 1992, it was business as usual. With the ruthless efficiency for which its country of origin is noted, my Braun alarm clock jolted me up at 8am precisely.

I was, as ever, the first mortal to stir in 36 Arundel Gardens.

This big, four-storey stucco house, which once would have been a fashionable abode for the well-to-do Victorian gent, his family, servants and faithful retainers, was now an assemblage of little cells, advertised as bedsits.

Cheap rents attracted a certain kind of tenant. I lived alongside ageing men of no fixed employment, who shuffled through what was left of their lives in a strange kind of perpetual twilight, an aura of bacon fat and sweat masked with talcum powder. Creeping death, I used to call them.

I lay in the bath with my hair up in rollers, dreaming up schemes while the rest of the house wheezed and snored fitfully, under their blankets of sleep.

I was Diana Kemp, age 26, journalist on the make. Working for a magazine called *Lux*, the product of over two years' graft, ducking between freelance gigs, shared offices and the oddest hours with my partners in crime, Barry Hudson and Neil Bambridge. We were unlikely bedfellows, but it worked.

Well, Barry and I weren't so unlikely. We were already friends, having met in a pub on Portobello three years earlier. He looked like a tattooed evil Elvis, while I was attempting a gothic Betty Page. We would have made a great couple, I suppose, but neither of us was looking for anything like that. I hadn't the inclination for entanglements and Barry was still recoiling from a sudden marriage break-up; what he really needed was a friend to have a laugh with. Seeing as I'd been collecting surrogate brothers since I left home, we formed a double act based on our appreciation of the more esoteric side of the arts world and our mutually morbid humour.

For months, we'd just plotted. I was still writing for *Melody Maker*, Barry had been working for the same rock management company for twelve years. We both wanted more and so, over many smoky nights watching gigs in Camden, or stretching All You Can Eat For £1 pizzas for hours on end in Notting Hill Gate, we tried to conjure up our perfect publication. He loved comix and deviant film-making; I loved crime-writing and rock'n'roll. We wanted a magazine that covered the lot.

Good at dreaming as I knew I was, in the end the magazine came to us, the result of a total fluke.

I had written a complimentary live review for *Melody Maker* of a rockabilly band with a Jacques Brel list, appearing at one of our usual Camden hangouts. The lead singer's best friend called me in the *Maker* office when the review came out, to say he had a proposition for me.

I met him in an artist's studio in Old Street. Neil Bambridge, entrepreneur, champion of transgressive art, wheeler-dealer public schoolboy with the smile of a contented shark. He wanted to create an alternative culture bible, a 'gun to the head in print' as he put it, and he needed co-conspirators. His ideas were far bigger and more audacious than anything Barry and I had even thought of – and he had the big money contacts to pull it off. And Neil was enchanted by us. Our unconventional appearances and Barry's blunt, Brummie wit gave him the sort of hard-on that lords get when they mix with gangsters. But even more, I think, he loved the fact that we were already established in the circles he wished to dominate.

At first we made the magazine hand-to-mouth, working out of Neil's studio after hours, putting the first year's issues together on the money we made from our other jobs and what Neil could raise from his chums for the print run. Then, just after Christmas,

Bambridge's festive season schmoozing paid off – he landed a backer willing to set us up in an office and pour in some serious money. A millionaire with a few bob to spare, who shared Neil's taste for esoterica.

The year had begun brightly: searches for proper premises, real budgets drawn up. Finally, two weeks ago, I'd been able to cash my first paycheck from *Lux*, buy myself the pair of maribou-trimmed black slingback slippers that now sat beside the bath. No longer did I have to scrape by on the crumbs of *Melody Maker*'s ten-pence-a-word payouts. At last, the dream had become a proper job.

I finished rinsing soap from between my toes. Although my bath had only filled up ten minutes ago, the steaming water was rapidly losing its battle to the dank chill of an unheated room. Now was the time I had to move suddenly and quickly. It was always the hardest part of the day.

Because I also had to run the gauntlet of Jerry.

Most of the creeping death were actually harmless, happy to pass on messages from the communal payphone in the hallway and nod away the time of day. But I happened to live next door to the one livewire.

Jerry was a blues musician who had been swinging, man, in the sixties, and hadn't quite got over the fact that that decade was over.

I had been stupid enough to introduce myself when I first moved in, about three years ago now. And to tell Jerry that I was working for the music press. I hadn't realised that his own cell was a lost world of valve amps and 8-track cartridges, antique mixing desks and mouldering music papers in stacks reaching up to the ceiling.

But now our mutual interest in music had been established in Jerry's mind, he felt free to intrude on me whenever the mood took him, waving a joint in his hairy hand while he banged on and on about the good old days.

This freedom also extended to 'accidentally' forcing the defective lock on our shared bathroom door on more than one occasion. I was relatively safe at this time of day, but still I felt uneasy being naked in here for more than a few seconds.

I stepped quickly onto the cracked floor tiles, which were also of Jerry's era, into my new slippers and a floor-length dressing gown. Out of the door to the gurgling suck of the emptying bath, and across the hall to my tiny kitchen. I necked cereal and orange juice standing up, washed the bowl and glass in similar haste and beat it back to my lair to get on with the job of applying the face I wanted the world to see.

Arched black eyebrows, pale foundation, black eyeliner, red lips. I undid the rollers, carefully brushed out the coils and wielded the hairspray until it resembled the tresses of one of those fifties femme fatales the hesitant male wouldn't know whether or not to trust.

The effect was completed by items from my specialist all-black wardrobe – a polo-necked jumper, tight trousers and pointy black boots.

I studied myself hard in the full-length mirror.

Satisfied, I swung my leopardskin coat off its hanger on the wall, snatched my bag from where it lay by the bed, locked up and climbed the staircase, through the weighted firedoor, into the hallway.

In the pale light filtered through a reinforced glass window above the front door, I picked through the pile of envelopes on the shelf by the payphone.

The one I'd been thinking about in the bath had come – an invitation to a crime writers' festival at the ICA. The Crimewave, no less. Better still, it came with a couple of paperback proofs – new writers making their debut at the event.

This was going to be sweet.

I shoved the lot into my bag, stepped outside and closed the front door on the rooms of shadowy men, still sleeping off their Sunday lunch hangovers in the distorted fish-eye of dreams.

The Crimewave was going to be my dream assignment. It was hard not to cackle out loud as I hurried down Ladbroke Grove, despite the weary cast of a March morning made especially for raincoats and brolleys.

I was headed for Edgware Road, just four stops down the Metropolitan Line and our office on Bell Street.

The new *Lux* office seemed to me the perfect set-up, although it was little more than a cupboard hidden underneath an art gallery owned by one of Bambridge's cronies. We'd crammed it to capacity with an assortment of Apple Macs in various stages of decrepitude, a photocopier, lightbox, fax and three phone lines. That and so many books piled on to sagging shelves, it looked like an overflowing library. But it was fully functional and, four well-received issues into *Lux*'s life, it felt as though we could conquer the world.

As if we were affecting the world.

As I stepped off the tube at Edgware Road, a couple of guys about my age, dressed like sixties gangsters, oiled hair, smart suits and cufflinks, gave me the wink. A definite improvement on Jerry, it had to be said. There were a lot of them about these days, and not just because the world was catching up with *Lux*'s aesthetic.

A young British film director called Jon Jackson was responsible for these armies of Kray Klones. He'd made a massively successful film called *Bent*, which pastiched the old gangster classics like *Get Carter* and *Villain*, and now everyone wanted to look like they worked for one of the old firms.

The soundtrack to that movie – roughly half Northern soul and half classic rockabilly – had been pumping across adverts and out of doorways all over London, ever since the film's release in May last year. It was a monster that kept on growing, with a cult of worshippers that swelled with the passing of its Christmas video release and Jackson's Golden Globe for Best First Time Director only a month ago.

One of the things that had so impressed Neil about Barry was that he'd been friends with Jon Jackson for years. They were part of the same rockabilly crowd in Camden, a clique of sharp-dressed guys who worshipped old movies and rare records. Neil had been begging for an introduction since the film had come out, but Barry had been keeping it back, like an ace of spades up his sleeve, realising the importance of always keeping Neil hungry.

On Bell Street, memories of the sixties lingered in more tangible form.

Like the café, where I ducked in for my morning coffee to go. It was crammed full of Formica table tops and creaky wooden chairs, encased in a fug of roll-up smoke and chip oil. The clientele was mostly builders and old men, some of whom had clearly had their own interactions with London's criminal history. Like the one with a Glasgow Smile, a livid, red scar, clean across his face. I wondered, as I waited at the counter, whether the Klones who went around repeating the dialogue from *Bent* like they were East End born and bred would be so impressed by Ronnie Kray's fondness for swordsmanship if that was their face.

Clattering down the metal catwalk steps to our office, the Kray Klones' latest recruit was stretched out on two legs of his chair, feet up on the imposing old wooden desk that faced the office entrance. The feet, so impudently plonked upon a mess of newspapers, press releases, photos and sandwich wrappers, were encased in a pair of big, glaringly white brothel creepers. With a strip of black diamonds around the laces. Soles about three inches thick. They clashed quite horribly with the trousers from a bottle green tonic suit and a pair of bright pink socks.

Neil was attempting trendy.

'Aha! Diana!' he boomed.

The rest of him was contained by jacket to said suit, and a pale yellow ruffled shirt. It hardly went with the floppy brown fringe, but I held my fire. The smugness radiating from his features signalled that whatever Bambridge had got up to during the past weekend, it had resulted in one of his coups.

As if on cue he said: 'You won't believe what I got up to at the weekend.'

'No?' I dropped my bag on my desk, invisible antennae twitching. 'Go on then, amaze me.'

His big white plates dropped back down on the floor and he leaned over the desk with his hands clamped together, pulsing uncontrollable glee. 'I got us an exclusive interview with Jon Jackson. Spent the whole of Saturday with him. Went to his *Guardian* lecture on the South Bank, even went to his party afterwards at the Deansgate Club. It's going to be our biggest front cover yet.'

I felt a tiny jolt of absolute rage deep in my chest.

He'd bloody done it. Barry's ace was no longer in the hole. Always, Neil had to do one better.

I must have let my feelings show. The triumph in his voice was like a lava flow.

'Don't you think that's excellent, though? He's not only totally right for our aesthetic, he's absolutely huge in the rest of the world. This is going to be our breakthrough, Diana, our big breakthrough.'

Thankfully for me, the upstairs door slammed right at that moment.

'Happy Monday, pop pickers!' screeched a loud Brummie voice, accompanied by heavy footfalls across the gallery floor. A large shape appeared at the top of the stairs.

Barry.

And he was a sight to behold. Camel hair coat and black suit over a lurid Hawaiian shirt, polished black pompadour and devilish goatee beard. Six foot two and stacked. The Klones at the station would've wept.

'Blimey!' he clocked Neil's new look. 'Been up Savile Row, have you? Something for the weekend, sir? Hoo! Hoo!'

He hurried down the steps, hooked his coat on the back of the bathroom door and fell into his swivel chair, wiping sweat from his brow and dropping his *Post* over his keyboard. Around his chunky frame, keychains clinked and rings in the shape of eyeballs and shark fins glittered.

Neil ignored the blatant sarcasm, safe in the knowledge he was about to puncture Barry's balloon as surely as he had mine. 'No, I spent the weekend with a famous film director, actually.'

'Oooo! Fellini, was it? Or maybe Truffaut?' Barry echoed Neil's accent, if not his perfect pronunciation.

'No, it was Jon Jackson actually.'

'You!' Barry practically spat the word.

We were both thinking, and for different reasons: 'How come?'

Jackson had promised Barry that interview weeks ago, over a game of pool in the Hop Poles in Camden, after he'd just handed over a load of videos the director had wanted to see. Barry had trusted him, was just waiting for the call, to do to Neil what Neil had just done to him.

'Andrew Pearson at the NFT sorted it out, really.' Neil's voice was like a big, fat, purring Cheshire cat. Pearson was one of Bambridge's Cambridge chums. What chance did the rest of us have?

'As I was telling Diana, I got to spend all day with him. Got masses of these…' he held up a bunch of cassettes, 'to transcribe. It really is going to be our best front cover ever.'

'He even got to go to the party,' I told Barry. 'At the Deansgate Club.'

'You knew I was working on that,' Barry glowered, like a just-lit fuse.

'Well, you took your time about it, didn't you? All's fair in love and journalism, old boy,' Neil beamed. 'Anyway, it's not important who did the interview. The important thing is we've got him. It's going to raise our profile immensely.'

'I know what I'd like to raise,' mumbled Barry, 'and where…'

'Well, I've got my invitation to the Crimewave,' I said, hoisting the package out of my bag and slamming it on the desktop. 'Which I suppose is off the front cover now.'

'You know, you two.' Neil surveyed us like a Victorian governess would eye her spoiled charges. 'I actually thought you'd be pleased about this. I've got us access to the biggest figure in the arts world right now. And we are working on the same team, remember?'

Barry and I exchanged glances.

We would bitch about this later.

To distract myself, I got on the phone to Lucy, the ICA press officer. Confirmed my attendance for the Crimewave and set up some interviews with my three favourite writers appearing, Luther Lang, Kay McLachlan and Jack Hall.

Lang was a criminal-turned-author from Texas, McLachlan a Scottish woman who specialised in the true cases of female killers, and Hall a street-smart Londoner with an acerbic wit.

'That should be no problem.' She ran out a list of times I could have to speak to them. 'Now, did you get those proofs I sent you?'

'Yes.' I thumbed the card covers. Simon Everill and Susie Beck, both on the Hard Ball imprint.

'I really think you should interview these two as well,' she continued. 'They're going to be big, big names.'

Another knock-on effect of the Jackson magic was that crime writing was the new rock'n'roll. All over the place, the 'nouveau noir' authors were muscling in on some style mag action, posing with flash motors and jawing on about the mean streets of their local manors.

'They're both really young,' said Lucy, as if reading my mind. 'Susie's only 25, and I hate to have to use this as a marketing point, but she's very good-looking. She's done a gangster novel with a twist.'

I looked at the title.

Slaughtered.

Hmmmmm.

'And Simon, well, he's out of nowhere. That's one of the most amazing books I've ever read in my life.'

This one was called *Weirdo*. I liked that title more.

'If you like Luther Lang, you'll love Simon. It's that sort of writing.'

Well, she knew the right buttons to push with me.

'And I really think it would be good for the magazine for you to do them.'

Well, you can't argue with the 'good of the magazine', as Bambridge had so kindly pointed out. 'That sounds great,' I told Lucy, and she pencilled me in for an hour with both of her protégés.

I had a lot of reading to do.

But now, I had to get on with my usual chores.

Except, as I fired my computer up and shuffled through my papers, I realised that today, nothing was as usual. Neil, for instance, was plugged into his Dictaphone and merrily clattering away at the keyboard. Never before – including the times he had interviewed people he claimed were his heroes – had he ever shown any interest in such tedious grind. Normally, he got me to do it.

Meanwhile, Barry hunched over the light box, ostensibly sizing pictures behind pieces of tracing paper. But he'd put Black Sabbath on our office ghetto blaster and the resultant drone was as ominous as the shape of his back, turned against our glorious editor. It would all come out at the end of the day.

Neither of them stirred at lunchtime. Each was secretly sizing up the other, waiting for the first move. Neil, I could tell, wanted nothing more than to spend an hour telling us how clever he was while enjoying our petulant expressions. Barry, on the other hand, would want to rip his head off and piss down his neck. It wouldn't be pleasant, either way, so I offered to get sandwiches. They both jumped up at this, stuffed my hands full of coins and then sat right back down and got on with the job of ignoring each other. But each tap, tap, tap on Bambridge's keyboard was a slow, grinding source of irritation that no amount of Ozzy's wailing and Tony Iommi's sheet-welding guitar could quite drown out.

To cap it all, at 6.30, Neil got up and made a show of putting his tapes into his bag. 'Right – must dash,' he announced. 'I've got rather a special meeting tonight – with a young lady.'

'Lucky her,' Barry grunted, eyes purposefully resting on the white shoes. 'She's bound to be impressed by those.'

'Just what I thought.' Bambridge smiled brightly and snapped his briefcase shut. 'See you all tomorrow.'

Clomp-clomp-clomp up the metal steps.

'Hope he breaks his fucking neck,' said Barry, charitably.

I rubbed my brow, eyes starting to blur after a day of staring at typeface on a computer screen.

'I don't know how he manages it,' my companion continued. 'Him and Mr Lah-Di-Dah Fucking Pearson, after I was so fucking close to getting it. And what kind of shit questions is he gonna ask anyway? He knows fuck all about gangster movies.'

'Not knowing never stopped Neil having an opinion on anything,' I mused. 'You told him enough about Jackson. He probably recycled everything you ever said to him.'

I'd often seen Neil do this, in conversations. He could remember the minutiae of other people's opinions and then unleash them as if he'd just come to these dazzling conclusions himself. He'd often expressed my own views to other people this way, while I listened on in amazement.

'What I can't get over,' Barry continued, 'is that Jon's supposed to be a mate. I thought he'd have some loyalty.'

Poor Barry. In all his years of looking after rock bands, his main task was to keep them sealed off from any bad publicity. Even now, despite Bambridge's best efforts, he wouldn't spill the beans on any of their bad behaviour. He staunchly believed in loyalty.

Well, so did I, but after a few years in the music press, I realised that those bands you championed when they were little always ran off with your biggest rival as soon as they had their first whiff of the green stuff. Jackson would be no different. He would have been happy to talk to Barry two years ago, when he was making pop promos and no one else was interested. Now, in a world of *Guardian* lectures, Barry Norman and the not-so-distant beckoning of Hollywood, he'd be more impressed by Neil the Publisher/Editor than Barry the mere Contributing Editor, no matter how much more empathy Barry had for him.

They all went funny when they first got famous. Most of them came back from it.

'Shall we go for a pizza?' I offered.

The solace of red wine and pepperoni was something Barry and I had often shared in times of need. By the end of the evening, we'd be laughing at Neil's shoes and chalking Jackson up to experience. Believing, as we parted halfway down Ladbroke Grove, that that would be an end to it.

But we couldn't have been more wrong about that.

It was just beginning.

3

One week later, it started to happen.

It was the same kind of foul March Monday morning, the sort of blank, drizzling greyness that makes you despair of ever seeing the sun again.

Only it wasn't the Great White Shoes that greeted me at the office door, nor the same smug expression.

Neil was sitting at his desk, looking stricken. A man sat opposite. He looked about fiftyish, with white hair, cropped close to the skull. Dressed in a tan leather jacket, jeans, open-necked black shirt, thick-soled shoes. A notepad stretched out in front of him, a pen poised in his hand. He swivelled around slowly at my entrance, fixed me with deep blue, saucer-shaped eyes that were at once penetrating but strangely benevolent, the shadow of a smile on a generous mouth.

One thought: he's Old Bill.

The voice came as soft and deep as the eyes, the melodious accent of southern Ireland.

'D. S. Linehan, Kentish Town CID.'

A storyteller's voice, a hand to go with it. Big, cool. Long fingers.

I stood like a slack-jawed fool.

'Don't worry, you're none of you in trouble.' Definite curve of a smile now, glinting back from his X-ray eyes.

But it didn't look like that from Neil's face.

Papers were strewn all over his desk, croissant crumbs in his hair, where nervous fingers raked back and forth. His smile was a tight line, a thin pretence of bonhomie.

'Your friend here is just helping me with a few enquiries.'

I looked at Bambridge and back at the policeman.

CID, he had said. Not Fraud Squad.

'We've just about finished up, haven't we?' the smiling detective continued, snapping his notebook shut. He looked like he was enjoying making Neil squirm.

'Yes, yes, I think so.'

He couldn't look at me, or at Linehan. Instead he rose hastily to his feet, brushing more crumbs off his jeans, offering his hand in the hope of hastening the end of the encounter.

Linehan rose likewise.

'I'll expect to see you at the station by the end of the day,' he said. 'If anything else occurs to you in the meantime, here's my number.' He pressed a card into Bambridge's open palm, strafing him with the X-rays on full beam as he did so. 'Don't go too far, now,' he quipped.

Neil looked at the floor. 'Er, quite,' he said, uncomfortably.

'I'll see myself out.' D. S. Linehan strode slowly up the catwalk, raising a hand as he reached the top and padded out of the front door, closing it softly. The strangest copper I'd ever seen.

'The plot thickens.' Neil flopped back into his seat and wiped his arm across his brow. 'This could either be really bad… or it could be really good.'

'What the fuck…' I began.

Upstairs, the front door slammed.

'Who the fuck was that?' screeched a Brummie echo of my thoughts, clomping towards the catwalk. 'He was in a bit of a hurry,' the voice went on. 'Was he one of your debtors?'

'It was a copper, Barry,' I said. 'Here to see Neil.'

'What the fuck for?'

'I'm not at liberty to say.' Neil was rapidly regaining his usual demeanour, a sly little smile forming on his lips.

'Get off!' chided Barry. 'Was it the Fraud Squad? Are you under investigation?'

Great minds and all that.

'No, it's nothing like that.' Neil got up and stretched.

'He's expecting him down the station later,' I told Barry.

'OK, I'll tell you – but not a word outside this office,' Neil was warming to his big secret. 'It's a missing person's investigation.'

'Ooo.' Barry tapped his finger on his chin. 'Anyone we know?'

'I really shouldn't say.'

Bambridge was really milking it now.

'But, if you must know,' he flopped down in his chair, giving us a haughty sweep with his eyes, 'he came about Jon Jackson. It seems he's disappeared.'

'You what?' Barry scrunched his brow. 'What do you mean missing?' A heartbeat and then: 'And what's it got to do with you?'

Neil raised his eyebrows. I just stood staring, catching flies.

'I really don't know why it's got anything to do with me,' he sighed, folding his hands behind his head. 'It's just that I was the last person to interview him, and for some reason that policeman wanted to hear what was on the tapes. I have to go down to Kentish Town cop shop and hand them in.'

He sounded more annoyed than upset by this prospect.

'Here,' admonished Barry. 'Never mind about that, what's happened to Jackson?'

'Yes, OK, Barry, I was just coming to that,' his voice becoming waspish now. 'He was supposed to go home for a family meal in Cambridge last Sunday, apparently he never turned up. Never rang. None of his friends, acquaintances or publicists have heard from him since. Which is, apparently, not like him. As you know, I spent the whole day with him – the day before he disappeared.'

'So do they think that something's happened to him?' Barry's words tumbled out quickly, like his brain was struggling to make the connection.

'I don't know what they think. That policeman wasn't very helpful. He just came in and virtually demanded my tapes.'

'Well, you'd better go over there and give them to him.' Barry sounded abrupt now. 'Have you still got them here?'

'Of course I have,' sniffed Bambridge. 'But I wasn't going to tell him that. I'm going to make damn sure I make copies of them before I take them anywhere.'

'What do you mean, copies?'

'Well, we need him for the front cover, don't we? And Christ, if something has happened to him, it's going to be a bloody good exclusive.'

Barry's eyes turned dark. Frown lines froze across his forehead.

'I might have done his last ever interview,' Bambridge babbled on, oblivious to the change in atmosphere. 'God, I haven't even finished transcribing them all yet. I've got one left.' He began rummaging around in his overstuffed briefcase.

'Well, hold on a minute.' I tried to shut him up. 'If something has happened to him, then it might not be a very good idea…'

'Here it is!' Neil pulled out a cassette from his junkpile. 'Fantastic!'

'Do you really want to listen to that now?' Barry's voice came out like machine-gun fire. Neil jumped so high in his seat he almost dropped his precious artefact.

'What?' he spluttered. 'Listen to it? 'Course I do. This could be the making of the magazine. We could have something here that no one else has got. And just think, if there is a clue on this tape, we'll have helped the police in the case of the year. This is fantastic!'

Barry got up, really, really slowly.

Neil suddenly looked apprehensive.

'I'm going to get a coffee,' Barry said, equally slowly, 'so that I don't punch you through that wall right now. When I get back, I don't want to hear any more about Jon Jackson, helping the police solve the case of the century or what you're going to do with your fucking tapes. Keep it to yourself, I'm warning you, and have a bit of fucking respect for people who actually care about the bloke.'

Neil looked up at the vicious curve of the shark fin ring on Barry's accusatory finger, a suitably stunned expression on his face.

He managed to keep it shut until he heard the front door slam.

Then he said: 'I don't know what he's so worked up about. OK, he vaguely knows the bloke, but be realistic – this could give us more publicity than anything we could have dreamed of.'

'Neil,' I advised, 'think very carefully about what you say to him, and what you do with those tapes. You already pissed him off by stealing his interview with Jackson in the first place. Now you're really pushing it. I don't want you to end up in hospital.'

'Well, really! If that's your attitude then I'll go and do it at home. You two can have the place to yourselves. See if you can come up with any better front cover ideas.'

And he got up, marched out and slammed the door behind him.

Alone in the office, the phones started to ring.

I didn't answer them. I was thinking about Jon Jackson.

Guardian lectures, Barry Norman, Kray Klones, *Bent*.

Bent, to be totally honest, had actually left me cold. I knew exactly what he was doing, and why everyone would love it. It was all so clever.

On the day we'd gone to see it, early last summer, Barry and Neil were practically foaming at the mouth. The audience in the packed cinema had spontaneously combusted with laughter and cheers. The most genius thing about it was the casting. Particularly that of long-forgotten sixties actor Niall Flynn: resurrected by Jackson as the ruthless ganglord Marley, he carved his way through a London constructed from pulp legend and swoonsome cinematography.

A contemporary of Richard Harris and Burton, Flynn had been eking out an existence in Galway before Jackson had come to the rescue. He couldn't have picked more astutely. Flynn's features had almost been improved with the passing of time: he still had those piercing eyes and a bristling head of hair, a feline grace that could turn in an instant to fearful menace. It was like Flynn had deliberately put his career on hold for this moment.

Bent's climax raised the roof. Marley, having discovered that his own brother was really the father of his beloved 'son', crucified his treacherous sibling upside down while the soundtrack shook to Wynder K. Frog's Hammond inferno version of 'Green Door'. Followed by Johnny Kidd and the Pirates' 'Shakin' All Over'.

Jackson was a legend overnight.

A world away from when I first saw him. At the Brunswick Club, summer 1983, on a Friday night in Great Yarmouth. Psychobilly bands were popular then, and I was among the converts. Ridiculously high flat-top hair, home-bleached jeans, T-shirt with the sleeves ripped off. Cider and black and John Player Specials. Trying to look as hard as nails.

A band called The Chevys up from Norwich. A figure in ripped-up jeans and bleached semi-mohican, leaping all over the tiny stage and spinning around his badly-strung upright bass. All the goth girls swooning.

A blue dawn after, rolling up from the sea.

I had to keep my distance when I saw him at the bar of the Hop Poles, just nodded and smiled politely when Barry introduced us. I couldn't believe it was the same person, didn't want to embarrass myself by asking.

But it was him. And before the film had even been released, Jackson owned the place. Surrounded by his cronies, half of them in bands, half of them working in local record shops or the Psychotronic video emporium, all of them suited and booted.

Like the last gang in town.

Jackson now with black hair and dark eyes, swarthy olive skin, big nose, wide-mouthed smile. His mother a Spaniard, giving him a look that belied his low counties roots.

No way he was going to remember me.

Boot steps on the stairs interrupted my reverie.

The phones were still ringing.

'You going to answer that?' said Barry.

Later, about 7.30, we decided to call it a day and head for the pub.

To no great surprise, Neil didn't return to the office. But then neither did the police, so we concluded that he must have done his Great British duty and handed over his precious tapes.

Outside, the wind had blown the rain out to the east, though the pavements still glittered with water under the sodium glow of the street lights. A pale streak of pink remained above the setting sun, promising tomorrow would be a different day. On Bell Street it was quiet, all the shops shut up for the night, the roar of the traffic on Edgware Road reduced to a comforting hum.

I was glad our office was here, in the road where time stood still. Give or take the electric street lights, parking-restriction notices and double yellow lines, Bell Street looked much as it had 100 years ago. Apart from the pub, the caff and the newsagents, its main commerce was art galleries and second-hand bookshops, all stuffed to capacity with cheap treasures.

The Bricklayers Arms was similarly unspoilt, a haven from the theme bars and video jukeboxes that seemed to be springing up like cold sores all over the city. We took cold lagers into the snug corner, sitting as comfortably as the name suggests, surrounded by green-and-white flocked wallpaper and framed photographs of Bell Street in Victorian times.

Barry took a sip, wiped foam from his black moustache and said aloud what I was thinking: 'Why does Bambridge have to be such a total cunt?'

'I don't know,' I almost whispered, staring into my pint. 'It's all just good business to him, I suppose. But this could be someone's life…'

I trailed off, not wanting to say more.

Barry patted his hand on my knee.

'It hasn't come to that yet, pet. He's probably just done one, sick of all the publicity.'

'Yes,' I tried to sound enthusiastic, 'all those fucking Klones everywhere.'

'All going up to him saying: "That is not the way I do business".'

Marley's tag-line. I couldn't help but laugh at Barry's appalling

Cockney accent, something Niall Flynn had managed a lot better.

It was true, they all went round saying that.

'See,' he was pleased he'd raised a chuckle, 'who wouldn't want to run away from that? Look, I'll give Woody a ring later, see what he's heard.'

I nodded.

Woody was the friend who'd introduced Barry to Jackson in the first place, the guy whose band Jon had made videos for.

'It's probably a bird,' he winked, draining his glass. 'Want another?'

To Barry, a lot of problems were usually down to 'probably a bird'. He hadn't been so lucky with them himself, despite his striking appearance. Especially his wife upping and leaving him, flouncing off to the States with a trail of bad ju-ju in her wake.

Well, we both had our scars.

We started discussing other things, bands playing that we wanted to see, my interviews for the Crimewave. But by the time he'd reached the end of his second pint, Barry's thoughts had turned back to Neil again.

'Typical of him,' he let rip. 'It wasn't bad enough that I spent weeks trying to sort an interview out. That he knew how much I wanted to do that interview. Oh no, "we're all on the same team".' He mocked Bambridge's plummy tones. 'The same load of old bollocks he always comes out with when he's stitching you up.'

'Poshos,' I noted, 'always have an innate ability not to care about anyone else's feelings. It comes with their blue blood and passion for buggery.'

I was trying to make him laugh now, but it didn't work. He just stared into the smoky distance.

'He ought to have some respect, Di,' he said. 'We ain't the fucking tabloids.'

Barry was rarely wrong. I contemplated this while I sipped my drink. Then I said: 'I wonder what he'll do with that transcript?'

'That,' intoned Barry gravely, 'is precisely what worries me.'

He let that hang for a few moments, then deliberately changed the subject back to my forthcoming tussle with Luther Lang; joking, piss-taking Barry returned.

And we banished our black thoughts into the bottom of a glass.

4

Two days later, sprawled across my bed, I was getting to grips with those book proofs. I had *Crime and the City Solution* on my stereo, Simon Bonney singing like a tortured angel, blurry words about rooms of light.

A run-in with Jerry had thankfully been avoided. He'd been in earlier; I could hear him crashing about and swearing, but I hadn't turned my music on, knowing it would only be an open invitation. Instead, I waited in silence, flicking through Susie Beck's *Slaughtered* until Jerry's door banged open.

I crossed my fingers and prayed.

I could tell from the commotion he was lugging his bass guitar up the stairs, cursing all the way. It meant he had a gig. Probably at the Station Tavern, the seven-days-a-week live 'Good Time' blues bar opposite Latimer Road station, where everyone knew his name. He'd be out till at least midnight, probably later.

Waiting a few heartbeats until he was out the front door, I dived into my record pile and selected something good. Wedging the door open so I could hear Rowland Howard's chiming guitars and Bonney's swoonsome croon, I made my extravagant supper: cheese and pickle sandwiches, ready-salted crisps, a cup of tea. Haute cuisine prepared, it was time for a wallow in books.

I picked Susie up and gave her my full attention. My initial suspicions of this title were quickly confirmed. There were as many of them about as Kray Klones: *Bent* Books.

Ms Beck waded in with aplomb, not bothering much with any credibility to her plot, East End parlance and bad boy behaviour transmogrified through the fantasies of a West London trust fund baby. The amazing twist revealed in the first page. The ganglord was no ganglord. She was a ganglady!

That was the future of British crime writing assured, then. I struggled with a few more pages. But she wasn't doing it for me. I flicked to the back page just to be sure: bloodbath dahn the old East End, ganglady sending in a double to the arms of the filth, while dressed as a man, she hastened away in her Daimler.

It took my mind back to unpleasantness. Two days of Neil banging in and out of the office, on constant 'business meetings' that had suddenly materialised out of the ether. Barry's watchful gaze, clipped comments: 'Given those tapes to the Old Bill yet?'

'Of course I have.'

'Made yourself the copies, though?'

'I haven't got time for this. I'll speak to you later.'

Out the door with his bulging briefcase, expression on his face like he'd sucked a lemon and the lemon had said 'Eewww!'

Barry saying later: 'Spoke to Woody. No cunt's seen him since that Saturday. That copper's been in the Hop Poles an' all, asking around…'

Not wanting to think any further. Nailing down the door to the room in my head where the secrets are kept.

I put Susie down, and turned instead to Simon Everill.

The book called *Weirdo*.

That was what the beer boys used to call me at school. 'You're one of them weirdos, in't ya?'

Pronouncing it *were*-do, like *were*-wolf.

Me with my big old flat top, trying to look as hard as nails.

The title made me want to read. I tried the first sentence:

'I realised, as a tiny turd, that I could become other people instead of me.'

Not what I'd expected. Off the edge of the next sentence, I'd been tipped into a different world.

Weirdo was the name of a little boy. You didn't get to know

whether he had a real name, because no one ever used it, and though the story unfurled through his eyes, he was unaware of having any other handle. He lived with his mother, his brothers and his sisters, in a ramshackle caravan that stood in a scrapyard by a farmer's field, on the outskirts of a village. Their closest neighbours were chickens and pigs. In the eyes of the villagers, the porkers and Weirdo's family were closely related. They were the lowest of the low.

The brood inside the van were a kind of modern-day freakshow, each member the product of a different biker, gypsy or general drunkard who passed in the night. Each with a different level of mental illness or feral cunning.

Everill wrote like he was some kind of Harry Crews or Flannery O'Connor, trapped in a colder but familiar climate.

Little England.

The oldest boy in Weirdo's family was the most stupid and brutal. His name was Fists and, when he wasn't trying to copulate with the poultry, he ruled over his siblings with these big, raw-knuckled weapons. When chicken was off the menu, he would turn his ferocious lust on his two little sisters – Mary, whose only possession was a Gideon Bible she could not put down, and Mong, who, unable to speak, could only dribble saliva and snot.

There was another brother, Jake, who was a gypsy's son and clever enough to deflect Fists' monotonous attacks on to Weirdo, who, although older than Jake, was weaker and more pitiful. Weirdo's mum was almost a spectral presence; always too drunk, too asleep, or too flat out in the back of the van to offer any protection.

Mary and Mong buried the evidence of their hideous reality in praying to Jesus and total mute blankness respectively. Jake spent all his time up the town, doing his best to continue the family line, suck on bags of glue, and con the 'normal' kids out of their pocket money. Weirdo's only escape was his imagination; so powerful it was practically hallucinogenic, opening the door through which he too could escape.

Like, I could leave myself inside the shell of me, lyin' on the caravan floor, on the end of Fists' hurtin' hands, an' I could float away outside, across the big field an' over the hedges, down the windy road to the town. That was where the real people lived. I liked to go down the river, near the bridge, there were a nice old tree down there, a weepin' willow that was called. That bent down to let its leaves drink there in the water, and let me sleep there underneath it, all hidden an' safe on the grass. An' when I lay there, I could think who to become next.

I liked watchin' the normal people. I liked them 'cos they looked clean an' shiny, an' they had nice clothes an' that. They smiled at me when I was feedin' the ducks, just like I was normal like them.

There was one boy I used to see down there, an' he came down the river a lot, he had a proper brown paper bag an' it were full of bread what he used to feed them ducks with. He stood there for ages, he did.

An' they could see him comin' before I could. 'Cos they all used to start honkin' and quackin' and waddlin' up the bank to see him, shakin' their tail feathers behind 'em. I liked the way them ducks walked, they looked funny. An' I liked the way they all honked and quacked together, that were funny too.

An' sometimes there were little ducks, baby ducks they were, all fluffy and golden and soft lookin', like you couldn't have held them in your hand for fear of crushin' 'em. They were a bit shy, mind, but the momma duck, she used to take care an' keep 'em all close, an' they all loved that bread an' all.

I wished I was a baby duck at first, so as I could have a ma like that. But then I wished I was that little boy an' I could get all them ducks to come up out of the water an' hustle an' waddle an' quack all around me. Like they were my friends.

An' so I used to wish myself into him. I had dark brown

hair that was short and clean and not all stuck together. An' I had blue trousers, a right nice, deep blue, an' they were clean an' all. An' a red puffer jacket and red plimsolls what went with it. But best of all I had that bag of bread. I could slowly open up that bag, an' feel them crusts of bread inside, pick 'em up in my fingers, an' then throw 'em across all that green grass down there by the river. Them ducks, they'd be up there like a shot. They'd love me they would. Especially them baby ones, all shy and soft and golden.

So instead of hearin' 'Bam! Bam! Bam!' My brother's bloody fucken fists in my back and pullin' my hair an' shoutin' down my fucken ears, I could just hear 'Quack! Quack! Quack!' Them ducks are glad I'm here, I've made their day haven't I, just look at them all waddlin' up to see me. I'm not in this stinkin' van, on this stinkin' patch of mud an' rusty old mangled up machines an' pig shit. I'm a nice boy now, got nice clothes – look at 'em! – bet my parents love me as much as them ducks do. Fists, you can't hurt me here, I'm safe.

An' that was how I first learned how to shift myself.

I had to stop there, and light a fag.

I started rooting around in my bag, looking for the press release that went with it to see if there was some kind of writer's biog about Simon Everill. It was a right mess in there, so I ended up turning it out on to the bed, just to add to the breadcrumbs and fag ash.

I found nothing.

I checked the envelope the package had arrived in. There was plenty of Susie Beck. Fuck all Simon Everill.

Oh well, I thought. I'll phone Lucy tomorrow, get her to fax one over.

I practically skipped over to the hi-fi and flipped the record over. Turned the volume up so I could get maximum enjoyment out of both record and book.

Turned it up so loud I never heard the phone.

Next thing I knew, someone was banging on my door.

Oh fuck, I thought, it's Jerry, come back pissed. But when I looked at my clock, it was only 10.15. It couldn't be him.

Shit, maybe I was annoying my upstairs neighbour.

I turned the stereo down, ran over to the door.

'Sorry to bother you.' It was indeed old Alan from upstairs. But he didn't look angry, more concerned. 'But there's just been a phone call for you, sounded urgent.'

Poor man was out of breath from rushing down the stairs. I immediately felt guilty. 'Are they still there?' I asked him.

'That's just it,' he said. 'He just said it was Barry, and for you to turn on the TV right now, ITV.'

'The TV?'

I didn't understand. But turned around anyway, switched on my decrepit black-and-white portable.

You could hear the voices before the picture cleared through the snow and static. '...was discovered early this morning by council workers in Camden Town, North London...'

With Alan standing behind me, peering at the set with concerned eyes.

'...investigating complaints of a severe stench coming from an area of railway arches used by market traders...'

Simon Bonney still singing on my stereo, singing about a room of lights.

'...the police have yet to issue a statement...'

But the picture coming through the cathode tubes was of Detective Sergeant Linehan, pushing a camera away from taped-up arches in Camden Town, North London.

Alan behind me saying: 'Well, what was that all about?'

Me trying to sound normal. Trying to nail my memories back down. 'I'm not really sure. I think I'll have to call him back.'

'Maybe you missed the item he wanted you to see. What with the phone being in the hall and me being so slow.'

Dear, sweet old man.

'It's not your fault, Alan.' My voice sounded unnaturally calm, as it always did when I was freaking out inside. 'I would have heard it myself if I hadn't had my music on so loud.'

'All right then, dear.' He ducked respectfully out of the door. 'So long as you're OK.'

'Yes, fine, thank you so much.'

Tears in my eyes as the door closed behind him.

No more nails left.

Thursday morning, ashes in my mouth.

I hadn't phoned Barry back last night, because I didn't know what to say. Didn't trust myself not to spill my one secret, my one memory of Jon Jackson that no one else had. Instead I sat on the bed, staring through the French doors at the end of my room, watching through the glass at the branches of the trees swaying and curling against the wind. Feeling a flat hollowness inside like I hadn't felt for years.

One million cigarettes later, I had finally fallen asleep.

My dreams fractured cut-ups of memories.

Sitting on a table in the Brunswick Club, round the corner of the stage, the gig over, watching my friend Lisa necking with a punk rocker called Lucas. A tap on my shoulder. A handsome face smiling, saying: 'All right girl?'

Dissolving into Neil, shovelling papers into his snazzy briefcase, saying: 'I haven't got time for this.' Dissolving into Detective Sergeant Linehan pushing a camera out of the way of taped-up arches in Camden Town.

I didn't watch the news at 8am. Preferred the silence instead. Gathering together those book proofs, thinking methodically, must ring Lucy and get that biog before Saturday. Packing them all in my bag.

Doing my make-up extra carefully, so that Barry and Neil wouldn't notice the shadows of a fitful night. Concealer stick and eyeliner doing the trick. Checking myself in the mirror again.

All the nails in place.

Outside, the bare trees still tossed and groaned, a slanting rain cut crosswards from the west. At the kiosk by the tube, the red-tops screamed the unavoidable –

CAMDEN CORPSE IS MISSING DIRECTOR

Unthinkingly, I grabbed a copy of one of the scandal rags, just like all the other punters. Underneath a picture of a grinning Jackson, the copy went:

> A man's body found in the early hours of yesterday morning by council workers in Camden Town, North London, is believed to be that of missing film director Jon Jackson. Although police refused to confirm the facts until the body has been formally identified, the *Post* has learned that the murder site in Camden resembled a vicious re-creation of a scene from *Bent*, the gangland thriller that shot Jackson to fame in May last year.

I looked up from the newsprint, down the train track that curved away from Ladbroke Grove around the bend of the Westway, framed by council tower blocks, like grim giant's teeth against the grey wash of sky. Willed the train to come quickly.

On the motorway, streams of cars speeding by, little blurs of colour with things to do, places to go. My eyes were drawn back to the black-and-white letters dancing out from the page.

> The writer and director was reported missing after he failed to show up to a family dinner in Cambridge on 12 March. The night before, he had been celebrating his *Guardian* lecture on the British Gangster Movie at London's National Film Theatre. Jackson and friends had moved on from the South Bank to the trendy Deansgate Club in Soho, where he was seen leaving, alone, at approximately 3am. No sightings of him have been reported since, and Interpol has been brought in to step up a widespread search after local CID and Scotland Yard failed to turn up any leads to his whereabouts…

Finally, like a great grey worm winding its way up the track, the tube rolled into view.

None of the other passengers look concerned. All with their heads stuck into the same paper as me, but flicking through nonchalantly, some of them even starting at the back with the sport section, more interested in Arsenal beating Spurs than some poncy film director getting snuffed. Their blank faces offering nothing but stoic indifference. 'Don't ask me, guv. I never saw nuffink.'

London through and through.

In Bell Street, I sat in silence staring at the paper. Not reading, just staring. Waiting for Barry to come in. Instead, I heard Neil's feet.

I pulled out the books and the ICA schedules, spread them all over my desk, my eyes scanning up and down the running order, taking in nothing at all.

'Suppose you've seen this?' Neil said, slapping the *Post* down on my desk.

'Mmmm.' I forced myself to meet his eye.

'Not looking good, is it?'

I shook my head, looked back down at my papers.

Neither of us made a move to turn on the radio. Just booted up our computers and tapped away, listening for footsteps on the pavement outside.

The front door slammed. Barry appeared on the top of the stairs, waving the very same tabloid over his head.

'Can you fucking believe this?' He clattered down the gangplank.

'They've not even identified the body yet and they're all over it like a fucking freakshow.'

'You reckon it's definitely him, then?' Bambridge sitting upright.

'I don't see how they can get away with printing this shit if it isn't.'

'Well, how do they know,' asked Neil, 'that it was done in the style of the film if the police aren't saying?'

Barry shot him a look.

'You don't think that council workers won't take a bung?'

'Hmmmm.' Neil pored over his paper as if trying to decipher a coded subtext between the black and white lines. He sipped from his Styrofoam coffee cup thoughtfully.

'But who would do such a thing?' I wanted to know.

'A nutter.' Barry determined.

'Yeah, but one who knew him?' My steady diet of crime novels now clicking thoughts into my head.

'Nah, a random nutter. As much as I knew the bloke, he just wasn't the type that could make that kind of enemy. Anyway, they reckon he left on his own.'

'You think it could be the taxi driver?' asked Neil, as if we were playing Cluedo. 'That would make it creepier still – the demon cabbie of Old London Town.'

Barry's eyes began to cloud over again.

Saved by the bell, the phones began to ring.

'I'll get that,' said Neil, snatching the receiver on his desk from its cradle. 'Bambridge speaking… Ah yes, Sergeant Linehan…' He turned his head away as if that meant we couldn't hear him. 'Yes, yes, I understand… No, no I won't do anything of the sort… You have my word, Sergeant. Yes, thank you. What? What now? Well, what have I… I see… I see… Well, yes, of course I will. Speak to you presently.'

He slammed the phone back down.

'Well?' Barry demanded.

'That policeman's playing games with me,' Neil snapped back. 'He said the tapes are now *sub judice* and if we print a word of it we'll be sued to hell and back by the good old Metropolitan Police.'

'It is him, then?' My voice a whisper.

'Yes! It's him all right. And they want me down the station for further questioning. Me of all people! Am I supposed to find the murderer for them too?'

Barry almost smiling. 'Hold the front page!'

5

The sunlight didn't penetrate the room he was in. Although the heat did, and it served to raise the sweetish stench in the dead air around him. Fastidious to the outside world, in here all was dust. Ghosts floating like motes on the ceiling.

The newspaper headlines returned him to memory.

Of his first visit to Camden Town, when he had tramped the streets all day. It had been in July of the year before, the height of the summer and just after he had made these quarters in Sodom his permanent home. A time of tracking, of finding his bearings up there in Camden, the place he needed to be. What he had found was an intersection, between commerce and misery.

Idly, he fingered a nickel medallion he held in his left hand. It was a St Christopher, the patron saint of travellers, a totem, a comfort, to its previous owner. A virtually incoherent Glaswegian, whom he had encountered on that first foray. St Christopher, who guards the path of the righteous.

At first, confused and upset, he hadn't realised quite why he had taken it with him. But in time, it had come to him – it was a sign. A signpost on his journey.

The men whom the saints had forgotten got an iron bed in the clamouring corridors of Temperance House, the alcoholic's refuge that sat in the middle of Arlington Road like a squat, red brick toad. A Victorian philanthropist had founded the institution and it remained, the last of its kind in the capital, to shelter the ragged shadows of men that everyone pretended not to see as they went about their business of buying from the market. Their only living philanthropist these days was the patient landlady in the Irish pub on the corner, a few yards' staggering distance away on the corner of Inverness Street.

Which was where he had found himself at about six o'clock that day. The market was starting to pack up as he stopped on the corner of the little street where the fruit and veg stalls stood, wondering what to do next. There had been so much to take in and see already, that now his feet were aching and the heat of the day was sharpening his thirst. He needed to find a café or a pub, but which one? There were so many, the choice was bewildering.

The tramp had come staggering out of a doorway to make his decision for him, his grimy hands clutched around the butt of a roll-up and a near-empty can of Special Brew.

'Escewz me, pal,' he slurred loudly. 'Cshud yeez shparze uza few boab fer uzsch stea?'

He had been taken aback. 'I'm sorry, mate, say that again.'

'Issszched, cshud yeez shparze uzscha few boab fur uzsch stea, pal? Issch goonan run oot.'

He tried to make sense of the pronouncement. 'I'm sorry, I can't understand what you're saying.'

The man's face suddenly grew resigned and, for some reason, his next words came out crystal clear. 'Ach, mon, nae one understands us. I'm a Camden Town drunk, eh.'

He smiled at this, and thought, well here's a kindred spirit, then. 'Let me buy you a drink,' he had said at once.

The tramp's face broke into a wide and toothless grin. 'Ach, yeez a gent,' he had proclaimed, leading the way down Inverness Street to the Hop Poles.

He had been most surprised by that pub. Of all the alehouses he had sampled in endless London town, this one most closely resembled those he had used as a teenager. The very old, hopeless winos occupied the lounge bar and the snug, in various stages of quiet decrepitude. But the saloon bar, where there was a pool table and a tiny stage for sporadic attempts at live music, was used by the rebel set.

And how rebellious they were – worshipping the same greasy

gods as their Teddy Boy forefathers, by the look of them. Boys with slicked-back hair and leather jackets, drape suits and loud shirts; girls with heavily styled hair and heavily made-up faces, pencil skirts, stiletto heels. They obviously had control over the contents of the jukebox as Elvis, Jerry Lee, Johnny Cash and Lee Hazlewood grunted and groaned, twanged and moaned their way through the smoky air. Which sat well with the old folks as well, gazing into their beers, their eyes misting over with memories of their youth, still burnished bright, even when the mundane details of the current week's events had already been dumped into the synaptic dustbin.

Two greasers playing pool in their dandified outfits looked up as they entered. They nudged each other and laughed, muttered something about another poor sucker.

He ignored them, stood tall.

'What you drinking?' he asked his new companion.

'Highland dew, eh.' The man's eyes misted. 'Ach, whisky, pal.'

'Landlord, a pint of your finest bitter and a malt whisky for my friend,' he said loudly.

He had always preferred the company of older, more alcohol-ravaged men anyway. It was easier to hide yourself in the company of those whom society had already written off. He could hear the greasers sniggering again, the click of the cue against balls, Tom Jones singing from the jukebox, dreaming of the cotton fields of home.

They found a quiet corner, on the other side of the bar, in the snug. The alcoholic, Glasgae Boab, babbled his life story into a line of whiskies, enjoying the rare novelty of unburdening himself to uncomplaining ears.

He pretended to listen, but all the while he was watching the greasers, prickles running up and down his spine. Eyes darting to the door, just in case the next person who walked in with a big oily quiff was the one he was looking for. Something told him this was the right sort of place.

But it got to closing time and there hadn't been a show.

Boab was boasting about his time in the gangs of Glasgow. It seemed a pretty low-life career of hoisting stolen goods and using a razor blade – everyone used them then, eh. If you didn't have one then you'd be the one bleeding in the gutter. A post office robbery gone wrong, one mate on the floor, blood pumping out of him so fast it was hard to believe it was real. The other running straight into the arms of the police. Not Boab, he was The Shadow, eh. But had to get away after that, y'ken? And the streets down here were all paved with gold, naturally.

He'd thought he'd pick some work up here, sooner or later. But sooner turned to much later, and his ambitions had long since been obliterated under the haze of cigarette smoke and whisky, the occasional golden slumber provided by smack, the feral, everyday survival of hostels and streets. The screaming in the night, by Christ, the noise they make in those places.

But still proud of his skill with the razor. That's why they left him alone, eh. The Terror of the Gorbals, he was in his prime.

Boab cackled and nudged him as he plied more lurid boasts into his tales, something that a lesser man might have found deeply annoying. But not him. He was enjoying the company of another human being, even one in this degraded state. Which was why, when time was called and they found themselves back on the pavements, he'd let Glasgae Boab lead him up to some dodgy Greek restaurant that sold under-the-counter whisky. Why he'd paid for a bottle and followed the tramp's ambling course along the winding canal, where Boab had his secret bash out there on the wasteland behind King's Cross, to stash anything he found of value. 'Cos you couldn't trust nae fucker in Temperance House, eh.

It was all very interesting, an insider's course on the local lowlife and how it operated.

Only, when they got to the shack Boab had constructed out of corrugated steel, discarded furniture and rusted barrels, the old bugger had suddenly got suspicious of him.

'Eh, you're nae one of these nancy boys, are yeez? Ye get any ideas like that on me an' all cut ye, ye bastid.'

The words popped in the back of his mind like sparks. Here he was, being kind to this unwashed bastard, and all the thanks he got was to be called a dirty poof. That was uncalled for. Ungrateful. He could feel a faint pounding starting up in his temples, but tried to push it away, wiping a hand across his brow.

'Ahh, don't be daft.' He forced a smile. 'I just don't want to head home yet. I feel like hearing more of your stories.' He waved the bottle of Scotch to underline his point and the cunning old eyes became bright.

'Ach, youze alreet. All reet, I'll tell ye some more o'me tales.'

He had realised then that he'd have to be careful. So he uncorked the whisky and they sat themselves down on what once had been a sofa, staring out at the canal. There had been a full moon that night, the edges blurred by the petrol fumes that rose out of the city, hanging low and orange in the cardboard-coloured sky.

He drank deep from the bottle, willing the tattoo in his head to subside.

At that point, his memory became hazy.

He thought, looking back on it now, that something the tramp said must have started it. Something about the wife and bairns he had deserted back there on the other side of the Border. He could remember him laughing, mocking the woman and wondering if she'd had to take to the streets herself to support the wee ones. Because that was all she was fit for anyway.

'Is that so?' he had said, and suddenly he'd found himself with a piece of wire in his hands. It must have been something he'd picked up from the tangled mess of the bash, something he'd been idly playing with. The pounding in his head was getting louder and louder, to the exception of all other noise, and as if walking through a dream he had moved quickly towards Glasgae Boab, and his hands and the wire had gone round the wino's neck.

Immediately, Boab's big, ham-like hands had reached for the noose, cutting into his greying old flesh, but it was as if his weight was nothing, like he could toss him around like a doll.

'Think you're a fucking hard man, do you?' The very idea seemed amusing.

Glasgae Boab twisted and lurched, one hand now scrabbling inside his coat for the trusty razor. A kick in the kidneys made him drop the blade, and as he did so, blood had started to gout out of his nose and mouth, while his eyeballs bulged out of their sockets. Blood started to come from there too, blinding him with its sticky darkness.

Boab let go of his bowels in a warm rush. He could no longer breathe and the stars swam brightly in one last white burst before his blackened eyes. Then the night and the pain caved in on Glasgae Boab. The Camden Town drunk whom no one understood was just as uncomprehending of his own savage fate.

It took him a while to realise the jerking now was only reflex spasms. And when he did, the strength drained straight back out of his arms, and he pushed the stinking bulk away, panting with exertion. Fell backwards on to the canal bank and lay there for minutes, his eyes shut, waiting for the red fog to lift.

When he came back to reality, he wondered why Glasgae Boab wasn't talking any more. Why he was lying at a funny angle, his head twisted round to one side like it shouldn't be, glassy eyes staring far beyond him into a never-ending night. Why his neck had opened up like a big, gaping, mocking smile.

The whisky bottle had tipped over and all the liquid had run out, forming a pool on the dry earth. The fumes mingled with a terrible stench emanating from the corpse.

It was a hideous scene. Carnage. And he must have been responsible. The thumping tattoo in his brain was replaced now with a more pure, violent pain, matched by that in his hands, which were cut from the wire and the force he had used. Hands that were shaking and covered in blood.

Nothing like this had come over him for so many years that he had thought he had got that side of himself under control. Thought that he was just honing that power now, keeping it stored up and in check, for when it was needed. But just look at this now. He howled then, long and hard, tears running down his face. Sat rocking on his heels, not wanting to look at the destruction he had wrought, wrought with his bare hands on an innocent man.

Eventually, as the sky began to lighten and pale streaks of pink started to seep over the spires of St Pancras station, he knew that whatever he had done, he had best be away. He knelt down by the corpse and tentatively fingered the wound. It was then that he noticed the St Christopher, strangely unbroken, still hooked around the dead man's neck. Gently, his long fingers found the clasp and undid it, curling the chain around the medallion. He examined it, dark with blood.

He'd better remember this, he had thought. Better keep this medal so that he did. Better count his blessings, too – although plenty of people had seen him in the pub, he doubted that anyone would come looking for a tramp. No one would care. Someone else would take Glasgae Boab's iron bed and not give a thought to what had become of its former occupant.

And the terrible thing was, he was right.

Gently, he knelt down by the body, almost tenderly he closed the man's eyelids, murmuring, 'It's all over now, Bob, all over.'

Despite the humidity, a colder breeze rose off the water, seeping through his splattered clothes. He took off his leather jacket, an item he still found it necessary to wear even as the temperatures hit the 80s, removed his T-shirt and dipped it into the canal. Washed his face and his hands, sponged down the leather. Rinsed again in the dark water, then rolled the clothing up into a ball, tucked it in his jacket pocket. The warm air would soon dry him. With his jacket folded over his right arm, he began to make his way back home, the St Christopher tight in his fist.

As he walked, he whistled to himself, although of this he wasn't aware.

Now, with the newspaper spread out on the bed before him, the headline announcing a 'Copycat killer' in 32-point bold type, he smiled at the medallion again.

A sign, no doubt about it.

St Christopher, lighting his path.

6

Thursday, Friday – two days passed in a blur.

Starting with Neil stomping out of the office, leaving us slack-jawed in his wake. There was just too much to take in: Jackson dead. Bambridge 'helping the police with their enquiries'.

Barry could barely wait until he'd got up the stairs and out the door before he flew over to Neil's desk.

'Where's that fucking tape?' he said. 'It must be here somewhere.' But Neil's desk was a Permanent Chaos Area, just like his briefcase. Papers everywhere, drawers full of cassettes. Barry pulled the lot out, a blur of tattooed arms and flying pages, put tape after tape into the ghetto blaster, found nothing but plummy Bambridge whittling on to his New York art mates about the role of the degenerate in overthrowing the establishment. Barry grew even angrier hearing things like that and threw them all on the floor in a rage. Then he had another idea:

'Let's look on his hard drive.'

Electronic files similarly ransacked, even ones with titles like JAN–APRIL BUDGET FORECAST, just in case he'd played a cunning trick to throw us off the scent. But there was nothing there either.

Barry finally flopped back down, spent. I hazarded a guess.

'I don't really think Neil's the killer, do you?'

'No!' Barry screamed. 'But there's something on that fucking tape he won't let on about, otherwise what the fuck's he doing down Kentish Town nick? What the fuck does he know? Him and his fucking copies. The cunt's got something, I know he has.' His eyes red-rimmed with frustration.

'I bet Bambridge has a safe at home,' I replied, softly. 'It'll all be in there. He wouldn't have left anything here. He knows us too well.'

I got up, slowly began picking up the tapes and papers from all corners of the room, hoped I was putting them back in the right drawers and that there was no order to Neil's chaos.

Barry banged into the bathroom and stayed in there ten minutes.

I did one more scan through Neil's hard drive. That was the most logical place to me. There was a transcriptions folder, but the documents in there were what they purported to be:

Richard Kern

Ted McKeever

Edward Gorey

Dame Darcy

Stuff we'd already run, or that was waiting to go into the new issue.

I checked one more thing. The wastebasket. But there were only some layouts for this issue that I'd already seen.

I was shutting it down as Barry came out of the bogs, looking sheepish. 'I didn't mean to go off like that, pet,' he began. 'I just can't believe what's going on here.'

'Neither can I,' I agreed, and tears suddenly threatened to spring from my eye sockets. I looked back down at the keyboard, composed myself. 'There's nothing here, I've double-checked. The place is empty. I reckon everything he has is at home.'

'He's never been that careful before,' Barry noted.

'I know. Well. None of this makes any sense to me. I don't know what it is that he's got, but I don't think it can incriminate him, otherwise that copper wouldn't have made such a show of ribbing him in front of me.'

'Did he?' Barry forced a smile.

'Yes. Talked to him like he was a naughty little schoolboy. Had his number all right.' I nodded to myself. 'I really thought he would be from the Fraud Squad. All this money flying around and fuck knows where he gets it from. If Neil's got anything to do with crime, it's money, not murder.'

Barry nodded.

I looked around the office, said: 'Look, what do you want to do? I don't know about you, but I can't concentrate on work today. Not with all this shit going on.'

'Me neither. What about him?' He nodded towards Neil's computer. 'Think he'll be back?'

'I doubt it. He'll probably have to go running to one of his Soho clubs for a stiff champagne to get over the indignity.'

'Me! Of all people!' Barry shrieked, laughing again.

'Let's go to the Hop Poles,' I suggested.

'That's where the wake will be.'

On the steps of Edgware Road tube, the first edition of the *Evening News* screamed a new headline:

FILM DIRECTOR SLAUGHTERED – it said – LIKE A PIG.

Inside the Hop Poles at 11am, the room was already full to the rafters. Barry's mate Woody, all five foot six of him – including pompadour quiff – pushed through the bodies towards us, Guinness in one hand, whisky in the other. He threw his arms around Barry, weeping uncontrollably. Other bodies thronged around, guys I vaguely knew, everyone hugging and drinking and crying and hugging and drinking some more.

The Dubliners on the jukebox, sounding melancholy.

I found a whisky in my hand without knowing how it got there, but it tasted like God's own medicine, burning down the back of my throat. I chased it with a Camel full strength and a pint of lager, trying to hear what everybody was saying. A guy called Mark, another one of those short, compact rockabillies with a dark blond flat-top and bandy legs in too-tight jeans, grabbed hold of my collar, shouting into my ear: 'He was the best! You know? The fucking king!'

I just nodded, trying to stay upright in the mass of bodies, my pint half gone already and most of it fed to the carpet.

Barry eventually steered us into a corner, where we perched around the pool table, which had been thoughtfully covered over to support a mass of glasses. Mike the landlord was trying his best to pick out the empties. More beers all round, more whiskies, fag packets doing the rounds, fog thicker than your traditional pea-soupers and The Pogues on the jukebox now, dreaming about the old canal, a dirty old town. Camden Town.

Woody so drunk by 12.30 they had to lie him down upstairs.

The old winos in the saloon and the snug looked on with wonder.

I found myself talking to Alex, the stuttering proprietor of Psychotronic Video and part-time band-leader. The last time I saw him, he was doing backflips off this pool table and landing in a perfect Elvis stance.

'When they catch the f-f-fucker who did this,' he said, waving his arms in agitation, beer flying everywhere, 'I'm f-f-f-fucking doing the f-f-f-fucker.' His girlfriend stood behind him, weeping quietly into her handkerchief, arm-in-arm with her best friend, who was doing likewise.

Mike came round with huge plates of cheese and corned beef sandwiches on the house. More beers appeared from nowhere. Barry shoved back through, saying: 'He's all right, I've put him on his side, he just needs to sleep it off.'

By now I was feeling giddy, trying to force down a cheese sandwich to see if that would make me feel better.

Nancy and Lee were on the jukebox now, sounding eerie: his dark baritone, her floaty, ethereal replies, a song about strangers in strange lands. I realised that half the songs on here were on the *Bent* soundtrack. Prayed to God 'Green Door' wasn't one of them.

Barry, seeing my expression, shoved a wrap into my hand. 'This'll make you feel better. Got it off Alex.'

I staggered through to the bogs, where a trail of mascara-stained tissue lined the floor, two girls cried all over each other, and someone else was loudly sick in one cubicle. The other one was mercifully free.

Putting the toilet lid down, I chopped out a big fat line of speed on top of it. Rolled up a fiver, snorting the vicious white powder right up my nose.

Bingo.

I flushed the bog and staggering out, bright-eyed, I recognised two brothers swaying in front of the gents, one from a brilliant band called the Suave Bastards, the other a writer for one of the broadsheets. Both of them had black quiffs, black suits, red shirts – only one of them with the height and build to pull it off.

'You fucking cunt!' the Suave Bastard was shouting.

'Look, it's a fucking obituary,' his shorter, rounder brother shouted back, trying to sound reasonable, respectable. 'Somebody's going to write it – they didn't have him on file. Surely it's better it gets written by a mate rather than some cunt who didn't know him.'

'Better you get your blood money, you mean, you conniving little cunt!'

I struggled past and saw Barry had got us a seat at last. He waved me over.

On we went into early evening, going strong on whisky, beer and speed. Woody staggered back from upstairs, launched straight into a pint of Guinness. Conspiracy theories started to form in the smoky air – copycat killers, nutters OD-ing on the film, fixating on Jon. No one was making much sense of anything, just glad to have a diversion. The usual clientele of winos appearing sporadically in the doorway, blinking uncomprehending in the gloom.

On and on with the whisky, beer and speed.

A figure appeared at the bar like Banquo's ghost. With a tan leather jacket and cropped white hair. I nudged Barry, saying: 'Is that Linehan?'

The X-ray eyes strafed down the bar, straight into my own.

'That's Bambridge released then,' Barry replied.

Linehan's eyes lingered on us, then flitted past. Last I saw him, he was attempting to talk to rockabillies, and the rockabillies were swerving away. Tapping his notebook on the bar, drinking a bottle of lager by the neck. Then he disappeared into the throng like he was part of a dream.

I can remember one last song from the jukebox. 'It'll Be Me' – Jerry Lee Lewis, piano pounding, voice threatening all sorts of violence.

Then nothing more.

7

I awoke in my bed, still in my clothes, the sheets all twisted around me, drenched in sweat and stinking like the Hop Poles' troughs. The contents of my ashtrays spilled all over the floor, shoes kicked off into different corners, posters ripped off the walls, total chaos all around.

How did I get here? I thought, clutching my pulsing head.

At least I was at home.

Upstairs the phone started ringing. I glanced at the clock, dreading what I'd see. It was 10am, Friday morning.

I heard the creak of Alan's door, his footsteps in the hall, the click of the receiver being lifted. There was a muffled response, then the fire door opening, footsteps coming down the stairs.

Oh God, here comes the payback.

I extracted myself from my tangled pit, knowing if I answered the door I would look like Medusa with her head of snakes, wearing yesterday's black trouser suit all crumpled and beer-stained. So I cowered behind the door instead, waiting for his knock.

'You in there, dear?'

'Yes, yes, just coming.'

'Phone for you.'

'Be up in a minute. Just getting decent.'

Decent. As if. There wasn't enough time in the world left for that. One thought making me smile through the grinding machinery in my head: I got my own back on Jerry at last. For once, I must have been making as much noise as he did.

I crept upstairs in bare feet, waiting for Alan to go back into his room. When I lifted the receiver, my voice came out as a dry croak: 'Hello?'

A force nine hurricane came back down the line. 'Where the fuck did you get to yesterday?'

It was Bambridge.

'Hello, Neil. Are you OK?'

'No I'm fucking not OK. I come back from the police station, expecting support, a bit of unity, and you two have gone out, left all the fucking phones ringing, all the business out of hand, me on my own, after that ordeal, managing a million phone calls all at once...'

'What did they say to you?' I moved the receiver an inch away from my ear.

'What do you care?'

'Look, Neil, I'm really sorry. It's just that Barry was really upset about Jon getting killed. He wanted to go down the pub to see his friends, you know, the firm that knew him. They were having a kind of wake in there. We should have waited for you, but it's my fault. I didn't think you'd feel like coming back, and we couldn't face working. Barry was all cut up, and I hate to see him like that.'

Neil started to relent. 'I see your point. It was a tough one on Hudson, I suppose.'

'Were they OK to you, the police?'

He sighed. 'They were civil. Just went through the tapes with me there. Don't know what they thought was on there but, honestly, it was no different from any other interview that we print. No revelations that I could see. I don't know what they were looking for, but I tell you, that Linehan gives me the creeps. He really seems to have it in for me.'

'What do you mean?' I mentally patted Linehan on the back.

'It's like he suspects me of something, even though it's plain I've got nothing to hide.'

'Well, you did copy the tapes.'

'Well, of course I did – I'm a journalist. And I don't see how it can be *sub judice* when no one's on trial. That's what *sub judice* means.'

I could see him now, poring over *Essential Law For Journalists*.

'Did they let you have them back?'

'Not for the moment. But I don't see how they can hang on to them much longer, they must have taken their own transcript by now. Anyway,' he changed the subject abruptly, 'how is Hudson? Bearing up?'

'I honestly don't know,' I said, shamed. 'I think he must have got me home last night, which I think means he's OK. We got pretty hammered in there. I can't remember leaving.'

'Ah, bit of a hangover then?' Bambridge sounded pleased.

'You could say that.'

'You coming in today?'

Jesus, no.

'Erm, well, you see, I've got that Crimewave thing tomorrow, that's going on all weekend. I've got five interviews and I wanted to prepare for them at home – got a bit of reading to do, you know.'

Another chuckle. 'I see. Well, OK, you stay there, I'll phone Hudson and make sure I get my money's worth out of him today at least.' That was Bambridge's idea of a joke. Then he became serious. 'But do me a favour, Diana. Do a bit of digging around at that conference thing you're going to. Must be a lot of people going there who knew him – see if there's any odd talk about it, will you? See if people know any more than that bastard Linehan. He can do his investigation, and I'll do mine.'

I tried not to laugh at Bambridge's pomposity. 'Yes, course I will, Neil. I'm sure there'll be a lot of people with a lot to say.'

Not that I wanted to hear any of it.

'Good. Well, you carry on then. I'll see you on Monday. But if you do hear anything in the meantime that you think I should know about, you give me a call, OK?'

'Right you are, Neil. See you Monday.'

I hung up, amazed by my own endurance and powers of

persuasion under pressure. Then I looked down, and noticed the vomit flecks on the bottom of my jacket. My stomach rolled like a tidal wave.

Back downstairs, spewing until I could only dry-heave over the splattered toilet bowl as my stomach lurched up into my throat. Sweating and sticky, I began to run a bath. Right now I didn't even care if Jerry walked in. I just needed to feel clean again.

In the cupboard in my kitchen, some Anadin Extras, thank God. My mum brought me a maximum-size bottle last time she was down, knowing I get headaches like she does, ones that go on for days and drive you up the wall. Sometimes you don't even need to drink to get them. I forced the pills down my throat with a glass of lukewarm, cloudy water.

Back in the bathroom, I peeled off my awful clothes, sank into the water's warm embrace. Ducking my head under, I tried to wash it all away. Not just the smell of stale tobacco, spilt pints and vomit. The bad memories of being dirty, the sickening fear of being vulnerable, of being out of control in public, of not knowing what had gone on. I needed soap and shampoo and more soap. Rinse it all away, send it down the plughole. I had been calm talking to Neil, but now, as I stepped into my dressing gown, realisation dawned. What I'd told him was actually true. The Crimewave was tomorrow and I didn't even have my questions ready. I had to sort myself out.

Back into my room, I threw the clothes into the laundry bag, fell back on the bed. Here my good intentions wavered. Just five minutes of sleep, I thought, just to clear my head. The next thing I knew, the phone was ringing again.

This time it was 3pm.

Feeling disorientated, I struggled up, knowing it was going to be for me. There were no other noises in the house now, no footfalls on the stair nor rattles of ancient water closets. Just the shrill, incessant ring.

It was Barry. 'You all right?' His voice was almost a whisper.

'Yes, are you?' Whispering too.

'Just about. Apart from me head, like.'

'How did I get home?'

'In a taxi, with me. You staggered in all right.'

'I was sick everywhere and I don't remember a thing.'

'Good girl.'

'Bambridge getting his money's worth?'

'I should cocoa. He's been on the phone to a load of Yanks today, wheeler-dealing. I can't really concentrate, tell you the truth. Just wanted to make sure you were OK.'

'Yes, I'm fine. I'd better do some work.'

'OK. See you soon. Love ya.'

'Love you too.'

I padded back downstairs in that strange interzone state of having slept too much but not well enough. There was no sign of Jerry, just the eerie stillness of an empty house. I put the kettle on, brewed myself up a big pot of coffee. Scratching around for food, I found some bread and shoved it into the toaster. Piled everything on to a tray – coffee, milk, toast, marge and Marmite – then returned to my pit.

As soon as I bit into the first slice of toast, I was suddenly ravenous. I wished it was a fry-up instead, but I couldn't face going out in the daylight to the caff around the corner to get one. That would mean running the gamut of builders yakking: 'Cheer up, luv! It may never happen!'

I drank more coffee instead, then attempted to clear up my room. Everything happened in hangover slow-motion, until my clock read 5.10pm. Right, I thought, I really must do this now.

Sitting down at my typewriter, wearing my dressing gown like a comfort blanket, I typed:

Twenty questions for Luther Lang.

Twenty questions for Kay McLachlan.

Twenty questions for Jack Hall.

My fingers flew over the keyboard. Questions came out of nowhere. Somehow I always worked really well like this, when

I was fucked; like something took me over, bypassing my brain and coming down through my fingertips instead. I didn't deserve it, but it happened. I couldn't be bothered with Susie Beck, I'd just busk that one. She'd only be the type to whittle on for an hour about nothing anyway. That only left Simon Everill. So I'd better finish reading his book. Flopping back on the bed with it, I opened the page where I left it and started to read…

> Mum came out of her private room and straight away she didn't look right. Her hair was all out on end and her housecoat was torn right across the chest. She had blood runnin' down her nose an' black rings around her eyes. First I didn't know what looked worse. Her old udders hangin' out where that housecoat was ripped, all covered in bite-marks and burns. Or the smell that come off her, that ashtray smell had become more like a dustbin, overflowin' with rotten old booze an' a thousand million fag ends, an' spit and spew, an' somewhere in there a horrible sweetness that reeked of death. An' somethin' worse. I see her eyes; all blank, dead, empty. Black holes in her face what don't reflect no light at all, like burnholes they were, goin' deeper than the skin, deeper than a river. An' she's singin', like, a funny little tune what really isn't a tune, and the words are all mumbled and hummy.

Everill's book got creepier and more horrific. Weirdo's sister Mong wandered off one day and fell into some farm machinery. She got baled and wrapped in twine while the farmer's son was off smoking a fag.

Weirdo related this fact in a curiously detached manner, like it didn't really affect him, his mind contained by the thought of shape-shifting into the boy who fed the ducks. One day he spoke to the little boy, and to his astonishment, the duck child didn't seem to mind that Weirdo lived on the caravan on the farm. He let him share the bread and feed the ducks, teaching him which were mallards and which were teal, pointing out the shy coots and moorhens as they darted in and out of the reeds.

Meanwhile, more and more bikers grunted their way up to the van. Maybe as a result of this ritual afternoon debasement, Mary began speaking in tongues. Despite all this, there was a frightening absence of teachers, social workers, police, clergy, concerned villagers or anyone else to look out for these children.

The farmer, who was so horrified by the baling incident he could no longer stand having this family of inbreds on his land, began to use the presence of the Hell's Angels to warn Weirdo's mum that she couldn't stay if she continued to entertain such lowlife on his property. He said it to assuage his guilt because, although his hands were far from clean, he could not intervene with this brood, fearing a malevolence there that was beyond his comprehension.

Weirdo's mum was too drunk to take any of this in.

Jake tricked Fists into peering into a septic tank to see the 'blue goldfish'. He pushed him, closed the lid in and ran away. As nobody bothered looking for the hated bully, there he stayed and rotted. Jake ran off himself after that – some gypsies camped nearby and he followed, his Romany blood calling. The pikeys knew he was one of their own and took him gladly, away from hell in the corner of a neglected field.

After this, Weirdo lost his ability to shift. Feeling his imagination deserting him, he could no longer bear to meet up with the duck boy. On a freezing Christmas Eve, while their mother thrashed and groaned with another oily charmer, Weirdo and Mary found a bottle of brandy and what Mary thought were communion wafers left unguarded in the pigsty of the van's 'front room' and decided to ask Jesus' help.

They took their holy host into the iron-cold fields, drank the brandy and let the 'wafers' dissolve on their tongues. As the acid kicked in, they were horrified to see the Messiah, his crown of thorns dug into his matted head, his hands and feet trailing blood, walk white and glowing towards them, his eyes full of terrible compassion they could not bear to look upon. The children fled, crying and screaming, across the ploughed soil to hide in the hay barn, the only place that offered warmth and sanctuary on a perversely horrific re-enactment of the First Night.

No shepherds for them. No wise men either.

After that, neither child could speak. But they didn't have long left to endure their silent torment. The farmer, kindly waiting until Boxing Day to do so, served an eviction order on Weirdo's mum and threatened that he and 'his boys' would help them to pack if they couldn't manage it sooner than tomorrow.

An' at first I think she must be sleep walkin', she's in a right old state, in't she, this time. An' she kind of drift over to Mary's bunk, still hummin' that watery tune, an' I see her take up a pillow an' I think: 'Cor, bloody hell, what's she doin' now?' An' she puts the pillow over Mary's face an' I'm thinkin: 'No mum, that's not what you're supposed to do with pillows, that don't make a lot of sense now do it, you're gonna stop her from breathin' you carry on doin' that.' An' then I realise that is what she's doin', she's murderin' my sister, poor little Mary, the only one I loved, the only one I got left.

An' I try to scream, like, or even move to stop her, but nothin' come out of my mouth an' I try to stretch out my arm but it won't move, like in one of them dreams when you're tryin' to run through quicksand. An' I realise my tracksuit bottoms are gettin' all warm, like, I realise I'm pissin' myself, lyin' there in bed an' I can't bloody move, an' that hummin' sound is gettin' louder, an' with it come other sounds, like a gurglin' noise an' I see Mary's little hands, they're like flappin' an' her legs are kickin' an' mum is singin' louder and louder and louder to her. I can't believe it, I must be makin' it up, I must be dreamin', but no, it's goin' on and on and Mary's legs are kickin' an' her hands are flappin' and them noises like an animal dyin', they keep goin' on and on and why can't I move? Why can't I stop my stupid fuckin' mother? She's gone completely barmpot, she's singin' an' I can't bear it, an' when at last Mary's legs stop kickin' an' her hands flop down I see my mother turn her head slowly round and she's smilin' right at me. Her teeth are all busted an' broken and blood's runnin' all over her face like one great big gapin' hole, an' she's singin' and she start walkin' toward me...

Weirdo's mother knew the game was up. In a zombie-like trance, she smothered her children and took their small bodies down to the river, where she tossed them over the bridge, the place where Weirdo had fed the ducks.

She followed them in.

And as he hit the icy currents, Weirdo finally did shift into the little boy, and watched himself floating past as he fed the ducks on the river bank.

I stared at the last page for about half an hour. It had gone midnight when I'd finished reading, so sucked into Everill's world I hadn't noticed time passing, whether Jerry was in next door, or that my tears had smudged some of the pages of the proof.

I finally put it down, set the alarm, put the light out, and fell fast asleep.

That night I dreamed I was lying on a tomb in a Victorian gothic cemetery, while a man who looked like Neil slowly drained all my blood through a plastic tube protruding from my neck. I couldn't move for fear.

8

The next morning's papers had two faces splashed across their covers: Jon Jackson, grinning, outside the NFT, on his last night on earth. Next to Niall Flynn, caught at the entrance to the Groucho Club, shielding his eyes with a paper, shaking a fist at the photographer.

A sudden heatwave had hit the capital. It was all blue skies and red death and, as my tube rattled towards Charing Cross, I wasn't the only one caught short in their winter coat.

I read the headlines sweating in fake fur, my bag heavy with tapes, notebooks, biogs and books resting uncomfortably on my knees. It was all too much, too early in the day. I folded my paper up, shoved it back inside my bag, and concentrated instead on the ICA schedule.

As I crunched up the Mall, figures were already swarming outside the Institute foyer, all of them waving newspapers, locked in animated discussion. I kept my head down, slid through to the front desk, to sign in and receive my own laminated pass. I was surrounded by publishers, publicists, journalists, a posse of half-familiar Kray Klones and a smattering of the authors themselves. All of them were talking about one thing and one thing only: what had happened to Jon Jackson.

I kept my head down, my eyes on the itinerary. Finally, the doors opened and everyone filed into the cinema for the forum to begin.

A curious hush fell upon the assembly as a lone figure walked to centre stage and picked up the mike. It was Bill Beauford, *Guardian* critic and London's Mr Crime. A tall, upright, stern-looking middle-aged man with crinkly grey hair and heavy horn-rimmed glasses perched over a drinker's nose. His tweed three-piece suit and yellow bow tie were all neat and buttoned up despite the heat, and his face was set in the grim folds of a preacher with bad news to share.

'As you are all aware,' he intoned sombrely, 'a great tragedy has befallen our world this week. A great young talent, taken from us in the most brutal of ways, just as he was setting out on what surely was only the beginning of a remarkable career. I am talking, of course, of Jon Jackson.

'A man responsible not only for reinvigorating British cinema, but British crime fiction itself with his remarkable debut film *Bent*. Jackson turned the focus of the world back on to our capital when all eyes had for so long been focused on America. He created excitement, a wave of followers,' the watery hazel eyes behind the thick lenses swept across the assembled Klones, 'and he gave our industry a massive boost at a time when, let's face it, things were frankly dull.

'I'm sure that all of you, like me, are shocked and horrified by the manner of this young man's death. Shocked and horrified too by the press's implications that this was the act of a maniac, so obsessed by Jackson's art that the boundaries between fact and fiction blurred. That, in some terrible way, Jackson was responsible for his own horrendous end. Responsible for...' Beauford drew back, holding on to that pause for maximum impact, before hissing the dread words '...encouraging violence.'

Across the packed auditorium came the crinkling sound of *Guardian*s pressed to panicking hearts.

'If that were the case,' Beauford now boomed, 'then we are all, in this room, responsible for murder.'

He reeled himself back in, spoke his next words in level tones.

'Of course, that is nonsense. It is not my intention, however, to provoke some vast political debate today, although none of us can afford to be complacent when the Rightist elements of the press seize on these matters. No. Today,' he continued, removing his glasses and wiping some moisture from his eyes with a large white handkerchief, 'I merely want to pay tribute to the life and the gifts of Jon Jackson. And it is also the intention of the organisers, and all the participants, of the 1992 ICA Crimewave, to dedicate this year's event to his memory.'

A loud round of applause greeted this statement, and Bill stood there, satisfied. 'Thank you all,' he acknowledged. 'And now, without further ado, I would like to introduce the writers for our inaugural panel discussion, American versus British crimewriting, and our guest of honour, Mr Luther Lang.'

More relieved clapping followed as the bad lads themselves took to the stage, led by the enormous Lang. The rest of the lads, in fact, didn't look so bad by comparison. Representing Britain was a middle-aged bloke who resembled a used-car salesman, and a much younger man I didn't recognise. He was tall, skinny, pulling on a cigarette. For America, behind Lang, was a mixed-race guy from Los Angeles who was currently being hailed as the black Raymond Chandler. Which must have been nice for him. They arranged themselves in a semicircle, two factions facing each other, all of them wired for sound. Beauford, as the compère, had to circle the tigers and prod them into a little controversy.

Well, the Yanks clearly had the muscle.

Lang was a great hulk of a man, biceps the size of bolsters covered in jailhouse tattoos, and a wide, stoic, crushed-about face. His hair was clipped, Marine-style, and from his top lip bristled a big grey moustache that no one, but no one would ever make Village People jokes about.

Luther was my literary hero. His writing was as immense as his frame: great seething tales of the American misfit – the carnival huckster, the hyperbolic street preacher, the outlaw mystic. He had been in prison most of his life, cheek-to-jowl with his fictional creations, and he conjured them so powerfully you could smell their breath, taste their paranoia, as they stalked through his pages.

He chose his words equally carefully today, taking his lead

from Beauford: 'Before we begin this discussion, I just want to extend my deep sympathies to the family and friends of the late Mr Jackson at this terrible time.' His voice was a sombre rumble.

'And I'd like to add something here to what Bill has been saying, about why y'all are here. And you can take this from an expert: there has never been any recorded evidence that any person has committed any crime because of what he saw at the cinema or read in a book.

'Likelihood is, most kids get into trouble ain't never read a book. They got parents, or a parent, that don't give a damn about 'em – don't talk to 'em, don't pay attention to 'em, leave 'em to make their own entertainment. Most kids locked up are there because no one cared to give 'em a moral centre. Not their parents, not society, not no one. Y'all know that cliché that society gets the criminals it deserves? Undoubtedly true.

'This is the way I came up,' he sighed, 'through the Belly of the Beast, as my fellow "prison writer" Jack Henry Abbott put it. This is the America I bring to you in my books. And the real psychos in the joint, your Henry Lee Lucases, your Ted Bundys, way I see it, they come up two ways.

'This here person is a fella had somethin' gone wrong in him a long ways back. His folks coulda had somethin' to do with that – Henry Lee got messed about with while he was a little bitty kid, an' ole Henry started his career on his own dear mom. However, you take someone like Ted Bundy. His folks were decent, white-collar people, he didn't see no hardship like Henry did, there's just somethin' plain wrong with that guy from the get-go. A *psych-o-path*,' he strung the word out, felt its weight on the audience's psyche, 'cannot relate to the world the way normal folks do. It's like they're kinda flat; they don't have emotions as such, they have to learn behaviour from observin' how other folks react – when to be angry, when to be sad. They sure don't connect to anythin' like love. Scientists now, they reckon it's all to do with the frontal lobe,' he tapped his own balding cranium for emphasis. 'This bit here don't get enough stimuli early in life. It don't develop properly, and that there's the part of your brain that controls your emotions. You don't have enough, you don't relate to anyone else.

'Now, this copycat killer, whatever you wanna call him, either he's been in trouble a lot of times before, or this murder's somethin' he's been buildin' up to for quite some time. I would hazard a guess that this is someone who knew the victim real well, had planned out precisely what he was gonna do, and carried it out for some psychosexual reason that was tied in with what he saw as vengeance.

'Y'all'll see if I'm wrong,' he shrugged, 'but I wouldn't wager on it goin' any other way.'

There was hushed reverence from audience and panel alike.

'Which kinda neatly brings me to the American way of life,' Luther smiled wryly. 'Death. Death, corruption, bootleggin', slavery. You name me a place that does it bigger, better. You can't, right?

'In America, crime fiction is the voice of the immigrant, the downtrodden, the guy at the bottom of the social ladder. And believe me, there are so many rungs in our goddamn Land of the Free it's kinda like a fire escape that leads the whole way down into hell...'

I sat mesmerised while Luther wove spells in the air with his mellifluous Texan tones, a voice with the same sort of gravity as the one that says, 'Hi, I'm Johnny Cash'. A voice that would flatten corn as it passed over the land.

He was certainly flattening the opposition.

So who will be bold enough to prosecute for Blighty?

The one I didn't recognise. The one I had a date with later.

Alone on the Brit side, Mr Simon Everill seemed completely at ease. He was probably digging the irony that he actually was a young British writer, whereas his fellow nouveau noir panellist would never see 45 again.

He was dressed, naturally, in black, with close-cropped pale brown hair, a stubbly outcrop of goatee beard, and hooded grey eyes that shifted non-stop between the other speakers like an adder sliding through the grass towards a jolly summer picnic. And he just couldn't wait for his turn to come.

'You can't really compare the experience,' he announced when finally asked. Slouched back in his seat, sucking insolently on a cigarette, he probably had a degree in existentialist anti-hero technique.

'In America,' he continued, 'you have the grand stage. You have Hollywood, you have the Mob, you have, as Luther says, an entire country built on Prohibition racketeering, illegal booze and slavery. Here, we have old creepy country houses with secrets hidden under the floorboards, tatty seaside towns and the faded sunset over the Empire. Little old ladies solving crimes that are crossword puzzles. The killers are all thwarted office workers, or maybe failed actors, but not the kind that would have been hand-picked by Howard Hughes.'

This raises a chuckle from the panellists and audience alike.

'But what you can't do,' he paused and leaned forward in his seat, so that his cigarette smoke swirled around him, 'what you really can't do… is transpose the car chase from *Bullitt* through Tottenham High Road.'

This was squarely aimed at his fellow Brit, Paul Carver, who set all his novels in norf Lahndan. The target responded with the maximum retaliatory force it had been primed for. 'If you want to be fucking boring you can't,' he exploded in a mushroom cloud of fag ash. 'The reason all American hardboiled is great, and all English tea-and-sympathy is fucking boring is because of narrow-minded fuckers like you.'

Eloquent to the last.

'I love *Bullitt*!' he spluttered, steaming up his brown-tinted aviator shades, 'I love car chases! I love shooters! I love birds with big tits and bad attitudes and I'm gonna write all about them! Fuck you!'

'Thank you, Mr Carver.' Beauford swiftly stepped in, perfect Englishman to the last. 'Shall we move on to the next panellist?'

◆

Luther Lang was no disappointment. Face-to-face, he was like some monument forged from nature; the Grand Canyon in chinos and an open-necked shirt.

My questions forgotten, I just sat there, staring into that craggy visage as he laid out his agenda, spun me his yarns. His Texas way of talking was just mesmerising: old-fashioned, respectful, yet wholly expressive.

'It's the Southern law of civility ma'am,' he told me with a smile. 'We all got guns there, so we don't need to act rude.'

Interview over, he stood up and winked at me. I shook a hand the size of a shank of lamb, bid my farewell and wandered, with that strange, inbred journalistic instinct, over to the bar.

There was a conspiratorial huddle propping up said edifice. As per usual for these dos, it was a frenzied orgy of backslapping and stabbing, everybody sucking up to everyone else while sizing up any visible signs of slippage down the greasy pole of notoriety. TV series? On LWT? Not bad. Did you hear about my phone call from David Lynch?

Today, the mob of perennially bubbling-under authors seemed to be aligning themselves with Paul Carver, lucky recipient of his own forthcoming TV serialisation, hoping that the Midas touch would rub off on them.

All except for Simon Everill.

He was lounging, some distance back from the fray, long limbs sprawled all over his chair, smiling to himself as his ever-moving eyes scanned the room and everybody in it. I could see what Everill was doing. He was laughing at them.

I wanted to approach him but somehow I didn't dare. I just watched him, and smiled too.

My time came later in the day. At 5.30, Lucy led me to a little room at the back of the press office, a little room where Simon Everill continued to lounge and smirk. I took one look and knew I wasn't in for an easy ride.

He was edgy.

He was slippery.

His lanky frame moved around in his designer chrome and pine chair, making the thing look frankly uncomfortable. He wasn't still for a moment. Long legs thrown over the arm of his seat one minute, long fingers scratching around his stubble the next. His curious eyes held the same shifting quality as they had had onstage, only up close it was much more unnerving. Like the reflections of heavy clouds over a still pool, they met mine only briefly before rolling on.

'What fascinates you about criminals and crime?' I began.

The chair teetered on three spindly legs.

'That's an original question.' His top lip curled. 'How long did it take you to come up with that?' He smiled nastily and continued rocking.

My heart dropped like a stone. Shit, I thought, is he this harsh to everyone? But I kept a smile plastered to my face as I tried to think of something more interesting to say. 'OK then. There's a very strong sense of place in your novel. The isolated rural community. You're obviously speaking from experience, aren't you?'

'Ah, the good old village in the middle of nowhere.' He laced his fingers. 'Where everyone knows each other's business but never minds their own.'

'Where was your particular middle of nowhere?'

The hoods over his cloudy eyes grew deeper. 'Does it matter? It would be the same in any village in any part of this country.'

I tried to shake off the impression that he was looking straight into my mind by attempting to place his accent. It was vaguely northern, the rounded vowels suggesting Yorkshire. Peter Sutcliffe, Donald Neilson, Ian Brady and Myra Hindley – a lot of queer folk in those dark hills. The sort of place that would give a young boy a lot of nightmares to dwell on.

'What is it about these people, then?'

'These people?' He looked at me like he was regarding an imbecile.

I could feel my hands start to shake. I'd never been very good at direct confrontation. 'The people who don't mind their own business. The bad guys in your book.'

He leaned forwards. 'Ah, the bad guys.'

Was he going to just repeat everything I said? But no, suddenly he was on a roll. 'They go to church and they gossip about the local fallen women afterwards. They smoke and drink but they go on and on about the horrors of drugs and what are these young people coming to? They smile at their neighbours while they size up their assets and smugly commend themselves on having better taste. It's what I said earlier about the secrets under the floorboards, the twitching net curtains. And if you're ever, ever different from them, they will make your life hell.'

'That's why your book is called *Weirdo*? Is it personal experience?'

He met my eyes properly for the first time.

'Sort of.' The chair rocked steadily. He retreated back to silence, looked down at his watch.

I felt sudden elation drain just as abruptly away. He'd foiled me. He wasn't going to give anything away. But I wasn't going to stop trying. 'So, how much of it is personal?'

'That's immaterial.' He shot me a look that plainly said: 'Shut the fuck up.'

What he actually said was: 'It's what you get out of the story that counts.' His thin lips curled into a semblance of a smile that never reached his eyes. 'And what did you get out of my story, Diana?'

The way he said my name almost made me shit.

'That small towns are very spooky places,' I mumbled pathetically.

He was looking into my head. I didn't like it.

'Which was just what I've said.'

The pause that followed was excruciating. I struggled for some kind of rejoinder, some kind of way to burst that arrogant, all-too-knowing veneer.

'But doesn't everyone come from a small town really?' I finally squeaked, despising my own meekness. 'I've never met anyone in London who actually comes from London.'

'That's the good thing about them,' Everill considered, throwing me an unexpected lifeline. 'It gives you something to escape from.'

'True. I totally agree.'

'And something to work with.'

I felt like a ruptured balloon as I heaved my heavy way back to the bar.

Well, that was a right royal fuck-up, and no mistake.

Tired of my day-long, goody-two-shoes orange juice routine, I ordered a pint, took it to a corner as far away from everyone else as possible and crashed down at a table. Was he completely arrogant, or am I just a crap interviewer? I wondered savagely to myself, lighting a fag and throwing the match into the ashtray as if it had personally offended me.

I took my crushed-up paper out of my bag and pretended to survey it, head down, elbows on the table, hands in my hair, trying to form a barrier between myself and the raucous guffaws still emanating from Paul Carver's side of the bar. Now I knew how it felt to be stitched up by the crime-writing equivalent of Johnny Rotten. Suddenly, a voice beside me said gently: 'You all right, Di?'

I look up, blinking. It was Peter Reid, a small-press publisher, whose dedicated imprint was testament to his second mortgage-busting determination to put out his favourite authors, whatever the cost.

I really liked Peter, admired his tenacity, and most of his writers too.

'I've just had a run-in with Simon Everill,' I admitted, motioning for him to sit down, which he did, plonking his flagon of real ale down so that it splashed all over my paper.

He didn't notice and I was past caring.

'Aha! The boy wonder,' he nodded. 'Making a bit of a show of himself, is he?'

'Making a show of everyone else more like,' I grunted. 'That was just about the worst interview I've ever done.'

'Well, he made Carver look like a right twat,' considered Reid. 'Which is always to be applauded.'

He raised his glass in the general direction of the noise and took a foaming gulp. Another reason I liked Peter. He always made me laugh.

'Where does he come from, Pete?' I asked him. 'Everill, I mean. Anyone ever heard of him before?'

'Fucked if I know,' Reid admitted, and it was an admission for him. He was normally the first for any gossip, real or made up. 'Think he came out of nowhere, don't know who found him. Hard Ball are keeping completely shtumm about it too, and Christ knows, I've tried. Wish the bugger had sent me his book first, it's fucking dynamite. I could do with some sales, I tell you.'

I nodded my agreement. 'They didn't have a biog for him,' I told Peter. 'And there's fuck all you can get out of him about where he came from either. It's weird.'

'Sounds like he's from up North,' Reid noted. 'But he's not from Lancashire, I can tell you that much. Never heard an accent like that up there. Maybe Yorkshire…'

'That's what I thought.'

'By way of Johnny Rotten.'

I couldn't help laughing out loud. 'What I thought too.'

Another figure approached our table.

'All right, you two?'

Another small publisher, but a more successful one. Ryan Smith's Short Fuse had star authors and American connections aplenty.

'All right, Ryan,' said Peter heartily. 'We're just discussing that mouthy one, Everill, the boy wonder. What do you know about him?'

Ryan placed a briefcase on one chair, himself on the other, while disentangling himself from a number of carrier bags.

'Nothing, actually,' he said. 'No one does. Not even his publishers, I think.'

'Gonna make a lot of money, though, no doubt,' said Peter wistfully.

'You finished for the day?' Ryan asked.

'Certainly am,' I nodded. 'My last interview, with that Everill, was a disaster. I feel like drowning my sorrows.'

'I've done all my touting for one day,' agreed Peter. 'Sun's over the yardarm now.'

''Cos I tell you what. I've got Kay McLachlan meeting me here in a minute. I was going to take her down the Deansgate, get away from the meat market a while. You're welcome to join us – you're interviewing her tomorrow, aren't you, Di? May be good to have a chat first?'

'I'd love to,' I smiled, warming quickly to the idea. 'Thanks.'

'Right you are, lad,' said Peter, draining his ale. 'Even if they do serve a poncy selection of bottled lager down there.'

The Deansgate. The vortex of the social whirl. The last known sighting of…

Fuck it, I thought. Bring it on.

9

It was not what I expected, the Deansgate Club.

Anywhere that major celebrities would hang out, I anticipated to be like the Groucho – big, ostentatious, full of coke-bingeing, loud-mouthed arseholes. No, the Deansgate was something else entirely.

Ryan pressed a buzzer on a well-concealed doorway, at the Shaftsbury Avenue end of Dean Street. A homeless Scouser was sharing the doorspace. He joked with us while we emptied our change into his hands, until a velvety male voice answered the intercom: 'Push the door, darling.'

Down a narrow, steep set of steps, dark green walls, lined with ancient theatre posters, into a tiny part of Soho that time had, thankfully, forgotten.

It was a little cellar, with a minute bar and leather-upholstered booths around tables with candles on them, all surrounded by a very un-celebrity-looking bunch of people, who obviously preferred to be heard and not seen. Actors' professional photographs hung from every available space, along the walls, above the bar. The air was alive with chatter that had reached the pitch where it sounds like waves; waves forming one loud, prolonged upper-class vowel: O.

Roy Orbison, the Big O, was in the air too, singing 'It's Over'. A bunch of men propping up the bar, waving large gin and tonics in even larger fists, attempted to sing along. They sounded like stray dogs in an alley, howling at the moon.

I was enchanted. It was perfect. It was another secret world.

Ryan was at the bar, ordering drinks. The man with the

velvety voice, the proprietor, sported a perfect white helmet of hair, matching beard and moustache. He introduced himself, his handshake smooth, his smile crinkling in his eyes: 'Hello, darling.'

Not wanting to look like a first-timer, I ask for a gin and tonic. Peter moaned in the background about the bottled Becks.

We found a table in the corner, next to an upright piano and a set of drums. 'Wait until later.' Ryan nodded in the direction of the instruments. 'They'll start up on all that, make a right old racket.'

'Yeah.' Peter nudged me, enjoying the joke. 'And all the old people will start waltzing.' Kay McLachlan, small, dark and vivacious, laughed her approval. 'What a fuckin' briiilliant place, Ryan. I cannae believe it. Have we fallen through some time tunnel or wha'?'

Kay McLachlan was hilarious. She kept up a steady stream of entertaining invective about all the other writers at Crimewave, interspersed with anecdotes about vicious women killers, comparing them to a couple of brazen blondes at the bar, tapping wobbling but well-heeled old men for a steady supply of free champagne. I laughed along with her, knowing that, at least, my next interview would be a good one.

An elegant-looking black man took to the piano and cooked up some jazz with a saxophonist friend and a little, stocky drummer. Just as Peter predicted, people started to waltz around in the tiny amount of available floorspace.

All at once, Kay and Peter headed for the lavs, while Ryan went up to the bar. Momentarily alone, I scanned the room. There were some priceless charmers in here. A fop like something out of P. G. Wodehouse brayed loudly to a small, agitated-looking chap in a safari suit. A long-haired Lord Byron sketched people's caricatures at the bar. The Roy Orbison singers attempted to drink each other into the ground while shrieking about the amount of property they owned.

'I've got FIVE houses!' the largest of them was bellowing.

And suddenly, I nearly jumped out of my skin. A pair of eyes were boring into me from the corner of the next table.

It looked like that actor, Niall Flynn.

It couldn't be.

But it was.

He couldn't be looking at me – could he?

As if to answer this unspoken question, the man lurched out of his seat, weaving unsteadily towards me. He was clearly pissed, but his eyes remained fixed on me. He extended a long bony finger and asked:

'Where the hell have you been, girl?'

'I'm sorry,' I stammered, looking into eyes as menacing as those of the screen ganglord Marley. 'I think you must have the wrong person.'

He sat down anyway, on the chair opposite, Peter's seat. 'God forgive me, so I have.' His voice was beautiful, his eyes terrible. He was shaking and he looked like he'd been crying non-stop for a week. His white hair stuck out at all angles. 'You can't be her, you're not Irish. But you look so much like her, Emily Davey.' He grabbed my hand, looked straight into my eyes. 'God forgive me, darlin', what's your name?'

'It's D-Diana,' I stuttered. 'Diana Kemp.'

'Diana, you're a beautiful girl and I'm a wretched old man,' he said. 'Will I get you a drink?'

I looked up to see Ryan standing behind him with a handful of glasses. Behind him, the landlord, looking concerned.

'It's all right,' I said, 'my friend is just bringing me one.'

'Are you all right, darling?' The landlord's hands were now on Flynn's shoulder. He was looking more concerned for me.

Flynn spun round, grabbed the landlord by the hand. 'Oh Gerry O'Brian, you're a fine man, now tell me, does she not look like Emily Davey?'

'Darling, Emily Davey would be sixty years old by now,' said the landlord gently. 'Come over to the bar and let me get you a drink. This young lady is with her friends. Come on, Niall.'

Flynn staggered to his feet, started weeping on Gerry O'Brian's shoulder. The landlord looked at me and said: 'Sorry, darling. But you know what he's been through.'

Who didn't?

'Getting them all today, Di,' noted Peter, eyebrows raised, reclaiming his seat. 'You're a nutjob magnet, love.'

We finally staggered out of the Deansgate Club at nearly 2am. As we went back up the steps, I couldn't help but look back and notice Niall Flynn, still swaying at the bar, fixing me with those tragic eyes, as if I had personally stabbed him through the heart. He raised his glass of champagne to toast me and screamed across the crowded room:

'God love you, Emily Davey. I'll always love you too.'

Of course, Ryan and Peter couldn't wait to relive the moment when I caught up with them in the ICA foyer, round about ten the next morning.

'What was that all about?' Peter demanded straight off.

'What, that actor?' I didn't want to say his name out loud.

'Yeah, Niall Flynn,' Peter boomed, 'was he off his head or what?'

'I don't know.' I was painfully aware of the earwigs this last comment has attracted. 'I think he thought I was somebody else.'

'So Emily Davey isn't your real name then?' Peter started, then clutched his head. 'Oooh, that bottled lager, I can't be doing with it.'

'Poor bastard,' said Ryan, but not meaning Peter. 'It must have done his head in, what happened to Jackson. I mean, he was in the wilderness before that film came out.'

'Imagine if the poor sod had had to sit through Beauford's speech an' all,' Peter added sagely. 'Not that Bill was sponsored by the *Guardian* to say all that, oh no. Still,' he dropped the sarcasm for a minute, thoughtfully adjusted his balls in his brown elephant cords, 'it's got to be a worry for him, that killer still being out there. Maybe he thinks he's next.'

'God, Pete, don't go all *Texas Chainsaw Massacre* on me,' said Ryan.

Luckily, their banter was suddenly interrupted by the arrival of the ever brisk and beaming Lucy.

'Sorry to interrupt,' she broke in, 'but we're changing one of our panel discussions today. You know what Bill was saying yesterday, about the pro-censorship elements of the press having a field day over the Jackson murder...'

'Yes love,' Peter put on his most concerned, angelic face. 'We were only just discussing that. Dead right he was, dead right.'

'I'm so glad you think so.' Her auto-beam smile was as dazzling as the headlights of an oncoming juggernaut. 'Because have you seen this?'

She brandished a copy of the *News of the Screws*. The front cover headline screamed:

JACKSON KILLER WAS FILM NUT, SAYS TOP SHRINK

'I've suggested we discuss the relationship of art with violence, and I've got all the major papers to attend. I've got Gareth Davies, who is a criminologist, Shaun Turner, who set up Jon Jackson's *Guardian* lecture, and George Dickinson, who was one of Scotland Yard's leading criminal psychologists until his retirement last year.'

'So he's better than their bloke, then?' Peter prodded the 'top shrink' headline.

'Obviously,' she said. 'Now, would either of you two,' she glanced brightly at Ryan, then more grudgingly at Peter, 'be up for joining in?'

It was my opportunity to lose the piss-takers for a while. Remembering my professional duties, I swiftly made my way to the phone by the toilets, dialled Neil's home number.

'Ah, Diana. Any progress?'

'Well, something interesting's going on here later,' I said, and told him about the panel. 'That old boy from Scotland Yard sounds like he'll know what he's talking about. But everyone's gone conspiracy-theory mad. I think you should come down and witness it for yourself.'

'Yes, excellent, thanks for the tip-off.' He sounded thrilled, as I knew he would. 'How do I get in?'

That's how they stay rich. They never willingly pay for anything.

'Meet me in the foyer at one,' I said. 'You can use my laminate. They won't check it, they never do. I'll meet you in the bar after.'

'Excellent, Diana. Thank you for this.'

'Oh, and Neil. Don't forget to buy Britain's Brightest Sunday on your way down here. It's what's got them all stoked up.'

'Right you are.'

Next I called Barry. He was much more up on his film facts than me.

'What do you know,' I asked him, 'about Niall Flynn?'

'What, before he was in *Bent*?'

'Yeah,' remembering Gerry O'Brian's line: Emily Davey would be sixty years old by now.

'When he was famous the first time round.'

'Why do you ask?'

'If I told you, you probably wouldn't believe me.'

'Go on.'

'I met him last night. Got taken to the Deansgate Club by a couple of the publishers here. He was down there and he went mental when he saw me. He thought I was someone called Emily Davey.'

'Emily Davey, that rings a bell,' Barry's voice crackled down the line. 'She was that actress from the 1960s, young British starlet. She was in a couple of films with him, let me think now... *The Slaves of Solitude* and *Next Door To Danger*, I think. He's right, you know. She did look a bit like you...'

'Great.' That's all I needed. 'Did he shag her?'

'Probably. Reckon he shagged half of London at the time. Tell you what, pet. I've got a couple of books I can dig out, see what I can find out about it for you.'

'Thanks.'

'How's it going, anyway?'

I told him about the sudden developments from the anti-censorship lobby. He sighed. 'Rather you than me, pet.'

'Well, rather Neil than either of us.'

'You're not wrong there.'

'Better go, I've got Kay McLachlan in ten minutes. She was there last night. No doubt I'll get a ribbing off her too.'

But thankfully, Kay hadn't a clue who Niall Flynn was, just took him for a typical Soho drunk. We rattled through our interview pleasantly, reiterating most of what we had talked about the night before. I traded phone numbers with her as the interview ended, then schlepped back to the bar in search of sustenance – cold chicken sarnies, a strong coffee and a discarded copy of this morning's *Screws*.

I met Neil in the foyer at the appointed hour. He was waving his copy of the same paper, and couldn't snatch my laminate from me fast enough.

There was an hour to kill before I met him again. It was still beautiful outside, the freak heatwave carrying on unabated, so I decided to go for a walk. Out into the sunshine, across the Mall and into St James's Park. Plenty of people were taking advantage of the rays, colourful bodies in various states of half-dress strewn all over the grass. I picked my way through them, subconsciously making my way towards the lake in the middle of the park.

Tourists were swarming near the water, while laughing children with ice-cream-smeared faces threw bread at the resident Canada geese. I got to the water's edge and looked down the curve of the lake. Further along, a familiar figure had also found sanctuary here.

He was still wearing his black uniform, despite the heat, and was hurling stones into the centre of the pool like an angry teenager.

I felt a real surge of annoyance. You made me feel like a twat yesterday, I thought. Now it's payback time. 'Feeding the ducks,' I called out to the back of Simon Everill. 'Is that something you actually like to do?'

He spun around, startled for a second. Then he fixed me with his hooded eyes. I could see his mind ticking over, trying to place me, remembering and remembering to sneer.

'It is, as it goes,' he said. His eyes shifted over me, as if weighing me up. He took a packet of cigarettes from his leather jacket, slowly lit one up. He didn't appear to be sweating, or in any way encumbered by the heat. 'That's part of the reason I put it in the book. I used to like doing it when I was a kid. I like being with animals.'

'Why's that?' I wanted to needle him. He thought I talked in clichés, so I used the oldest cliché in the book. ''Cos they don't let you down like people?'

'Something like that.' He hurled another stone as far as he could. His eyes followed the projectile, skimming the surface of the lake.

I tried a different tack. Flattery usually worked with difficult people in the end, but this was something I really did want to know. After yesterday, it didn't seem to matter if I got a metaphorical bloody nose for asking. He could only add to the sarcasm, or he could prove to me that the person who wrote *Weirdo* was in there somewhere.

'There seems to be a lot of empathy in your book,' I remarked quietly. 'A lot of compassion.'

'You think so, do you?' he said abruptly, turning back to face me, the far-away eyes now locking straight on to target.

'It wouldn't be so powerful if there wasn't that feeling there,' I continued, staring straight back. 'It would be a gratuitous pornography of violence. And you'd have to wonder about the mind of someone who came up with it.'

Everill's eyes narrowed right down and a thin smile played on his lips. He was considering me in a way he hadn't before. I'd got him interested.

'The reason I wanted more than a few journalists to read this book,' he explained, as if addressing a small child, 'is because I wanted people to know how it feels to be invisible. An invisible man, drowning, while all around him people like this,' he gestured at the happy campers around us, 'walk on by. Don't even notice.' His voice had become almost a whisper. 'Because I have had some personal experience of feeling that way.'

A wind stirred up out of nowhere, rippling the surface of the lake. A cloud passed across the sun.

'I might feel like telling you more about it,' he said, sucking in his bottom lip, chewing on it a while. 'But not today.'

And with that, he strode briskly away from me, back across the park, through the carefree sunbathers. A tall, thin scarecrow dressed in black on the hottest day of the year.

I lit a fag and watched him go. The armour plating did have its chinks, then. The person who wrote the book was under there somewhere. And now he'd shown himself, I had to know more.

Neil had already collected an ensemble of acolytes by the time I got back. They were well into discussion on how outraged they all were by the fake newspaper shrink and the attacks of the Tory press on their liberal beliefs.

'I think we'll dedicate the next issue to it,' Neil was saying. 'Make it an anti-censorship issue.' I could just imagine what was coming next: 'It's what he would have wanted.'

'Ah, Diana, there you are,' he said, standing up and waving. 'You should have been here for that panel. You missed a real treat. But from what I've been hearing, so have I. What's all this about Niall Flynn then?'

Good news travels fast.

'Nothing, Neil, honestly.' I felt embarrassed and angry at the same time. Just as I was feeling I had some kind of breakthrough with Everill, Bambridge was about to make me the laughing stock. 'I don't know who's been saying what,' I looked him straight in the eye, 'but he was just a sad, drunk man at the bar. I think he's been through a lot, lately.'

But my sarcasm was lost on the loudspeaker who'd obviously been broadcasting his version of events to everybody.

'He thinks she's an actress called Emily Davey,' announced Peter Reid.

'Emily Davey?' said a thoughtful-looking, thin man I had never encountered before. 'Ah. Old squeeze of Flynn's she was. They made a couple of films together and I think they got engaged. But she died. Suspicious circumstances too, if I remember rightly. Jumped out of a window – or was pushed. They never quite worked out which.' The thin man, much older than the rest of the gaggle, stared hard into space, as if trying to picture the scene.

'Right, well, I think it's nearly time for my next interview, if I could have my pass back now, Neil?' I said, holding my hand out.

'Oh, you sure you haven't got time for a quick one?' He looked puzzled.

'Yes,' the thin man nodded and continued his reverie. 'They found her on the pavement, outside the Hilton, it was. Window was broken too, makes for a bit of a suspicious suicide if you ask me.'

I took my laminate back from Neil.

'D'you think it was Flynn who pushed her then?' asked Peter, clearly delighted.

'That's what the rumour was, in those days. That was why he went back to Ireland and disappeared. Out of guilt, they said.'

'I've got an interview in a minute,' I told Neil, wishing they would all shut up while the thin man was talking. 'I'll catch up with you on Monday.'

'Well, I might hang around a bit myself,' Neil said, annoyingly. 'You never know. Maybe we'll bump into each other later.'

'You want to be careful.' The thin man looked up at me. 'You want to stay away from that one, dear.' He put a paper-thin hand on my arm and looked up at me with watery eyes.

'Thank you,' I mumbled.

'Tell you what, Di,' Bambridge the bloodhound cut in, 'if the old boy fancies you so much, you should try and get an interview. He's notorious for not doing them, but if you've got special favours there you could grab us another exclusive. It would be great for our...'

'Yes, Neil, I'm sure it would.' I cut him off with a look I hoped would chill his blood. He merely raised his glass and smiled demurely.

'Jolly good. You do that. Don't take too long about it.'

I stumbled off to my next interview, still feeling the thin man's touch.

Susie Beck was as boring as I had anticipated. The ganglady had French manicured nails, a Louis Vuitton handbag and long, honey-blonde hair that she flicked around self-consciously as she droned on. Channel 4 were really interested in her, apparently, because she was breaking such barriers. Wasn't it funny, she giggled, how all the other women crime writers she'd met were lesbians.

I didn't bother to even turn on the tape.

But it hadn't ended up all bad. The last interview with Jack Hall was hilarious. Being about the only openly gay male crime writer in the country, he had especially liked Susie Beck's ignorant comments about dykes, and had added to them a selection of his own fantasies on the secret homosexuality of Paul Carver and Bill Beauford. Like Luther Lang, all you had to do with Jack Hall was press play and let him get on with it. We got on so well, we ended up in the bar. Sadly, Bambridge was as good as his word, and had spent the day cultivating a new set of media friends. Within seconds of our arrival, he was all over my new friend. Jack had kudos, he had Savile Row suits, and that was the equivalent of a Belisha beacon over his head, flashing and winking at moth-like Neil.

So, at the fag end of the festivities I was left talking to Peter, the last standing drunk at the bar. And bless him, he really had tried to divert attention away from Jon Jackson at this festival. He attempted to make me the centre of all the gossip instead.

'Emily Davey!' he slurred into his pint. 'Who would have thought it?'

I thought that instead of hitting Peter with my extremely

heavy handbag, I would have one last try at extracting some useful information out of him. 'Who was that old guy at the bar earlier? The one who knew her?'

'Robin Ainsley,' he replied, the fount of all knowledge. 'He works for *Time Out*. He's been their theatre critic nigh on twenty-five year.'

'Jesus,' I said, 'so he knows what he's talking about, then?'

'Oh yes,' Peter nodded sagely. 'He's known them all, you know. Actors, artists, you name them, he's rubbed shoulders with the lot of them. Apparently his dad was a peer of the realm, worth a fucking fortune, and Robin pissed all his inheritance away in Soho with Francis Bacon and the like. Oh yes.'

His eyes were misting over, and the barman was calling time.

Bambridge came over, rubbing his hands with glee.

'Coming to the Groucho with me and Jack?'

'Neil.' I stared at him in red-eyed exhaustion. 'I've had more than enough for one weekend.'

'I should say you have,' he laughed approvingly.

'Finish your drinks, ladieeees and gennnelmen!' roared the barman.

Which was enough of a hint for me.

10

He hadn't gone back to Camden for a while after that. He had to come to terms with what he had done, to feel sure that it wouldn't happen again. So he concentrated on reading his clippings and making his plans, venturing out occasionally to check the local papers for any news of Glasgae Boab. Only the tiniest footnote for the former Terror of the Gorbals, a paragraph in the *Camden New Journal*:

> The badly decomposed body of a homeless man has been discovered by the Grand Union Canal in wasteland near the back of King's Cross Station. It is believed that the man had been murdered some time in the past few weeks but, owing to the level of decay, the pathologist could not be sure. The man has not yet been identified.

After he saw it in black and white, the panic subsided and he felt the place calling him back for more. Although his initial reasons for going there were personal, he found an unexpected upside to his investigations: he liked it. Despite its down-at-heel appearance, Camden had a carnival atmosphere that set it apart, made him feel he was really in the centre of a city that was alive, not tacked on to some suburb of endless estates and congested roads that spread into the grey infinity of London.

And it was full of music.

He had always been a one for music and throughout his teenage years his search for new sounds had led him to begin a bit of a record collection. Because there were no decent shops where he came from, he had ended up scouring the music press and *Record Collector* for dealers who had what he wanted – mainly Krautrock and psychedelia, the obscurer the better. Here it was a different matter. Not only were there countless record shops, pubs full of live bands and legendary venues like Dingwalls and the now boarded-up Roundhouse, there were stalls and stalls full of vinyl on the market. He couldn't resist riffling through the racks, and most of the stallholders were happy to shoot the breeze, talk the obsessive's language of real record collectors. Gradually, he felt his way in, shelling out now and then for something he really wanted, but actually becoming more fascinated by the traders themselves. One stall in particular really attracted him: Big Tony's Sounds for Swingers, which specialised in records from the sixties.

Tone himself was more of the magnet. A bear-shaped, second-generation Italian in his early forties, he radiated benign good cheer, and seemed to genuinely enjoy the conversations they had over his prog rock section.

Actually, Tony was impressed by the amount of knowledge held by the shy young man who kept coming back to his stall. He had been looking out for someone to give him a hand now and then, but he needed someone who was an expert – who knew what the records were worth and could up the price according to the gullibility of the punter. This fella seemed to know it all.

He also divined, from all the shows of enthusiasm and willingness to please, that here was someone who was a bit lonely and lost in this city. You can't have much else in your life, figured Tone, if you know so much about music. So, having a heart as big as his belly, he decided to take this loner under his wing, and asked if he fancied putting in a few hours now and then.

He was shocked by the trader's kindness and inordinately pleased – it was as if Camden itself was welcoming him in. There was only one awkward moment – when Tony asked the simple question, 'What's your name, by the way?'

He'd had to hesitate for a moment before he remembered someone he went to school with and vaguely liked: Andy Smith.

Afterwards, he congratulated himself of the simplicity of his choice. Only a step up from the ubiquitous John, it was bland and easy to remember. Exactly like the person he wanted to be. The work was all cash in hand anyway, so he didn't have to have any legitimate ID. Becoming Andy Smith was like a fresh start.

To Tony's pleasure, Andy was a good, uncomplaining worker, who always put the hours in and never turned up late. He didn't even mind covering for some of Tone's mates – Mitch, off the video stall, and Lee, who sold overpriced African carvings. At 6 o'clock, he would help with the packing up, shifting the boxes on trolleys down to Tone's lock-up under the railway arches.

There was a lot to discover in those arches. Some of them had been turned into cafés, some into rehearsal studios. A lot of them were used by the market traders, but at that time, a lot of them were still empty and, Big Tony warned him, not particularly safe.

'They haven't been shored up in years,' he explained. 'And they're full of rats and shit. Don't go poking around in there.'

Gradually, as Tone's bond of affection deepened with the geezer, he gave Andy a spare set of keys. And if Tony thought he'd made a good find, his protégé also knew he'd been fortunate. It was, perhaps, the happiest time he had ever known. Not only did he suddenly have some friends and a job that he actually enjoyed, but he was precisely in the place where he wanted to be.

For Camden, the many articles he had collected kept repeating, was the place his prey hung out. When you got used to London, you broke down the homogeneous mass of it into individual districts, villages almost. Camden was a showy and intriguing village, but much like any other: the longer you spent there, the smaller it got. The record stall was perfect cover. He knew it couldn't take long.

Though the first time it happened, it sent a jolt right through him. For all his careful planning, he hadn't expected to react the way he did.

The greasers from that pub were always hanging around the record stall and they really put his nerves on edge. It wasn't because he thought they'd even remember the night he'd been in with Glasgae Boab. It was because of their attitude. They had a ready affection for Tony, but they always looked at him as if they were about to burst out laughing. They reminded him of the bikers back home, the ones that used to snigger at him in the pub and bump into him on purpose to spill his beer, knowing that he'd never fight back.

One day in August, they came with a special guest.

He was checking some stock, his back to the punters, when he heard Tone exclaim, much louder than usual: 'All right, Jon? Good to see ya, mate.'

His voice resounded with pleasure.

Andy turned round slowly.

'All right, mate, how's yourself?'

The accent had changed, completely. All traces of the past wiped out in one bright Cockney chirp. But his face hadn't altered much. Those dark eyes, that big nose, that cocksure tilt of the head, like he owned the place. All present and correct. Jon Jackson was shaking hands with Big Tony, stupid big grin plastered all over his face. He was wearing a ludicrous Hawaiian shirt, bright red and white flowers all over it, obviously couldn't attract enough attention to himself. Bold as brass, in the middle of Camden market.

'Good, good,' Tone was beaming like a five-year-old. 'Well, it's all taken off for you, hasn't it?'

'Not half, mate, but I tell you what, it's good to be back in the real world.'

Jackson's magnanimous gaze swept down the back of the stall, to where Tone's assistant stood in the shadows under the tarpaulin.

Stock-still, trapped in the headlights of that gaze. Waiting for the recognition to show in the other man's eyes.

'This is me new assistant,' Tony was blithering on, oblivious.

Time was standing still for Andy Smith as he stared into those dark eyes. Falling away, like the pit of his stomach.

'Mr Jon Jackson, this is Mr Andy Smith. What he don't know about records ain't been written yet.'

'All right, Andy?'

Jackson was leaning towards him, offering him his hand.

Andy stared back, like an idiot, waiting for that foolish grin to break. Waiting for the director to see further into his icy eyes and tremble at what he saw there. Waiting for him to realise…

'Andy?' Tone swivelled round, mildly concerned now.

Nothing. Not a glimmer.

'Don't be shy, he's an old mate. He ain't forgot where he comes from.'

The big man's words couldn't have been more ironic. But they seemed to shake him out of his reverie.

'How do?' Andy's voice came out strained, like his throat was clogged. He reached his own arm over, shook hands briefly but hard. That made Jackson wince, just for a second, before he was raising his eyebrows and piling on the false platitudes as quickly as he dropped his grip.

'Nice to meet you.' His eyes darted back to Tony, who looked embarrassed.

'So you back for a while now, Jon?' The stallholder seemed equally eager to change the subject.

'Yeah, back for the rest of the year, I hope. Got more projects to work on, gotta get stuck into the new stuff, if they'll let me. It was mental in the States, I'll tell you, but they're gonna have to get along without me till the spring now.'

'Bet you picked up some good gear there though, yeah?'

'Phew,' Jackson crinkled his forehead and whistled. 'Did I ever. Had to have it all shipped back, too much to carry. Crates of good records out there…'

It was as if Andy Smith didn't exist, he thought. As if he had never existed.

Jackson and Tony gabbled on about records, rare labels, vinyl-only warehouses they had known in the USA. As they did so, the last vestiges of true happiness in Camden Town slipped away from the quiet man at the back of the stall, like the sun setting on his perfect day and darkness seeping in.

That familiar darkness, that veil of his obsession which separated him from the rest of the world, from the light-hearted chatter and silly summer clothes around him. It hardened in him then, tougher and stronger than it had been before.

'You coming down the boozer later?' said Jackson as he prepared to depart, £50 lighter from the pick of the stall's Northern soul vaults.

'You betcha!' Tone clapped his hands together. 'It's been a good day.'

'Nice one. See you later.' Jackson raised his arm to wave as he gathered his posse and turned away. A red-faced clone of himself who had been nervously hanging around the stall while they had been speaking stopped him for an autograph, which he signed with that same ready smile. As if the very aroma of fame hung heady in the air, others soon noticed, moved in on him. He had nothing but laughter and handshakes for all.

'T'riffic bloke,' said Tone admiringly, staring after him. 'Really, there's no need to be shy of him. Sound as a pound that one.'

'Seems like it.' Andy tried to make his voice sound jocular, pleased his benefactor had hold of the wrong end of the stick. 'Does he come up here often?'

'Every week, usually, only he's been doing promo in the States for the last month. Expect we'll see him regular again now.'

'That's nice.' The voice was authentic now, the enthusiasm sounded real.

Regular was good. Regular would let him get his bearings, feel out for the right moment and be prepared for it when it came.

For now, he had to concentrate on acting as normal as possible.

11

Monday morning and the office strangely deserted. Maybe it was Neil's turn to do battle with the hangover of nightmares, to reflect sombrely on all the Ponce Tax he'd paid for his night at the Groucho. Myself, I'd had a dreamless night. Woken really early with no trace of tiredness, just an urge to get in and get on with it. I unpacked my wedge of interview cassettes with a clatter on to the table.

The heatwave was over. As if the glorious sun of the weekend had drained all the city's reserves of colour, it was left to recover now in shades of monotonous grey, while the temperature dropped several degrees in sympathy. All in all, the ideal day for the laborious process of transcription.

I went for the Luther Lang tape first. I wanted to kick off with his Lucky Strike-seasoned rumble; it'd be a balm, easing me into the task until soon I'd be carried away, eager to relive the moment.

That was the funny thing about transcribing tapes. Often the conversations you'd had that left you with a real buzz would end up coming out flat, a succession of missed opportunities for diverting the talk down more interesting avenues. You'd see that you were too carried away with your own notions to notice your subject was hinting at other things. Even worse, you talked over them the minute they were about to say something really interesting. Conversely, though, the ones that seemed like a real effort at the time, or even downright dull, could throw up the sparks, make you see you had actually hit a nerve. But Luther, I knew, would be a solid bet.

Besides, I could hardly stand to listen to that Everill tape first.

And so, I was tapping away, lost in the Southern heat and dust, when Barry clattered in, an hour later.

'You're in early,' he noted, as if this was something of an anomaly.

I pressed STOP on the Dictaphone, unplugged my ears from my headphones.

'Got a lot to get on with. You wouldn't believe the weekend I've had.'

Barry raised his eyebrows.

'Oh yeah? Any more old actors throwing themselves at you?' He had a couple of plastic bags with him, and from one, he extracted a big A3 hardback black-and-white photo book. He handed it over.

British Film Noir of the Fifties and Sixties.

A Post-It note was stuck to one corner, marking a page he obviously wanted me to see. I let it flop open. A spread with one full-page photo to the right, three more stills placed horizontally to the left. The big picture was of a breathtakingly handsome young man, dressed in a US Army uniform, all razor-sharp cheekbones and a shock of black hair, greased back and shining. His left hand was raised, tilting up the chin of an equally stunning, equally raven-haired young woman, her hair dressed in a wartime roll.

'Emily Davey and Niall Flynn in *The Slaves of Solitude*,' read the caption.

I could see him now, or the echoes of him that were still left in the ravaged face I had encountered at the weekend. But to look at her in profile, even with a virtually identical hairstyle to my own and the stark make-up of the era, I couldn't see the resemblance Flynn had. She was far too beautiful.

'That one,' Barry tapped on the page opposite. You could see her full-face.

Now I got it.

The eyes, the shape of the face, it was the same. Her nose and mouth were different – the former much smaller, the latter more generous – which had made her look different in profile. It was the combination of that and her expression in this particular still.

She looked terrified.

She looked like me.

'I can see what he was getting at there,' Barry said.

'So can I,' I nodded, biting my bottom lip. 'And I found out what happened to her at the weekend.'

'Suicide,' he said.

'Maybe. Some old guy was there, who's worked for *Time Out* for twenty-five years, according to Peter Bigmouth Reid. He reckoned it was never sure whether she jumped or was pushed. And after that, Niall Flynn went back to Ireland to drown his sorrows for nearly thirty years.'

'Well, he never got nicked for it, did he?' Barry sounded doubtful. 'I wouldn't pay it too much attention, pet, they were probably winding you up.'

I considered this statement for a moment. Barry was probably right, they'd spent the whole weekend sending me up for their own entertainment. If Ainsley was a lifelong lush, his memories were probably addled. I shut the book, placed it to one side.

'You can borrow that,' Barry said, sitting himself down and organising his desk. 'How was the rest of it anyway?' he asked.

I told him the highlights, finished up with Everill.

'Sounds like a wanker to me,' was Barry's pronouncement.

'Well, he got to me,' I admitted.

'Let's see his book.' He gestured over. 'Have you got it with you?'

'Mmmm…' It was at the bottom of my pile, a right state now, the spine all broken from excessive re-reading.

'*Werrrdo*,' Barry gave his approximation of a Norfolk accent. 'Mind if I have a read?'

'Not at all. I've got shitloads of transcribing to do.'

'Where's his nibs anyway?'

I scowled. 'He went off to the Groucho last night with Jack Hall. After he'd spent all day hanging around, taking the piss out of me.'

'That would be about right,' Barry mused. 'Nosing around like usual.'

'Hmmm. I didn't tell you, but he intends to do his own investigation into the Jackson murder.'

'Yeah?' Barry's nose didn't rise from the book, although his eyebrows did. 'Well, he can count me out.'

He put his feet up on the desk, and carried on reading. He hadn't even taken his coat off. I plugged myself back in, carried on with Luther. Pages of text flew under my fingertips in the pleasant silence of an office without Neil. Nothing but the patter of rain on the window panes above our heads, the slight whisk of pages being turned. Even the phones kept their silence that morning.

After an hour or so, as the first half of the tape finished, I was drawn back to the pages of Barry's book:

Niall Flynn and Emily Davey first played opposite each other in Peter Steele's 1959 adaptation of Patrick Hamilton's wartime drama. Taking a few liberties with the original, Davey, as the beleaguered Miss Roach, was, at 29, ten years younger than her character in the book and a good deal more attractive. Flynn played the American Lieutenant who brings the first glimmer of romance into her life, leading to conflict with her untrustworthy friend, the German femme fatale Vicki Kugelmann, played in this version by Veronica Stone. The romance between Flynn and Davey was real enough; they played opposite each other in Roland Pickard's Next Door To Danger *one year later, and were engaged in 1961. Davey, on the brink of marriage and offers from Hollywood, mysteriously committed suicide in January 1962. The film world lost a little-remembered but luminous talent. Flynn subsequently made one more film, which many consider his best work, 1963's* Ganglord *(Dir. Don Hill), before slipping into obscurity.*

Ganglord was the one Jackson had seen that persuaded him Flynn was coming back as Marley. Barry and I had gone to see it at the Scala, when they did a season of Flynn films after *Bent* had made him famous again. An amazingly violent picture, by British standards at the time, it had hardly had the same magical effect on Don Hill's career as what amounted to the same character had done for Jackson's, some thirty years later. Hill had died an alcoholic in 1979. I liked his effort a lot more than *Bent*. Now I wished we had stuck around to see Flynn's other movies.

I studied the pictures. Poor Emily. What a handsome couple they made. No wonder Flynn wanted her back from the dead.

'Barry,' I began, 'do you think we can rent those movies from that video shop near you?'

'Uhhh?' Barry was still deep inside *Weirdo*.

'The two that Emily Davey was in. Do you reckon they'll have them?'

'We can try it, pet.' He put the book down. He had read roughly half.

'Enjoying it?' I asked him.

'It's fucking brilliant,' he nodded. 'I can see what you see in him.'

I laughed. 'I don't see anything in him, if that's what you mean.'

Barry gave a slow, sly wink. 'That's what you say. Fancy some lunch? All this hard work's making me hungry.'

We sauntered back from the caff via the second-hand bookshops. Interest piqued, I rummaged in the loosely contained film sections until I had found decrepit copies of both *Film Guide 1963*, with a chapter on *Ganglord*, and *The Angry Young Men*, with a chapter on Flynn. Nothing on Davey was to be found at all. So much for her luminous talent. Back in the office, still no sign of Bambridge either.

Perhaps he wasn't sleeping off his hangover, maybe he was out scamming some deals instead. He could have made a few more important connections over the weekend, while I was elsewhere. He often disappeared without warning when things like that happened, only to return slapping his palms over another few thousand quid in the kitty from some altruistic collector or would-be media tycoon.

Just as I was pondering on this, the phone rang.

'Hello, *Lux*, how may I help you?' Barry picked it up, affecting a Bambridge accent. Then his expression changed, an exaggerated look of surprise crossed his features. 'Just one moment, please.'

He covered the receiver with his hand.

'It's for you,' he said. 'Simon Everill.'

I took the phone from him, my heartbeat quickening.

'Diana Kemp.'

'Hello there, it's Simon. Listen, I hope you don't mind, but I got your number off Lucy and I thought I'd better give you a call…'

His tone was completely different from the sneering punk of Saturday and the existentialist loner of Sunday. The voice that came down the other end of the phone was altogether more relaxed, chummy even.

'Oh yes?' I said.

'Yes, I wanted to apologise. I realise I was a bit off with you yesterday and I didn't mean to be. It's just that I've had a lot of interest in this book, a lot of people sniffing around, but you're the first person who's actually seemed genuinely, I dunno, moved,' he emphasised the word carefully, 'by it. Like I say, I'm quite a private person, and it's sometimes hard to know how to react properly. I didn't mean to be quite so rude. And I wondered if I could take you out for a drink or something and try and behave a bit better? I don't want you to think I'm a complete arsehole.'

He sounded so genuine that he took me totally by surprise.

But I must admit, I was pleased. My plan had worked. He did want to see me again. And he had gone to all the trouble of finding out my number to do so.

'Well… That would be lovely. When do you want to do it?'

'Er, tomorrow would be OK.' He seemed very eager. 'If you're not busy, that is.'

I couldn't work out whether I was supposed to be busy tomorrow or not. But I didn't want to lose the moment. If everyone else was 'sniffing around' then it was a matter of personal pride to get a better interview than they did.

'No, tomorrow would be fine. Where do you want to go?'

'Where are you based?'

'Up near Edgware Road – I can make the West End pretty easily if that's good for you?'

'Well, what's that pub called where all the reprobates are supposed to hang out –the Coach and Horses, is it?'

'Oh yes.' I liked the idea. Home of the perennial delinquent. That would be about right for him.

'See you there about eight?'

'Great. See you there.'

I put the phone down. 'Unbelievable,' I told Barry. 'He's as nice as pie now. Wants to do a proper interview.'

'Wants a date, you mean.' Barry raked his fingers through his goatee, eyeing me speculatively. 'You sure you don't fancy him?'

'Yes! He's not exactly pretty, you know.'

But, to my horror, I could feel myself going red. Was I sure I didn't fancy him? Well, yes. The way he squirmed about and licked his lips like that, it wasn't attractive. In fact, it was mildly repellent. But yesterday at the park, I had felt a connection with him. Felt almost sorry for him. And his book was a work of genius. That was the important thing.

Barry was smiling at me, fanning himself with my copy of *Weirdo*.

'Mind if I take this home tonight?' he asked. 'You can have it back tomorrow. I want to know how it ends now.'

'Of course.' I looked away, aware his smile was challenging that flush of red travelling up my neck and round my face.

The phones started ringing again. This time I pounced before Barry could, and was rewarded with a familiar voice. My old friend Hugh Fielding was on the end of the line, sounding like he was in the middle of a party.

'Hello, duckie,' he trilled, 'you'll never guess what's happened.'

'Are you on the Royal Yacht *Britannia*?'

This was a game we had played since we first met at art college in Yarmouth. It had started out innocently enough at some fancy dress party back then and got progressively more ridiculous as the years went by.

Hugh had come up to London two years after me, settled himself in with a job at a PR agency and a flat in West Hampstead. Or at least he had up until now.

'Not yet,' he giggled, 'I'm only in some old winos' pub on the Harrow Road, but I've just landed myself a job at Dove Records.'

'How excellent! How did that happen?'

'Head-hunted, naturally.' He put on his snobbiest of tones and then chortled. 'Well, one of the bands we did work for at PRQ have signed to Dove and they wangled me in here. There was a job going in the press office. And now it's mine! All mine!'

'Well, well done you. And you're celebrating in West London?'

'That's why I thought I'd call you – what time are you home tonight?'

I looked at the clock on the corner of my Mac. It was going on five. I wasn't going to stay too late after the weekend I'd had. And the prospect of seeing Hugh was a much cheerier one than the night I had envisioned.

'I can be back at about 6.30 if you want to come over.'

'Hoorah! Shall I bring some food with me?'

'No, don't worry. I'll have cook rustle up something.'

'All right, I'll bring the wine.'

So I had forgotten all about my blushes by the time I got out of the tube that evening. My bag was heavy with Barry's book and my new purchases, along with the tape machine and interview cassettes. A further bag of shopping, picked up in Marks & Spencer by Edgware Road station, banged around my calves.

Ladbroke Grove was thronging with rush-hour foot traffic. As ever, a few stray loonies milled around the twenty-four-hour shop by the station, clutching cans of Special Brew, staring out blankly on to a world that had no time for them. One man passed out against the wall, looking like nothing so much as a few bags of spuds with a worn-out broom for a head, a trail of piss leaking from his tattered trousers out across the paving stones. A black man, thin as a reed, with layers of ill-fitting clothes coming off him like unravelling bandages from a mummy, reeling dangerously in front of the bus stop, arms wide, as if in the grip of some biblical revelation. A couple of black kids on BMX bikes were laughing at him. I hurried past, not wanting to make eye contact with any of them, sensing hurricanes of rage within that twisting form and those mocking children that the slightest blink in the wrong direction could unleash.

Everyone else was obviously thinking the same, hurrying home, bags held close, heads held down, checking the cracks on the pavement. All the way past the rowdy Elgin pub on the corner of Westbourne Park Road, where the sly figures sneaked up on you mumbling: 'Hashish, speed, hashish,' waiting to relieve you of your cash for a lump of Oxo or a packet of Ajax.

Crossing Westbourne Park Road quickly, up the hill to where the stucco houses demarcated the change in territory. Nowhere else in London did so much wealth shack up quite so near to so much poverty. A police car screeched past as I reached the corner of Arundel Gardens, sirens howling north down the Grove.

Down the stairs to the basement, dropping bags to the floor as I fumbled the keys into the lock. Inside the bedsitter, the air was chillier than outside. I switched the stinking fan heater on straight away, and left the room to heat up while I unpacked the shopping in the kitchen. I'd bought pasta and salad, easy and quick, for when Hugh arrived. I was boiling the kettle, slicing some onions, when the doorbell rang.

My Fairy Godfather was clearly already merry as he stood on the doorstep, waving a bottle of wine, shouting, 'Cooeee!'

'Dinner won't be long,' I informed him as I ushered him inside. 'Cook's working on the menu right now. Swan stuffed with wigeon be all right with you?'

'Of course. That's why I brought the three-thousand-year-old port with me. Just had my young boy dust it off from the cellar this morning.'

He followed me into the kitchen, inspected what was going on and started shuffling through the cupboards and the fridge to find more ingredients. What was to have been tomato and onion pasta with a bit of lettuce and a tomato on the side became penne arrabbiata, with avocado, spinach and pine nut salad and some hastily whipped-up garlic bread. He took over the entire operation, leaving me to sip wine and watch him spin around the foot-wide kitchen like a dervish. Nothing, with Hugh, was ever going to be plain or boring.

As he cooked, he told me all about his new job. He was going to be a press officer, with a much better salary, and a host of interesting artists to work with. His excitement was tangible, overflowing into the food.

'That's better,' he sighed, eyeing the results of his efforts.

We took our plates and glasses back to my room. The temperature had now risen to a comfortable degree. Hugh perched on the end of my bed, picking delicately at his meal while I rammed this unexpectedly delicious feast into my mouth as fast as I possibly could. After watching him transform into Fanny Craddock for the past half an hour, I was starving.

'Ahhh.' He finally put his plate on the floor, and picked up his glass. 'That was delicious. Now you tell me what you've been up to? What's all this?' He was examining my new books, nothing passing his sharp brain by.

'You see him.' I found the page in Barry's book that showed Niall Flynn off to his most beautiful, youthful advantage. 'He's in love with me.'

'How dare you?' Hugh squealed. 'He's gorgeous!'

'Not really,' I laughed. 'Anyway, he's an old man now. No, I met him at the weekend. He was in that film Jon Jackson made.'

'Ah, he's the old guy, the ganglord,' Hugh clicked. Then his tone became serious: 'I've got to admit, I didn't just come here to show off. When I saw what happened on the news, I really wanted to see you. Are you all right?'

Hugh was the only person who knew all my secrets. Had been around when some of them happened. If I wanted someone to talk to about everything that had occurred over the past week, well, here he was.

My eyes dropped and so did my smile.

'Not really. I've been trying to keep busy, but everything comes back to him.' When I looked back up, I could feel the tears welling.

'Have you ever told anyone else?' he asked.

I shook my head. 'What am I gonna say? It was only a one-night stand, nine years ago. I've been in the same room as him since, he didn't recognise me, why would he?'

'No,' Hugh nodded agreement, 'when you look so much better now.'

I smiled, despite myself. Hugh had never approved of my psychobilly look. He said it was positively distasteful.

'When he had much more beautiful girls to look at, you mean.' I tried to shrug him off.

'Well, it meant more than a one-night stand to you,' Hugh said quietly.

'I know.' I looked down, fiddling with the bedspread.

He realised I was on the verge of sobbing and took pity

on me. 'So how did you get to meet Mr Handsome here?' He gestured at the film book.

'I was at this crime writers' convention at the weekend. Met all sorts of mad people there, including a husband for you, until that bastard Bambridge ran off with him.'

'Neil's not gay.' Hugh frowned. 'What was he after?'

'His money. They spent last night at the Groucho, don't you know?'

'Ughh, how common. And who is my husband-to-be?'

'Jack Hall. You'd love him. He looks like an Italian spiv. He was the only bloke at the whole convention who was intelligent, good-looking and well dressed.'

'Had to be gay then,' Hugh considered. 'Nothing for you?'

'No...' My thoughts went back to Everill. Then decided better. 'But I did get taken to this excellent club, the Deansgate, which is where I met our friend here. It's like the land that time forgot, like a portal opening up into the sixties or something. All these excellent...' I struggled for the right word, 'piss-artistes down there. And there's a jazz band and they all waltz and jive around, showing up the young people. I must find a way of getting us back in. You'd love it.'

'How did you meet him?' Hugh enquired, tapping the picture.

'He met me. He thought I was her.' I pointed at the page opposite.

'Oh my God!' His eyes widened and he held the book right up to his face. 'She is you! Who is she?'

'His old fiancée who committed suicide.'

We looked at each other for a minute, both biting our bottom lips. When we knew we shouldn't this always happened. We burst into hysterical laughter, smothering our faces in the pillows and rolling round the bed for a good ten minutes.

'Oh dear.' Hugh finally sat up, reaching in his jacket pocket for a handkerchief, and blowing his nose loudly. 'I think we need some more wine. What time is it?'

I checked the Braun. 'Ten o'clock. Let's go to the offie round the corner.'

I followed him out on to the street, feeling like a weight had been lifted. We didn't have far to go, to the Peppermill by the boarded-up Electric Cinema on Portobello Road. A long, thin, convenience store with a selection of overpriced wines of dubious vintage. Hugh selected a Soave, pronouncing it deliberately a 'suave' because that was one of our favourite words.

When we got back and opened it, he insisted on playing Dean Martin records for us to dance around the room to. We were performing the 'Mambo Italiano' for the edification of anyone watching with field glasses from the houses opposite when there was a loud banging at my door.

'Shit!' I said. 'We've been playing the music too loud.'

Hugh leaned over to turn the record player down. 'I'll get it,' he said.

He opened the door and in his politest voice said: 'Can I help you?'

'Is there a party going on?'

Jerry burst into the room, eyes bulging, neck swivelling around like Linda Blair, desperate to take in any evidence of a swinging orgy.

'No,' said Hugh, sniffily. 'We were just playing music. Sorry if we disturbed you, we'll turn it down.'

Jerry was hankering for an invitation to join in. When he became aware none would be forthcoming, he decided to try another tack. A deeply bizarre one.

'What are they?' he demanded, pointing at my two coats, hanging from the picture rail.

'My coats?' I suggested.

'You're a murderer!' he yelled.

'What?' I couldn't take in what he was saying.

'They're real fur!' he foamed. I had never seen him this fighting drunk before. He'd obviously stumbled back from the

Station Tavern, hoping that his luck was in, and was disgusted to see I already had a man with me.

Hugh pulled the leopardskin coat down from its hanger, shoved it under Jerry's nose.

'Yes,' he said sombrely. 'We killed real cuddly toys to make them. Twenty little toy leopards and twenty little toy zebras met their deaths here. At our hands. And you will be next if you don't kindly leave. Now.'

Jerry was turning purple.

'Come on.' Hugh propelled him out. 'Go and sleep it off.'

He managed to get him through the other side and slam the door in his face, double-locking it behind him.

'Murderer!' Jerry screamed again.

I could hear Alan starting to shuffle above our heads.

Hugh put his finger to his lips.

Jerry stomped his feet a bit, said 'Murderer!' again, a lot more quietly, and banged back into his own room. Above, Alan retreated back to his bed.

'What a twat!' Hugh exclaimed. We started laughing again, but halfway through, I wasn't laughing any more. Something had taken me over, something triggered by Jerry's shouting, and I started crying hysterically, tears streaming down my face, clinging on to Hugh, blubbering one word over and over again: 'Why?'

He rocked me in his arms until the grief had abated, until that face in my memory had faded back into the shadows and the knife's thrust subsided into a dull ache. Held me close like none of my boyfriends ever had.

'I'm sorry,' I said eventually.

'Shhhh,' he shook his head. 'It had to come out sometime. Better now than when you're on your own.'

He passed me his handkerchief and I did my best to clear the trails of black from down my face while he poured us another glass each of suave and lit us some cigarettes.

'Here.' He passed mine over.

'Thank you.' We clinked glasses.

The wine hit the back of my throat and made my eyes burn. A blast from the cigarette held down any further tears.

'I'll stay here tonight,' Hugh decided. 'I'm not leaving you on your own with that idiot next door.'

'Thank you so much.'

'It's OK.' He smiled. 'Really.'

He kept the demons at bay for the rest of the night, until the cool calm of morning delivered us.

12

'Wake up, petal, it's half past eight.'

'Hmmmmm?'

My eyes flicked open on Hugh, a teapot and a stack of buttered toast.

I shuffled upright. Must have forgotten to stick on the alarm clock. How nice to wake up to something other than the usual relentless electronic *gütenmorgen*. How nice to wake up with somebody else there. Someone using pet names and bringing me my breakfast. I had forgotten what closeness could feel like.

'How lovely of you,' I told him.

'Don't worry, I cemented up his door while I was making it.' He nodded towards the dividing wall between mine and Jerry's rooms, giggled at his own lightning wit. 'Have this, then I'll do dawn patrol on the bathroom.'

I took my time, enjoying each warm and runny mouthful, each sip of perfectly brewed tea. Even my bed felt unnaturally warm and comfortable.

'Have you transported us to a different world?'

'Yes. When I throw back the curtains you will see we are in the royal suite of the *QE2*, enjoying a commanding view of the ocean. You will probably just be able to make out the coastline of China from our bearings. Da-nah!'

Sadly, it was still the concrete patio overlooking the communal gardens, but patches of pale blue were emerging hopefully in the sky.

'I had a word about the weather as well.' Hugh stared up at

it. 'Should be pleasantly sunny, with light variable breezes from the east.'

'Excellent. Things really are looking up.'

Even better when I'd come back from the bathroom. Not only had he packed up the sofa bed, he seemed to have cleaned the rest of the room too, leaving it orderly and almost sparkling in the shaft of sunlight that now slanted straight in from the French doors. It must have been the fairy dust.

He left me at the border of Westbourne Park Road, where he'd detour right to catch the 28 back to West Hampstead. We agreed to meet up again on Friday night, try and busk it into the Deansgate. After everything he'd done for me, he deserved a bit of a treat.

When I got to the office, Neil was already waiting, fidgeting in his seat, drumming his fingers on top of his desk with a surfeit of nervous energy.

'Hello, there!' he boomed as I walked down the steps. His eyes looked somewhat mad.

'Hello, Neil. What have you been up to?'

'I had an excellent meeting yesterday,' he said, standing up and stretching. 'I'll wait till Barry gets in to tell you all about it – but we've got something to celebrate. How did your interviews come out, by the way?'

'Pretty good, on the whole,' I considered, sitting myself down. 'Apart from that stick-on Susie Beck. I don't want to put her in the piece, she's not good enough.'

Neil nodded agreement. One good thing about him, he took your word for it on subjects that were out of his area.

'I thought Luther Lang was gonna be the best,' I continued, 'and the tape's come out fine. But there was another writer there who I think is even more interesting. Simon Everill. He's written a book called *Weirdo.*'

'I heard about that.' Neil's brow furrowed. 'Now, where did I hear it?'

'At the bar, probably, from Peter Reid, no doubt.'

'No, it wasn't there, funnily enough, though you would think...' he paused, flicking through his mental Roll-O-Dex. 'I'm sure someone told me about him ages ago...'

'Really? I thought he had come out of nowhere...'

Typical of Neil. He always had to claim to have been there first, even when he wasn't. Peter Reid, the biggest gossip in the book world, didn't know, but Bambridge did.

'Anyway, I've got a second interview with him tonight. I wanted to go in deeper than the time at the ICA allowed.'

On second thoughts, thank God Peter didn't spill anything about that first disaster. 'We've got to get a better story on him than anyone else.'

'Quite right,' said Neil absently, still checking the files. 'I wish I could remember who told me about him. That's going to bug me...'

The sound of the front door slamming announced the arrival of Barry. Neil's train of thought was soon lost.

'Barry!' he announced excitedly. 'I have some excellent news.'

'Oh yeah?' Barry looked astonished. It was probably sarcasm.

'Yes, I had a meeting yesterday with one of the major distributors in New York. They picked up a copy of *Lux* and they loved it. They asked me to come in and see if we could work out a deal.'

'Right,' said Barry brightly, 'nice of you to share that with us first.'

Neil ignored this slight. 'Well, I didn't want to get anyone's hopes up if nothing happened. But anyway, it seems they want to buy 10,000 issues which they will put the whole way across America.'

'Sale or return?' Barry shot at him.

'No, bulk. No returns. They're buying the lot! I thought I'd take us out to dinner to celebrate.'

When things were going very, very well, Neil would occasionally treat us to a meal out and a couple of bottles of wine. In the days before he could pay us salaries, we used to grumble that we'd rather have the money. Now that things were healthy, I guessed this was going to be rather better than the usual Pizza Express'n'Chianti.

'I didn't want to take the chance with tonight, in case you were busy, but how about tomorrow?'

We were both flabbergasted. Even Barry's voice sounded high-pitched and delicate as he responded: 'Yeah, yeah, that's great.'

'Good. I thought we'd go to the Criterion. I reserved a table on the off-chance. Now it's official I'll confirm it.'

We mouthed it to each other as Neil turned to pick up the phone, make a show of keeping good his word. 'The Cri-ter-ion!'

That was the first time we'd ever been invited to step into the inner vortex of the Bambridge social whirl.

'Now that's settled,' he proceeded brightly as he replaced the receiver, 'there's something I'd like you to write for the next issue, Barry. It's something we've talked about before, but with what's happened in the past few weeks, this really is the time to run it.'

Barry started to look worried again. 'Oh yeah,' he said carefully. 'What is it?'

'That piece on film censorship you always wanted to do.' He caught the frown forming on Barry's brow, was smoothness itself in reassurance. 'Now, it was something that came up at the weekend, over the papers, and at the convention. I know it's affected you personally, but now is the time to get it all off your chest.' Barry nodded, shifted uncomfortably from one foot to the other. 'Go on,' he said.

'Well, what the reactionary tabloid press were spouting at the weekend was that Jon Jackson's killer was inspired by watching his films, a knock-on effect that the violence of modern movies and TV is having on society.'

'Bullshit!' spat Barry.

'Quite so,' Neil assented. 'So I want you to write a long critique on why this line is totally wrong. I want you to write a history of violent cinema, banned films, directors like Peckinpah and Ferrara, going right up to Jackson.'

This was clever, bloody clever. Neil the politician was about to get exactly what he wanted – the What He Would Have Wanted piece – and in the process turn Barry from Doubting Thomas into Deadline Joe.

'Any directors you want to speak to, try your best to get hold of them and ask their opinion,' he carried on, giving the final carte blanche to Barry's dream feature. 'Then find out the statistics behind what the politicians say. I got the number of George Dickinson, that retired Scotland Yard specialist who spoke at the panel I saw, and he's happy to do interviews. He basically explains the psyche of the psychopath and how it's unrelated to external influences like film and television. Speak to him too and present the ultimate defence against the censor.'

Barry's scowl had come 180 degrees round. 'Fucking top one!' he beamed. 'I'll get on it straight away. I've got a mate who's worked with Abel Ferrara, that'd be a good place to start...'

I shook my head in wonder. Neil was a born player. God help us all if he'd chosen to be a Tory MP and not an art terrorist. I only hoped I could do a fraction as well with Everill that night.

Hugh's forecast had held firm to the last rays of the sun. It was still pleasantly mild as I cut across Soho towards the Coach and Horses.

No surprise that Everill would want to align himself with the elder league of The Bad Men of Letters. I knew about this pub mainly from the columns of its loyal patron Jeffrey Bernard, which I read not in *The Spectator*, but the cheapskate's alternative, the free *Midweek* magazine.

Ever since I moved to London, Jeffrey's grouchy Wednesday missives had always cheered me up. His self-deprecating style was one thing, but it was a line about Suffolk that really stayed with me. Jeffrey had once tried to lure himself into exile there, vainly dreaming of a healthy lifestyle, but the vast weight of the 'frozen East Anglian skies', under which he had attempted to toil like an honest man, had broken his resolve and sent him scuttling back to the comforts of Old Smoky. Better to do battle with bar bills than nature. I could sympathise.

Jeffrey sadly wasn't propping up a corner of the bar when I arrived. But I did get to watch Norman, the legendarily rude landlord of whom I had also learned from the pages of *Midweek*, pull off an extraordinary move. Some very blonde and tanned young girls were trying to find a table – a hard enough job at any hour – and they were obviously more attractive customers to him than the bunch of beer boys settled by the door nearest his present quarter of the bar. Norman stalked over.

'You lot,' he addressed the throng, 'are all barred. Fuck off.'

Amazed, they meekly complied. A satisfied Norman put on his most avuncular face and turned towards the women. 'You can sit here now, my dears,' he cooed.

I was chortling at this spectacle as Everill came through the door.

'Hello there!' he hailed loudly, attracting some supercilious eyebrow-raising from a bunch of venomous luvvies skulking near the Gents.

'Hi, Simon,' I replied. 'How are you?'

'Good, good. Much better since you agreed to this drink. What will you have, by the way?'

I hardly ever drank the same thing regularly. It depended on my mood. Tonight I decided lager shandy would be just fine. It meant I wouldn't get pissed and fuck things up, while still maintaining the illusion that I could hold my own with the best of them. Everill managed to find a spot where it was possible to get an elbow on the bar, fetch the drinks and pass mine over.

'Shall we stand outside?' I said. 'And mingle with the gutterarti?'

He laughed at that one. He wasn't at all like the cocksure Simon Everill facing down his rivals at the ICA. He seemed a lot more natural.

Outside, the bag ladies hit like flies to a windscreen.

'Got a few pence for a drink, luv? I'm not gonna pretend it's for a cuppa tea...'

Simon rummaged in his jeans pocket.

'Got a spare fag, luv?' another buzzed in.

Eventually, we were able to have a conversation.

'Who are all the people who've been hitting on you, then?' I asked.

'Oh, you know. Broadsheets. *Time Out*. Even the music press. And I'm starting to get a few film offers,' he grimaced.

'That's good, though, isn't it?'

'Well, it should be. But I have a hard time seeing this as a film.'

'But that's where all the money is, for writers.'

'I don't really care about that.' He sounded blasé. 'I guess I just don't want them to take my baby away. I mean, you like the book. Can you really see it up on the big screen?'

'Not really,' I pondered. 'It's all about the dialogue, isn't it? The way it's written is why it's powerful. I doubt there's a director alive who could do it justice...'

He looked at me expectantly.

'What about dead ones?' he said, amused.

'Well, Sam Peckinpah was the only one I was thinking of who would have had the understanding. And you're not gonna get him, are you?'

He laughed. 'I see what you mean. Yeah, Uncle Sam. He would have been good. Hadn't thought of him.'

'Well, I guess it's like us doing our own magazine,' I continued, glad to have made him smile. 'We don't make much money – I still had to freelance up until a few months ago – but at least it means that we get to put in exactly what we want. We have total control. And I think that's why we get some good contributors, 'cos they know we're not going to fuck about with their work.'

'*Lux*, eh?' He looked at me contemplatively. 'How long have you been doing it?'

'About two years. We've managed to come out four times – even though it's supposed to be a quarterly. But we've got enough backing to set up our own office now, and we can pay ourselves just enough to live on. So it's good.'

'That's probably why you don't stink like normal journalists do.' That sneering voice was back, but he checked himself.

'You know what I mean.'

'The ones whose bylines are more important than what they're writing about,' I sighed. 'I know exactly what you mean. I've worked for the music press.'

'So who are your favourite writers?'

The conversation wandered down that pleasant path for a while. We discussed everyone from Dashiell Hammett to Jim Thompson while the winos stumbled up and down and the luvvies got louder and louder. Talking about books was one of my favourite things, and Simon seemed pretty knowledgeable.

'Books and songs,' I finally said, 'I would have gone mad without them.' Which then led nicely on to our favourite bands and singers. There our tastes diverged. He liked Hawkwind for a start. But his enthusiasm was infectious. The rounds went by and we never really spoke about his book again. Aware that I was only supposed to be here to do an interview, I was also conscious that he was deliberately avoiding coming back to the subject of his novel, either by talking about something else entirely or insisting on further drinks. I realised what he was doing, though. He was sussing me out.

At last orders, he started getting a bit twitchy. 'I'd better go,' he announced, as if he'd been enjoying himself too much and had to put a stop to it.

'Yeah, me too.' I made light of it. 'Thanks for this.'

'No, thank you.' He seemed sincere. 'And thanks for not bringing up the book again. I really didn't feel like talking about it, but I did feel like talking to you.'

It had been a test.

He leaned over, awkwardly, and brushed my cheek with wet lips. I could feel that stupid blush coming back again. Could see Barry fanning himself with the book he still hadn't handed back, giving me that slo-mo wink that suggested he knew more than I did. Shit, what was I playing at?

'Well, I hope to see you again soon,' I said, embarrassed, pulling myself clear of his embrace, starting towards Tottenham Court Road tube.

'Yeah, you will,' he smiled, and seemed pleased by what had just occurred. 'I think I can trust you to write my story.' And, with that, he ducked in the opposite direction, down Charing Cross Road, towards Leicester Square.

I didn't watch him go.

13

Barry did give me the book back the next day. Choosing a moment when Neil was engrossed on the phone, he slapped it down on my desk and pronounced:

'Fucking brilliant. How did it go last night?'

I cringed inwardly. I didn't want Neil to know the interview I'd been boasting to him about hadn't exactly happened. Neither did I want Barry to think he was right about me secretly thinking Everill was hot stuff.

'It was strange,' I said instead. 'He spent the whole evening discussing everything but his book. Then when it got to last orders, he thanked me for not asking him about it.' Barry's eyebrows shot up.

'Then, and this is even stranger.' I swivelled round to make sure Neil hadn't started to listen, turned back to face Barry's gaze. 'When he left he said: "I think I can trust you to write my story." I've been wondering about it all night.'

'Sounds like he's trying to lead you on,' said Barry bluntly.

'What did you think of him?' I purposefully ignored this. 'From reading the book?'

He eyed me strangely. 'I thought it was a brilliant book, but that doesn't mean he's going to be a brilliant person,' he said. 'It's some fucking twisted shit he's got into there.'

'That's just it,' I said. 'I wonder how much of it is real.'

'None of it's real,' Barry retorted. 'It's a fairy tale!'

'No, listen. When I first tried to interview him, he wouldn't tell me where he came from. He got really angry when I pushed it. He obviously doesn't want anyone to find out too much about him. So there must be something real in it.'

'C'mon, Di.' Barry tried to blunt the edge of his voice. 'All right, something nasty probably happened in his past, maybe there was a mad old bag in his village who killed all her kids – it happens. But this story is a fantasy worked around it; it's an exaggeration.'

What he said made perfect sense. Maybe I was seeing too much in all of this. Which made me feel pretty stupid.

'Whatever you say.' I plugged my headphones back in, turned my back on Barry so he wouldn't see me looking annoyed. He made me feel like I *was* a teenager with a crush. But I would prove him wrong.

I tapped on in silence for the next hour, working away on Kay McLachlan, letting my fingers do the work while Barry sang snatches of 'My Chérie Amour' loudly, trying to get me to laugh. I ignored him, concentrated on nailing Kay's words to the page.

The Everill tape still lay at the bottom of the pile.

It was getting towards the end of the day when he called me again.

'Thanks for last night,' he said, breezy as you like. 'I know it's a bit short notice, but I wondered if you fancied meeting up again tonight?'

'Tonight?' I remembered that wet kiss on the cheek and felt slightly uneasy. I really didn't want him to fancy me, or think that I fancied him. 'I'm sorry, I've got a work thing I have to go to, we've just had a bit of good news.'

'Yeah, right. I thought I might be pushing it.' He sounded like he was really pissed off, but straining to disguise the fact. With an effort, his voice got lighter. 'What about some time next week? The thing is, I've given it a lot of thought and I've decided you are right. I need to tell someone the real story behind my story and that someone is you.'

What a charmer. And it worked.

'That would be brilliant,' I exclaimed. 'Are you sure?'

'I liked what you said about the integrity of your magazine,' he replied smoothly, 'and I think it would be the best place to put it. All the corporate mags are fighting over me, so I thought I'd fuck them all off as well.'

'I like your sentiments,' I said, 'and you're right. What day shall it be?'

'Next Tuesday?'

I flicked through my dog-eared Fil-o-fax pages. 'That looks fine. Want to make it the Coach again?'

'No, I think we should make it somewhere quieter. I don't think you can really do an interview properly in that place.'

He had a point.

'Where do you suggest?'

'Is there anywhere you normally do interviews?' he asked.

I considered my local. 'There's a pub on Portobello Road that's nice and quiet and you can always get a table,' I said. 'The Earl of Lonsdale, on the corner of Westbourne Grove. Would that be convenient for you?'

'Yeah, that's fine. Meet you there at eight?'

'Perfect. See you then.'

'Him again?' asked Barry as soon as I'd clicked the receiver down. Then to Neil: 'Di's got a new admirer. Funny fella. He writes twisted stories about murderous inbred children. But he's got a lovely smile.'

'Hey, shut it, you.' I smacked him, but all real annoyance had evaporated in the triumph of getting another chance to show him what this was really all about. We laughed, both of us, in a relieved sort of way.

'Who is it?' Neil enquired.

'That writer, Simon Everill. Only, he's not my fella, OK?'

'So that's why you wanted to write a long story on him.' Eyebrows arched. They would proceed to take the piss out of me for the rest of the day, and our posh evening at the Criterion, I was sure of that. But Neil's brow furrowed again. 'I have heard his name somewhere before, though. I just wish I could remember who told me about him.'

But he couldn't, so the moment passed.

The Criterion was by far the most splendid place Neil had ever taken us to. It had a fantastic arch of blue and gilded ceiling which had been hidden for years behind plaster and now gleamed and glittered like St Mark's cathedral through the Venice fog. Smart tables underneath the pleasure dome, starched white tablecloths, cutlery and glassware gleaming like something from the era of Cunard liners and debutante balls, something more refined and distant.

I immediately felt under-dressed, grubby somehow; not a beautiful enough person to glide easily through such grandiose portals.

Neil and Barry had no such feelings, Neil because this was the pool he swam in: he was a shark who bit cheque-book-sized pieces out of beautiful people. Barry because he was always comfortable with himself, and his oiled hair and savage rings glimmered as magnificently as our surroundings.

'Champagne, I think,' ordered Neil at a surly-looking waiter, who obviously didn't share my sentiments about Barry. 'Laurent Perrier,' he continued without consulting the list, 'rosé, if you will.'

'Very posh,' noted Barry.

'Well, we deserve it. We,' Neil leaned back in his chair with the contentment of a hunting dog that had just managed to floor an elephant, 'are going to be big. We've come a long way in a short time, you know. And now all that hard work is about to pay off. There's a goldmine for us in America.'

'Well, I always thought the Yanks would go for it in a big way.' Barry tore a piece of ciabatta from the chic little basket of warm, fresh bread, and dunked it in the discreet dish of olive oil. 'It's the world capital of twisted weird shit. If they don't get it, no one will.'

'Exactly', said Neil.

'I'll drink to that', I said, as the impressive bottle of bubbles was proffered, popped open and shimmied into our crystal flute glasses.

'Cheers!' we clinked on it.

Neil continued to dazzle us with figures as we ordered food. It seemed that there was to be an all-expenses-paid launch party in New York, where a lot of our contributors lived and, according to Neil, it would be the talk of the town. Of this, I had no doubt. There was very little he couldn't achieve when his mind was fixed. I enjoyed the novelty feeling of champagne and success, let it wash over me in a pleasant haze. And then Barry said: 'So what was on those Jackson tapes in the end?'

'Barry', said Neil, casting his eyes down on to his plate. 'It wasn't easy for me to listen to a man who had just died. I spent the whole day with him, I really liked him, and to think it was the last night he had is a hard thing to deal with.' He looked up, meeting Barry's eyes with his sincerest expression. 'Even for me. I know you think I was cashing in on misfortune. In a way, I was, I admit, it was a gold carrot to dangle at the Americans. We have the last ever interview with the victim of the most sensational murder since the Manson Family, was how I pitched it to them, and they knew it would sell shit loads, introduce us in a big way to our new audience. But, you have to understand, there is more to it than that.'

Barry nodded, fork poised in mid-air.

'The fans will want to read it,' Bambridge continued. 'It will be a tribute to him and all he ever stood for. After all, we weren't the ones that killed him.'

I had to agree with him. 'I would want to read it,' I said.

'Fair enough.' Barry's tone was lighter than I expected. Whether he'd come to terms with it more, or whether it was his Feature of Dreams mixed in with the champagne, I couldn't make out.

'When can we read it?' I added.

Neil sighed. 'I haven't finished the transcription yet. I know

I went through it all at the police station, I have heard it all, but when you're alone with it, it gets to you.'

'Blimey!' Barry winked at me. 'He has got a conscience.'

'Why don't you do it in the office?' I asked. 'You started off doing it in there. You might not feel so weird with us two around.'

Neil laughed. 'That is actually very true. How could anyone feel strange compared with you two? No, honestly, that's a good idea. I'll bring the tapes with me tomorrow.'

There was a pause as he leaned back in his chair, scanned the room with his eyes, wanting to let the subject drop.

'Wonder when they'll find the fucker what did it.' Barry wiped his mouth with a crisp white napkin, not letting it go so easily. 'They're taking their time about it. You heard any more from your copper friend?'

'No, thank God,' Bambridge said quickly. 'I mean, good luck to him, but I have no idea why he wanted to treat me like that. Like I'd had something to do with it.'

'Well, whoever it was, they knew what they were doing,' Barry considered. 'It said in the *Post* that the whole scene had been drenched in disinfectant. No hairs, no fibres. Must have had it all worked out in advance, they reckon. They might come after you next,' he turned to Neil, 'when we run the interview.'

Bambridge laughed, a trifle nervously. 'Come on, the cops will have caught him by then. If someone hated him that much, one of his friends would know. Maybe he was being blackmailed or threatened. Lunatics who do things like this always give themselves away in the end,' he reasoned.

'Well, fingers crossed, Neil,' Barry laughed.

'Look,' Neil almost snapped, 'let's change the subject. This is supposed to be a night of celebration.' He picked up the empty bottle from the ice bucket, returned to the matey tone of earlier. 'Now I don't know about you, but I could do with another one of these. I say, waiter...'

14

He didn't take up Tony's offer to join him and his famous friend in the Hop Poles that night. It would be hard enough to stay aloof in that pub without being confronted with the further arrogance of Jon Jackson. Instead, he trailed off home early, back to study his files, to feed and shape his rage into a plan.

He decided that Tony's reaction had worked to his advantage. If the big man thought he was in awe of the film director, then he would use that. Be obsequious to Jackson when he visited the stall. He'd be well used to that by now, and it would put him even more at his ease, make Andy Smith seem even more a believable character.

It would give him the edge.

He gave it a couple of weeks, and sure enough, it worked. Tony's prediction was accurate; Jackson dropped by on a regular basis, like he couldn't get enough of the colourful Cockney locals and their wares, like he really wanted to be at one with them. Andy was careful to be as fawning as possible whenever his opinion was sought on whatever obscure Wigan Casino 7-inch they were banging on about that day, and was rewarded by an apparent respect for his knowledge. Even if the bastard did betray in his gestures a slight surprise that he knew so much.

It was working. He could feel the power growing. His illusion was so complete now that he had everything to gain from dropping the cloak away, making his quarry realise that all along, his eyes had deceived him.

It was the weekend of the August bank holiday when he

sensed the time was right. When everyone was in a light-hearted mood, ready to party.

They packed up as usual at six o'clock, lugging the boxes of records down to the railway arches on steel trolleys, already swigging from the cold cans of lager that Lee had thoughtfully nipped out for when the end of the day's trading was in sight. Andy was in particularly high spirits as they navigated the pot-holed back alleys, singing songs like footie boys after a win.

Tone had made a monkey that day and upped Andy's wages accordingly. 'You gotta come to the pub tonight,' he told him, slapping his back as they locked up their arch, draining the dregs from their cans and stretching from all the lifting and humping. 'It wouldn't be proper not to.'

'Too nice a night to miss,' he agreed, to the cheers of Lee and Mitch.

They strolled back down the High Street, into Inverness Street, where the fruit stalls had been packed up and the street cleaners were hosing down the road so that it shone like a glass lake. As ever, the winos stumbled about the street clutching their Special Brew or Thunderbird, eyeing up likely benefactors as they emerged from the comix shops, record stores and cafés, eager to join in the celebrity mix at the Hop Poles bar.

Only they didn't come up to Andy any more. It was as if by some secret code they knew he was much worse than stingy.

The pub was half full when Tone's troops arrived, balls clicking across the pool table where the greasers he now knew as Woody and Alex were taking shots with cigarettes dangling from the corners of their mouths, singing along to the jukebox to Dean Martin's 'Little Ole Wine Drinker Me'.

The girlfriends sat around the tables, immaculate in their reconstruction of Dino's era, right down to their diamanté earrings and helmets of beehived hair. Jackson sat in the middle of the girls, their eyes all glittering at him as he held court, making them laugh, lighting their cigarettes. Hanging on his every word with their boyfriends only feet away.

It might have got to him any other time, but this evening Andy was light on his feet. He insisted on buying the first round, passing over the deliciously cold pints as the foursome assembled round the bar, shouting over to the greasers and receiving the thumbs-up in reply.

It didn't take long before Mr Bigshot was striding over towards them, buying cocktails for all the ladies and lagers for all the boys, upping his show-off ante with tequila shots for all.

Andy didn't mind. He was riding his luck, and sure enough, once Jackson had distributed his beneficence around the pool table, he swaggered on back to chat with Big Tony.

Andy lounged beside him, leaning on the bar, taking in the room, savouring each moment. He'd worked out how to begin the conversation when it eventually came, and, because Jackson couldn't resist being friends to everyone, sure enough it did.

'So, Andy,' Jon began. 'You know a lot about Northern soul. When did you first get into it?'

'When I was a teenager,' Andy shrugged, 'about fifteen. Used to be a lot of scooter boys where I came from, and a lot of Northern soul all-nighters out on the coast. Used to blag a lift with some of them, buy up the records at the shows. Sometimes they even had the old stars playing. Geno Washington, he was quite a regular, but where I come from, it used to be his manor. He was posted there in the Air Force in World War II.'

He saw the glimmer in Jackson's eye.

'You mean Norfolk,' the director snapped his fingers. 'That's where I'm from.'

Andy couldn't help sniggering into his pint.

'I know.' Jackson suddenly seemed aware that his Cockney accent was ringing a little untrue. 'It's a bit of an embarrassment coming from there. Mind you, I was up near Cambridge way, didn't really pick up much of an accent. How about you?'

Andy swung round to face him, the laughter still on his lips, if not exactly reaching up to his eyes.

'I was up near Cambridge way too, Jonny boy.' He lowered his voice so it would only be audible to the man it was directed at. 'East Melsham. Ring any bells with you?'

Something passed across Jackson's face. A frown, and then his pupils began dilating. Instinctively, he dropped the volume of his conversation too.

'Did I know you before somewhere?' There was still the vestige of chumminess in his smile, but his eyebrows were beginning to knot together.

'You ought to,' Andy smiled back. 'We've got a lot of shared history.'

He watched the humour slowly dissolve from Jackson's lips, and at the same time, the recognition grow in his eyes. With it came a tremor of something else – guilt? Fear? Embarrassment?

Whatever it was, it was enough to send a jolt of power surging through his companion. At last, he thought, wanting to laugh out loud. At last he realised.

'What did you say your name was?' Jackson asked him, 'Andy Smith?'

Andy snorted. 'But you knew me as...'

'Don't say another word!' Jackson boomed. 'Jeremy Beadle!'

It shocked the other, for a moment.

The director laughed out loud but his eyes were saying something else. 'All right, you win,' he carried on, making sure he had eye contact with Big Tony as he did so. 'Come on then.'

He tapped the side of his nose and winked.

Andy's thoughts reeled. Had Jackson just gone totally mad? Then he twigged it. The director was pretending they should go to the bogs together and do a line of coke. So as to get him out of earshot.

Tony laughed from behind them, slapped Andy round the back. 'Didn't think you were the sort, son.' He gave a leering wink, then let it be known he was joking. 'Go on, fill yer boots. You've bloody earned it today.'

Jackson winked at him again and strode off in the direction of the Gents.

The swiftness of the turnaround had wrongfooted him. He could only grin inanely at Tony and follow meekly behind.

Jackson was waiting for him, and as if the luck had now turned to be on his side, the rest of the Gents was empty. The director swiftly shut the door behind them, leaned against it so no one else could follow.

His face had gone poker straight, his eyes hard like black coals. They locked into Andy's.

'Jamie Merritt,' he said. 'After all this time. It's you, isn't it?'

15

I agreed to meet Hugh in the French House at 8.30 that Friday.

Somehow, I didn't want to go back to the Coach, just in case Everill was there. I had no reason to think he would be, but no desire to go back to his old haunts and be caught out unaware. So I picked the French House instead, another long-time holding tank for the dissolute of Soho. I had a feeling that this would be the place to hook up with someone who could get us back into the Deansgate.

As with the Coach, most of the customers stood out on the pavement, clutching half-pints and braying loudly into the night. Step inside and you find out why – the place was tiny, and crammed. Three bar staff were attempting to cope with a constant screeching of orders:

'Glass of Aligoté, over here, my man.'

'Let's have one of those cocktail things you whipped up earlier. Damn fine stuff.'

'Packet of Gauloises, could I? And put another one in here.'

As if desperate to make communion with the Soho Saints that had passed before, those who still remained packed their bodies against the circular bar and made raucous conversation in a smog of authentically French cigarette smoke. From John Deakin's photographs on the wall, the past stared back at them, approvingly. A lot of them were familiar from my excursion to the Deansgate. The sketching man, having a loud argument with the man with Five Houses:

'I'm a true, blue Anglo-Saxon!' spluttered Five Houses.

'In that case, you're a fucking Kraut,' the sketcher pointed out.

'Whaaat?' Five Houses turned for confirmation to his flock of lesser-bellied hangers-on.

''Fraid he's right, old chap,' smiled a tall, sandy-haired one, whom I vaguely recognised from various Charles Dickens adaptations on BBC1.

'Is nothing sacred!' Five Houses bellowed.

After ten minutes, I managed to angle myself in. There were two Kray Klones at the bar. I noticed one of them eyeing me up. Well, I reckoned, they have to be good for something.

'Wanter gerrin?' The one with the roving eyes motioned to me.

He was a short-arse, with plastered-back, heavily dyed black hair, a shirt with a collar that was too tight for his neck and eyes that bulged like a rabbit with myxomatosis.

'Thank you.' I slipped between him and his mate with as much dignity as I could muster, waved a tenner in the air in the hope that someone else would notice me. His mate looked a whole lot nicer. Tall and thin, dark red hair, heavy with Black'n'White wax, Ronnie Kray-style horn-rimmed specs, offset by a beautifully cut, emerald-green tonic suit.

But of course, it had to be the ugly one that persisted in speaking to me.

'Come 'ere often, gel?' He elbowed me in the ribs, guffawed loudly at his unremarkable command of the cliché.

'No, not often,' I replied politely, hoping his friend would help me out.

'S'funny, 'cos I recognise you from somewhere,' Bug-Eyes continued.

Christ, not another one.

'You drink dahn the Hop Poles, do yer?' he eyed me up, from top to bottom, like a farmer assessing a pig for prime cuts.

'Sometimes.' I managed to catch the barmaid's eye. She slipped a look at Bug-Eyes like this was his usual routine, then back at me with a wink. 'What'll it be?'

'Pint of lager, please,' I offered.

'We only do halves here,' she explained, looking back at Bug-Eyes in a manner that made me want to laugh out loud.

'Half will be fine. Kronenbourg, please.'

''Ere, I'll get this.' Bug-Eyes flapped a crumpled fiver in the barmaid's general direction.

'No, it's OK.' I was desperate not to have to prolong conversation with this moron.

'Go on, gel, you can get the next one,' he insisted.

'It's quite all right.' I felt my mother's teacher voice coming on.

'Suit yourself,' he snorted, shovelling the greenfold back into his pocket, looking most put out.

His stoic companion clocked this and was finally moved to remark: 'Leave it out now, Darrell. She don't want to drink with you, and who can blame her?'

I smiled gratefully at him, he nodded back.

'She's a slag anyway,' decided Bug-Eyes. 'Stuck-up cow.'

Delightful. I took my half-pint and my change, squeezed out of there as quickly as I could, thinking, where's my Fairy Godfather?

Just as the question flashed through my mind, another familiar figure stepped through the door. Or rather, glided. It was the snowy-haired proprietor of the Deansgate, Gerry O'Brian, and he recognised me immediately.

'Hello, darling!' he said. 'How are you? I hope that encounter with Mr Flynn hasn't put you off visiting again?'

This was more of a result than I could have dreamed of. I looked back to see Bug-Eyes swearing in disgust, his friend smiling at him.

'Well, I'd love to,' I said. 'Only I thought you had to have membership.'

'For you, any time,' twinkled Gerry O'Brian. 'Can I get you a drink?'

'It's OK, I just got one.'

'Well, excuse me for one moment.'

I watched the waves part as O'Brian approached the bar. A glass of champagne was immediately proffered, and Five Houses was round the bar to slap him heartily on the back.

'Hello, petal.' Hugh was behind me. 'God, you know how to pick them. It took me about an hour to get round from the other side of the room.'

He looked immaculate in grey Sta-prest and a blue Hawaiian shirt. I doubted that Bug-Eyes would realise Hugh was gay and hoped the spectacle brought on some early angina.

Luckily, he'd already purchased himself a half, so we didn't have to go through all that again.

'I think we're in,' I told Hugh. 'The landlord is over there, he told me I was welcome any time.'

'Hugh Fielding,' came a loud voice from behind us. It was the sketcher. 'Thought it was you.' He reached out to pump Hugh's hand heartily. 'How are you, old boy?'

'Mark, how lovely to see you.' Hugh was clearly delighted, and I could see why. The sketcher, with his long brown hair and faux Victorian velvet waistcoat and trousers, was a proper Lord Byron. With maybe a smidgen of Marc Bolan and Jimmy Page thrown in for good measure.

'This is my friend Diana Kemp,' Hugh introduced us. 'Diana, Mark Miller. Mark did some album sleeves for us when I was at PRQ. I'm at Dove now, Mark, I'll have to see if I can get you in there too.'

'I know you.' Miller lit up as he eyed me. 'You're that one old Flynn was chasing round the room last Saturday. Christ!'

He shook my hand firmly. He had the longest eyelashes I'd ever seen on a man.

'Hope you've recovered.' He echoed Gerry O'Brian's sentiments. 'Mind you, he has been off his tree lately, poor bastard. Not the luckiest man in the world. So Hugh, Dove you say? Excellent, that's a step up the old ladder.'

'How about you? Have you had any good commissions?'

'Not bad,' the sketcher considered. '*Punch*, *Scallywag*. I've got a meeting with the *Mail on Sunday* next week, you never know.'

I suddenly remembered the name Miller under the satirical cartoon on the *Scallywag* letters page. His stuff was seriously savage.

'I've seen your stuff in *Scallywag*,' I said. 'That one of Ian Paisley…'

'Ah, don't mention that too loudly,' he said, finger to his lips. 'I've had death threats from that one. People with Ulster accents phoning up the office, saying they're old friends of mine, if they could just have my address…'

'Fucking hell!' Hugh exclaimed.

'Well, you know you're hitting them where it hurts,' I considered.

'You should show Di your stuff,' Hugh prompted. 'She works for a magazine. *Lux*, don't know if you've seen it.'

'Christ! You work there! That's an excellent magazine.'

'Well, my editor's well up on his art,' I explained. 'You should come in with your portfolio. I bet he'd be impressed.'

'Well, that calls for a drink,' Miller suggested. 'Tell you what, it's a bit crowded in here. Fancy going next door to the Deansgate? It'll be empty in there till closing time.'

Hugh winked at me.

Miller was spot on. The only customers at the Deansgate were a couple of old men, staring vacantly into their drinks. Upon hearing our footsteps on the stairs, one of them promptly fell backwards off his stool.

Miller rushed to help him up. 'Oh dear, old boy, is it time to call a cab?'

The barmaid looked mildly exasperated, as if this was a regular occurrence. 'I'll call him one,' she said. 'You get him out of the way.'

Mark and Hugh laid the old man out on the long seats in one of the booths. Before long he was snoring.

'Well, there you are, old chap,' Miller told Hugh. 'That's the Deansgate for you.'

He bought us a bottle of red wine, insisted on the booth in the far right corner.

'This is an amazing place,' I remarked, scanning the photographs of actors ancient and modern. 'You would never know it was here.'

'That's the thing I like about it,' Mark nodded.

'Last Saturday was the first time I've been here,' I continued. 'I really wanted Hugh to see it too.'

'Well, it's a happy coincidence, us meeting,' Miller raised his glass and we all clinked together. 'Now tell me a bit more about your magazine.'

I filled him in on the history, and the latest progress, the inroads into America. Several bottles of red wine flew by and suddenly, as the clock hit half past eleven, the place was swamped by the post-pub bar-rush; the same figures from the French and plenty more reassembling themselves in whatever space they could find, Gerry O'Brian gliding back down the steps to his place behind the bar, cigar on his lips, champagne flute in his hand. This, I decided, was the best place ever.

It was my round next, so I wobbled past the bodies to the bar, no mean feat when half of them were doing the geriatric jitterbug. I was amazed by their stamina. In fact, I was so busy looking at them that I hadn't noticed Bug-Eyes was propping up this bar too, and I had pushed in right next to him.

'So what makes you such a snotty bitch?' was his intro.

Startled, I turned round to face him. He was clearly arseholed, all red and sweaty with it, his hair grease making tracks down the sides of his ears and across his plump brow. Unfortunately, there was no sign of his friend here to save me. 'Jesus Christ,' I said before I could stop myself.

In every dream home, a heartache.

'Fancy yourself, do you?' He prodded me with one of his

sharp little fingers, spitting phlegm into my face as he did so. 'You fucking tart.'

A hand clapped on to his shoulder. A voice, deep with restrained menace, said: 'You don't talk to a lady like that.'

Niall Flynn.

He didn't look so ravaged as last time. In fact, with his hair swept back, his eyes clear, his black suit as well cut as a shark's fin, he looked exactly like the character Bug-Eyes was trying so desperately to emulate.

'Mr Marley,' the fat fiend choked, hardly believing what was happening.

Flynn pulled him round by the shoulder, so that he was staring him straight in the eye.

'Mr Flynn to you, you nonce,' he hissed, but he was putting on Marley's Cockney accent all the same, obviously wanting to give Bug-Eyes the fright of his tiny life. 'I don't like the cut of your jib.'

'I'm s-sorry, Mr Flynn, I didn't mean no offence.'

'Like hell you didn't. You're a worm, aren't you? A little, lowlife worm. I don't like drinking in the same place as worms, not when you should be where you belong, six feet under the earth.'

Bug-Eyes shook his head, and his body wobbled along with it, like this was precisely where he really wished to be.

'S-sorry,' he repeated, almost in tears.

'Good,' Flynn sneered at him. 'Then get out of my sight.'

Bug-Eyes practically ran all the way up the stairs out of the door. Flynn and I watched him go, then turned to each other and burst out laughing.

'What a command performance,' I said.

He stuck out his hand, spoke in his natural Galway accent. 'Hope it makes up for my behaviour last week. I owed you one. And it's always been my pleasure to deflate scum like him.'

We shook on it.

'Will you let me pay for that?' Flynn nodded at my bottle of wine.

This time, I knew it was OK to say yes.

He handed the money across to Gerry O'Brian, who smiled and winked at me. So this was why I was always welcome. He wanted to broker the peace.

'Do you want to join us?' I asked him. 'We've got a table in the corner.'

Flynn smiled and mock-bowed. 'If you can indulge an old man, then I'll make sure you have safe passage through the rest of these eejits.'

Mark was on his feet immediately as Flynn came over.

'Flynn, how are you, man? Great to see you.'

'I'm not doing too bad,' he said, seating himself down next to Miller, opposite Hugh and me. 'Glad to have the chance to apologise to this one.'

'Don't worry about it, really.' I felt myself blush, not wanting to be centre of attention. 'Anyway, I saw some stills of Miss Davey. I can see the resemblance.'

'There you go.' He lit a Silk Cut and proffered the pack. 'God rest her.'

We made a toast to my absent lookalike, then Miller excitedly led the conversation on. When Flynn got up to get another bottle, Hugh leaned across to me and whispered: 'Phwor, I'd still give him one even if he is a hundred. What a beautiful man. Then again,' he nodded towards Miller, 'I'd give him one too.'

'I noticed,' I laughed.

'No success so far,' he continued, 'but I'm going to keep on trying.'

So it continued, until Gerry O'Brian was walking around shouting out to all and sundry: 'Bedtime! Bedtime for boys and girls! My bed requires my presence!'

When he got to our corner, though, he shook his head. 'Not you, darlings. You can stay.'

And once he'd got rid of the worst of them he came to join our table, bringing a bottle of champagne with him. Before long, he,

Mark and Hugh were deep in discussion about Francis Bacon. It was at this moment I found myself telling Niall Flynn: 'I used to know Jon Jackson. Ages ago.'

His voice was soft and his expression concerned. 'So you have your own ghosts too?'

'You could say that.' I didn't know why I was telling him but, suddenly, it all came out. 'When Hugh and I were at art college, Jon was in a band called The Chevys. They used to play at what passed for our end of term balls. You know, they were from Norwich, we were in Yarmouth, they were the local heroes at the time. Anyway, they played one night, and he just started talking to me. I couldn't really believe it, and neither could any of the other girls there, who all wanted to rip my eyes out. But one thing led to another, and...' I stared into my glass, watching the little bubbles minnow their way up to the surface only to break as they reached the air. Telling him this felt oddly easy, even the hardest part of it. 'The thing was, it was the first time I had ever been with a man, properly, I mean. I was raped when I was 14, and I never thought I'd be able to do it.'

Flynn sighed deeply, put his hand on mine.

'And they still keep coming after you, the dogs,' he said. 'When something is beautiful and out of the reach, they'd rather destroy it than let anyone else have it. When Emily died, a lot of them were talking behind my back. I know what they were saying, that I had something to do with it. That I coulda pushed her...' He looked down at his hands. 'Somebody pushed her, but the Old Bill, they couldn't give a damn over a piece of Irish trash like her. Or like me. That's the way they were in those days. I know someone must have been up there with her, someone like that bastard at the bar tonight, someone she turned down. It was the story of her life. I thought I was going to make things safe for her. I got there too late.'

He looked up at me with bleary eyes. 'You see, you're more like her than you know. And you see now why I liked that character I played. The one that cuts down bastards and fucks with the Old

Bill like bejaysus. Perfect for me. I thought I'd only play him once, but God love him, Mr Jackson let me have another shot. And now the curse repeats itself.'

'There isn't a curse!' I exclaimed. 'Surely not?'

'I'm a fucking curse, I tell you.' He stretched back on his seat, his eyes misting over, staring into space.

'Well, you saved me tonight,' I told him, thinking of the pudgy face of Bug-Eyes, scowled up with the ugliness I had inspired in him merely by existing.

He patted my hand. 'I did that.'

'You all right, darling?' O'Brian noticed Flynn's discomfort.

'Ah, I'm fine, Gerry, don't you worry. Just feeling sorry for myself, as usual.'

'Well, you don't,' Gerry commanded. 'You've got nothing to be sorry for.'

I understood something then. In this room, so many secrets were hidden, guarded well by Gerry O'Brian and the Soho faithful. And Robin Ainsley was wrong. I didn't have to be careful with Niall Flynn. My secrets would be hidden here too. I decided to make something official, something I could go back and tell Neil.

'Do you ever do interviews?' I asked Flynn.

He smiled at me. 'Not ever,' he said, blowing out a smoke-ring. 'Not even to beautiful ladies like yourself.'

I clinked glasses with him and he winked and said: 'That way, we can always be friends.'

16

By 3pm on Saturday I had finally roused myself out of my pit.

Strangely, not as hungover as I should have been. Starving instead, and in no mood for cooking. I took myself down the street to the paper shop, bought a wedge of the broadsheets and took them to the greasy spoon.

Full English, hot milky coffee, and every arts supplement full of murder.

Jon Jackson's, naturally.

Every one of them edgy about the police's efforts. Every one of them trying to pick up on a different angle. Was Neil's boast correct – did we have something more than they did?

It appeared so. Had any of them had a 'last interview' to speak of, they would surely have run it by now.

The *Guardian* had a meticulous timeline of everything Jackson had been up to in his final twenty-four hours – apart from the fact he was in the company of cutting edge publisher Neil Bambridge, of course. Because the director's last public engagement had been a *Guardian* lecture, a sense of guilt hung over the piece. Was the killer, the article suggested, someone who had attended that very lecture? Someone who had managed to stalk Jackson from the NFT to the party at the Deansgate and then intercepted him on the way home? Could he have delivered a message, somehow, to Jackson while at the lecture, telling him to meet up with someone later? If so, the director hadn't told a single person about it. Not his agent, not his PR, not any of his friends. But it had been noted that he was clockwatching from the moment he arrived at the Deansgate, he hadn't engaged in any real conversation with anyone, which had seemed at odds, to those close to him, with the magnificent oration he had given to the audience at the NFT.

Did he know it was the last speech of the condemned man?

There was a list of places where he liked to hang out. Jackson wasn't a Soho scenester. He disliked the hysterical world of professional luvvies, preferred to keep the company of the same group of friends he had made when he had first arrived in London. The paper had discovered that his favourite haunt was a pub in Camden. It wasn't named in the piece, but it was obviously the Hop Poles. The *Guardian*'s crime reporters had attempted to speak to some of the regulars there, but no one who knew Jackson was saying anything. There was a picture of Woody and Alex, staring grimly from the bar. A caption noted Jon had made videos for both of their bands.

Then there was a description of Marley's scene in *Bent*. No one actually had full disclosure of the exact forensics but, the tabloids having whipped up a frenzy with their copycat angle, it seemed certain that Jackson's death had been a staged re-creation of the cinematic carnage.

Now, all sorts of conspiracy theories were being written into that scene. Was Jackson the secret father of somebody's son, someone who wasn't too happy to find out the truth – was that why he wrote the scene in the first place? Had he betrayed someone who now came looking for revenge, to cut him down in his prime? The *Guardian* wanted to look further than the copycat angle so rabidly pursued by their tabloid rivals.

So, the newshounds checked Jackson's childhood and his love life for clues.

He was born and brought up in a small town on the borders of Norfolk and Cambridgeshire, the bleak, reclaimed lands of the Fens. East Melsham had once been a profitable port town, eroded into decline over the past 100 years. The splendid Georgian residences set up by rich traders now sat uncomfortably next to gypsy encampments, the tourist industry was failing and unemployment was high. Up until twenty years ago, East Melsham had been a desirable place to live, a place where the rich could dock their yachts and commute easily to nearby Cambridge and Ely. But now it seemed more like an Old West frontier town, where youths raced rusty motorbikes down the high street at night and the police were conspicuous by their absence.

The reporters who had followed his trail down there had attempted to speak to some locals, but were taken into the back room of the pub they had entered, made to swallow their drinks down in one and told by the stern-voiced landlord not to come back. They likened it to the scene in *An American Werewolf in London*, where Brian Glover sends the hapless backpacking Yanks to their death on the moors. Which was a pretty accurate analogy. Strangers were never welcome in isolated Norfolk towns.

But Jackson, growing up as a resident of one of those remnants of prosperity, had the advantage of a top surgeon father who practised in Cambridge, and an academic mother who worked at King's College. The parents had been too upset to give interviews, but friends of the family had said this much: they thought their son would benefit from growing up in the country, rather than Cambridge or Ely, and it seemed their theories had worked. The boy, driven from an early age, was bright and popular at school. His parents noted his artistic bent and didn't hold him back or force him into academia. Maybe because he was an only child, who had come along late in life, he was their golden boy and they knew he'd excel at anything he turned his hand to. They wanted him to be happy.

So, the youthful Jackson studied graphic design at Norwich Art College in the early 1980s and, during his time as an OND student, had formed his own psychobilly band – The Chevys – who became local legends in the two years he fronted them.

But sleepy, picture-perfect Norwich was not going to hold someone like Jackson for long. He was accepted to St Martin's School of Art at eighteen and, soon after he arrived, diverted himself away from graphic design into film and video. Fascinated by the emergent pop promos and their ability to shock and provoke, he made a number of attention-grabbing music videos for bands he knocked about with, before his first ever feature film made him the saviour of British cinema.

He'd had a lot of girlfriends too; couldn't seem to stay the course with any of them for too long, probably because of that urgent inner drive. Or maybe he was too much of a lad's lad. However, here too, none of them had a bad word to say about him. The testimonies of tears proved that mostly they were still in love with him to this day. His last flame, a stunning, waif-like model, was still in shock after he suddenly broke things off with her, six months prior to his body being found.

The *Guardian*'s conclusion was that Jon Jackson was a man it would be easy to be jealous of. But no one they had contacted had anything remotely bad to say about him. No one could imagine who he could have offended in such a way. Because he had always been so outgoing and gregarious, it really didn't seem like he could have a secret to hide.

I wondered what would come out on Neil's tapes. He still hadn't managed to finish his transcribing, or even offered to show us what he had got. Would there be some clue lurking there in the spools, a casual comment that was actually loaded with meaning?

If so, why hadn't D. S. Linehan been knocking again?

I finished my food, supped the dregs of my now cold coffee. Limp bacon rinds lay like pale worms on my greasy plate. It was time to go.

I collected my papers together, paid for the food and stepped out into another drizzly early evening. All along this end of the market, the traders were calling out their special end-of-day offers:

'Two pahnds a pahnd yer strawberries.'

'Larverly ripe tomaters, pahnd a box, get 'em while they last, ladies.'

'Two fer a pahnd yer collies, won't get 'em cheaper than this.'

Stalls surrounded by ladies in plastic raincaps, queuing up for the offers that were slung rapidly into blue carrier bags, the callers not missing a beat as they served. Outside the Salvation Army office, a solitary fat man in uniform shook his collection box forlornly, the happy shoppers surrounding his patch more interested in cut-rate vegetables than saving lost souls.

I rattled the last of my change into his plastic receptacle. It was worth it to see the fat man smile. All weathers, all year round, I saw him standing here, carrying out his task with the patience of Job.

Up the drizzle of Kensington Park Road towards home, the street lights coming on in one quick buzz, leaving blurred amber trails in the gutters. I wondered if Barry was home.

Of course, having spent all my coppers on Cuppa Soups for the homeless, I had to go back down to my room and fish about in the bottoms of bags for stray 2p pieces. When I got up to ten of them, I took them back upstairs, into the murky hallway, dropped them into the slot and dialled.

He answered on the third ring, sounding sleepy. ''Ello, pet, how are you?'

'Not too bad, just wondered if you fancied some company. You sound knackered.'

'Umm, yeah, I stayed up till four interviewing Abel Ferrara.' He paused to yawn. 'Fuckin' brilliant, mind. He talked a lot about *I Spit On Your Grave*. Got everything I needed for me feature, so it was well worth it. I've just been pulling all me books out about video nasties and Sam Peckinpah and that. Wish he was still around to talk to.'

'That's really good news,' I enthused. 'So, d'you need an early night?'

'Nah, I'm all right. I've done enough for one day. Come over, if you like. I tell you what, give me an hour and I'll go down the video shop, see if they've got those movies you wanted to see.'

'Excellent.' This was what I'd been hoping for. 'I'll bring us a bottle of wine.'

'All right, pet, I'll see you,' he paused to check his watch, 'about seven.'

'Deal.'

I went back down to the kitchen, made myself another coffee to go with the rest of the papers, and switched on the TV to the early evening news.

'Kentish Town CID have arrested a man in connection with the murder of film director Jon Jackson,' said the stony-faced newscaster. 'The man, who has not been named, was apparently picked up after repeated surveillance on the late director's home in Primrose Hill and the murder site in Camden Town. It is now thirteen days since Jackson's body was discovered, and pressure had been mounting on police to find their suspect...'

My cup of coffee slid out of my hand and tipped itself all over the floor.

17

Jackson leaned across the Gents' cubicle door, his right hand holding it shut, bunched into a fist. His bicep flexed; it was as hard as his eyes, testament to daily workouts down the gym. His body was in good shape, that much he clearly wanted to make evident. But at the same time, a muscle was starting to flicker under his left eye.

'What's going on here?' His voice a low rumble. 'What are you playing at?'

His tone was as vexed as that twitch, as if the man who'd intruded into his normal, cheery Saturday night was the one in the wrong.

But the man who wasn't Andy Smith didn't get riled. Now he could clearly read the annoyance in the other, he felt as if a cape of cool self-assurance had been placed across his shoulders. He looked calmly across at Jackson. He was just playing for time. It was a bluff, and he knew it.

'Turned out well, didn't it?' He enjoyed each moment of finally being able to say it. 'The idea for that film?'

'I don't know what you're talking about?'

Someone pushed against the door from the other side. For all his muscles, Jackson was momentarily jolted.

'Just a minute, mate, I'll be straight out,' he called, pushing himself back upright. He heard his companion chuckle, and it was a sound that travelled down his nerve endings like the edge of a razor blade.

'Oh really,' the other man was saying. 'So we don't need to

be standing in here then. You might as well open the door. You won't mind talking to me in public? Back in there?'

He motioned with his head beyond the toilet door.

Jackson's eyes darted furtively from the mocking gaze to the floor and back again.

'I'll talk to you all right,' he seethed. 'But not in there. I think we need some privacy for this, don't you?'

'As you like.' The other man was expansive, generous even, he thought. He'd work out a scenario to save Jackson's blushes. 'Why don't you invite me back to yours after the pub? To look at your Northern soul records?'

Jackson hesitated for a moment, clenched his jaw. It was obvious he didn't like the idea, but it seemed he had no choice.

'Yeah,' he agreed, not quite meeting the other's eye. 'That sounds like a plan.'

He opened the toilet door, ushered Andy through, back to the bar.

''Bout time too,' an aggrieved-looking wino snarled as they emerged.

To the outside world, the pair were all smiles. And just a bit hopped up, edgy. The way you would be after a couple of lines of the white stuff.

Smith returned to Tony, Mitch and Lee. Jackson got his pint off the bar, ambled back to the pool table, where he laid down a twenty-pence piece and announced: 'I'm on.'

It wasn't long before he got his turn. He picked up a cue, chalked the end thoughtfully. Jackson was good at pool, like he was good at most things. Look at him, thought Andy, still showing off, even at a time like this.

Jackson broke strongly, accurately, sending two red balls into opposite pockets.

He looked up and across at Andy, to see if he was watching.

Andy smiled and raised his pint.

'Jammy sod,' said Woody, not fancying his chances of winning this game.

Jackson smiled back at his adversary.

For appearance's sake, he was careful to move back over to Tony's group about half an hour before closing time. Needless to say, the conversation came back down to rare records; they scarcely talked about anything else. And so it seemed to everyone else present, that when Mike the landlord called time and everyone began to swill back the contents of their glasses, Jackson's comments to Smith were only a natural extension of their conversation.

'Tell you what,' the director was saying, as he placed his empty glass back down on the bar. 'D'you fancy coming back to mine and having a look at some of the stuff I got in the States? I wouldn't mind your opinion on it. I think I found a goldmine in this place in Detroit. Car City Records it's called. It's about the size of a car plant, stuffed full of vinyl. I'm pretty sure I got away with some bargains, but I'd like to know for sure.'

'Really?' Andy feigned delighted surprise. 'That would be great.'

'Nice one,' Jackson winked. 'I'll just get my stuff.'

Outside, on Arlington Road, the director walked quickly, past Temperance House, away from prying ears. His companion kept the pace easily, enjoying every moment of the mounting sense of power within him.

'So, come on then, what are you doing here?' Jackson finally muttered.

'It's a free country,' the other man mused. 'You never thought you'd see me again, did you?'

'No,' Jackson admitted.

They passed some sacks of litter in a doorway. The sacks moved and groaned: 'Got ten pence on ya, guv?'

Jackson jerked away, spooked.

'Like it round here, do you?' his companion relished asking. 'I do. I've enjoyed working for Big Tony. I must say, you get a better class of people round here. Honest, they are. More decent than I'm used to. Funny thing is, that's exactly what they think of you.'

Jackson stopped stock-still at this. 'How long have you been stalking me?' he snapped.

'A couple of months, probably three,' Smith replied, as casually as if he was discussing the weather. 'Since I first went to the pictures to see your movie. After that I thought I'd come down to London to find you. Congratulate you on what sterling work you did.'

'Look, I think I know what you've come to say,' Jackson blurted now, angry all of a sudden at the veiled menace implicit in his companion's voice. 'But I don't know what you expect me to do about it.'

He heard a low, satisfied chuckle in response. Then: 'Well, first of all, you can show me what you bought with the money from that film. I want to know how well you're living from it.'

'Look.' The calmness he had shown over the pool table was escaping Jackson. He felt the edge of the razor again. 'There's an after-hours club on the end of this road. I think we should go in there. People will leave us alone in there, we'll be able to talk.'

'Ah, Jonny boy, you're so modest. You're a famous man now. Of course they're not going to leave you alone. They never do, do they? I've seen you, on the market, in the pub. And they're going to hear things, aren't they? Things that could be embarrassing to a man in your position. No, no, no, Jonny. That won't do. I think we should go to your house, get some real privacy. Just like you said.'

Jackson's mouth fell open.

'Otherwise, I could just leave you here and start talking to the press instead. I mean, I could have done that anyway. But out of respect for the past, I thought I'd speak to you about it first.'

Smith could see Jackson weighing it up, could see that twitch under his eye again betraying his smooth exterior. A couple of seconds and Jackson capitulated. 'OK,' he said meekly, 'it's up here.'

It was a big, comfortable flat, up on Primrose Hill. A place renowned for its literary heritage – Rimbaud and Verlaine, Sylvia Plath and Ted Hughes, they'd all lived, loved, fought and gassed themselves up here. All the doomed romantics.

'Nice place,' Smith said, letting his eyes travel languidly around the designer furniture, the stripped and polished floorboards, the pop art and cinema posters all framed up nicely, hanging on the shiny white walls. Jackson ushered him left, into the spacious front room. Inside was a brand-new TV, a wall of videos, a top-of-the-range sound system and another wall of records and CDs.

'Paid for all of this, did it?' the inquisitor asked.

'Not entirely. I made quite a bit doing pop videos.'

'I see.' He plopped himself down on the red leather sofa, which was designed to replicate the rear seats of a fifties Cadillac.

'I fancy a beer,' he said. 'And I'm sure you're not short of a few. Get us one, will you?'

Just then though, as Jackson went back through the door towards his kitchen, Smith felt his control of the situation slipping away. Smith looked down at the copy of *GQ* lying on the coffee table, and suddenly it seemed to get further and further away from him, as if a tunnel was opening up before his eyes. He began to hear a roaring noise, like the wind rushing by him, filling his ears. He shut his eyes for a second and when he opened them, he wasn't seeing a glossy magazine on a table any more, but a small boy standing under a bridge.

The small boy was doing something. Something disgusting. He was slowly and determinedly tearing a tiny duckling apart with his bare hands. Whistling while he did it. Throwing the feathers and bloody parts into the river, then putting his fingers inside his trousers. And as he watched, Smith realised just who that small boy really was. It was him, Jamie Merritt, at the age of nine.

'Fuck.' He wiped his hand across his brow, felt the cold sweat that had formed there. What was going on here? What was seeing Jackson again doing to him, bringing back this unwelcome memory from out of nowhere? Leaning back on the director's sofa, he screwed his eyes shut, shook the memory out of his head. Heard the clunk of a can of lager being placed on the table before him. Opened his eyes and fell back through the tunnel, up through the table, until things were back where they should be. Jon Jackson standing there, looking nervous.

He reached for the tin, flashes of light still crackling round the corners of his vision as his pupils contracted rapidly.

'Cheers, mate.' He cracked the can open and knocked it back noisily, smacking his lips.

Jackson slumped down on a matching, facing chair, totally transfixed by the intruder on the sofa.

Smith was returning to himself as the cold beer hit the spot. He lounged more comfortably against the leather seat, lit a cigarette.

'The thing is,' he finally said, 'if you'd have just left it as an idea two little kids had and done the rest yourself, that would have been fine. But you know I sent you a script and I know you must have got it.' He put his can down on the table and started to chuckle, his shoulders shaking up and down.

'What's so funny?' Jackson said.

'Before I sent you that film script, I sent a copy to myself. With a date stamp on the envelope and everything. So I've got all the evidence I need that you stole from me. You hardly changed a thing about it, did you?'

He could see from the reaction on the director's face how woefully Jackson had underestimated him.

'No.' Jackson's voice came out as a whisper.

'Did you think I wouldn't find you again?' The voice sounded genuinely interested. 'Did you think I was gonna stay in that place, mouldering away, while you got all rich and famous off of my work?'

'OK,' Jackson said, staring at the floor. 'I admit I got your script. And until I did, I had forgotten about those stories we used to make up. And you did give me an idea, but it wasn't a proper script you sent me, not one you can work from in the real world. It was an idea we already had, you admit that yourself, but it was the most clichéd, ridiculous idea. I thought if I made it look stylish, made it look knowing, put in a load of wisecracks from older, better movies, it would prove that all the public want *is* clichéd, ridiculous shit. It was a joke. And the joke was, it worked.'

Smith couldn't believe what he was hearing now.

'My ideas, shit?' he screamed. 'What's all this?' He flung his arm around the spacious room. 'Is this shit? Well, if it is, I'll have some of that shit too.' He stood up, loomed over Jackson, who squirmed back in his chair.

'I saw you,' Jackson murmured, 'killing a little duckling. I saw what you got up to when you thought I wasn't around.'

Smith's head swam. For a second, he thought he was going to faint. This was outrageous! Jackson had put that memory in his head! Put it there, just when he had him where he wanted him! Put it there to try and trick him!

But he couldn't let him see that, couldn't let him know. 'What,' he demanded instead, 'are you talking about?'

'Listen.' Jackson held his face back so far that veins bulged in his neck. 'Listen, I know what happened to you. I know how terrible things were for you. I wanted to make it up to you some other way. But, honest to God, I was too scared of you to do it directly.'

'But you were my friend!' Smith's voice was shrill. 'My only friend. That's why I sent you the script, you bastard. I trusted you. And you ripped me off.' Tears glittered in the corners of his eyes, his thousand-yard stare receding.

'But there is a way I can make it back up to you,' Jackson spoke quickly. 'There is something I can do for you that would mean you could have a place like this, and all the things that come with it. Getting stopped on the market by fans. Having people do you favours, giving you stuff for nothing when you already have more things than you could possibly need. It's a good life, as you've already realised. And it could be yours too.'

'Oh yeah?'

Smith looked at Jackson, the way a small boy had looked at another more confident boy all those years ago, waiting under the bridge. And, just like before, he wondered if Jon Jackson could save him.

18

I could hardly wait to get myself up to Barry's.

By seven o'clock, the drizzle had turned into a downpour, and a nasty wind came with it, blowing my umbrella inside out as I sludged up the Grove towards St Charles Square. Here Barry's flat was situated, on the second floor of a Victorian house, less grand than my own in demeanour, but a great deal more roomy inside. I picked up a bottle of red in the shop by the tube, which was crammed with steaming itinerants, all cursing and muttering about the weather. The rain had washed away the label by the time I reached Barry's door. Even my shoes were filling up.

I pressed the doorbell shivering. It was April Fool's Day all right.

A light came on and I heard Barry clatter down the stairs. He swung the door open on a hallway awash with the comforting orange glow of shaded light as I folded down my brolly in a pool of water.

'Get in quick,' he said. 'What a fuckin' night.'

'You can say that again. Have you seen the news?'

'No.' He led the way back upstairs. The hallway pulsated to the sound of industrial music, emanating from his flat. 'I've just been listening to records while I cleared up. Why? What's happened?'

'They've got someone,' I told him.

'You what?'

'They've arrested someone for Jon Jackson. Caught him in his flat.'

'Fuckin' 'ell, let me put the telly on quick.'

As I hung up my coat in the hallway of his flat, I could see that Barry's front room was full of the signs of recent activity. Books and videos piled up on his low coffee table, a pen rested on his bulging notepad, a further stack of magazines, most of them fastidiously kept inside plastic sleeves, had been placed underneath. Even in the midst of research, he arranged his things neatly, carefully.

The piledriver sounds of Ministry's 'Stigmata' were suddenly silenced.

''Ere, d'you want to stick your brolly in the sink until it dries out?' Barry called out.

'Er, yeah.' I moved across the entrance hall quickly, switched the light on in his bathroom. What appeared to be a bleached bison's skull was resting in the bath. Collecting the remains of animals was one of Barry's favourite hobbies; he'd really had a result with this one.

Channel 4 news was on as I entered the front room, Barry stood watching it, still holding the remote. Scenes on the screen of a country in chaos: flash floods had hit the Midlands and Wales, in a mirror of the monsoon raging down the Grove. Rivers had burst their banks and householders were stranded. We watched people sitting on top of their roofs, staring uncomprehendingly at fast, brown water rushing through the ground floors of their houses. To compound the Midlands' misery, lightning had struck the roof of a council block in Dudley, setting the entire building ablaze.

'Good job it weren't Birmingham,' Barry noted, nipping into the kitchen to fetch a corkscrew and some glasses. 'Otherwise I'd have to build a fuckin' ark and go and save me folks.'

Michael Portillo was sniping at John Smith by the time he got back, a wet weekend for the government too.

'I hope we haven't missed it,' I said, as he handed me a glass.

Then suddenly, late news.

A crowd of newsmen outside Scotland Yard, umbrellas and floodlights, the constant pop of flashbulbs. D. S. Linehan and some top brass assembled for an impromptu newscast, their hands upturned, their expressions placatory. Except for Linehan, who looked wired. 'I can confirm that we have arrested a man in connection with the Jackson case,' said Chief Inspector Phil Benson of the Yard, as flashbulbs popped around his head. 'He is helping us with a new line of enquiry and we'll be holding him overnight.'

'D'you have a name?' one of the press was shouting.

'No names at present,' Benson was saying as Linehan stared into the camera as if daring it to ask him outside.

'Is it correct that you caught him at the murder site?' Another voice discernible from the throng.

'We have no comment to make on that at present.' Linehan cutting in over his superior.

'Have you charged him?'

'At the moment he is helping us with our enquiries.' Benson smoothness itself, leaning into the frame and obscuring his mad-looking D. S. from view. 'When we have any more news, you gentlemen will be the first to know.'

'Was it a stalker?'

'Thank you, everyone.' Three figures sweeping back into the station, the hacks still baying.

Cut back to the studio and world news.

'Sounds serious,' whispered Barry. 'Christ, I hope they've nailed him.'

'I'll drink to that.' We clinked glasses. 'That Linehan looked deranged.'

Barry turned the sound down. 'Shall I ring Bambridge, make sure it's not him?' He was only half-joking, but I laughed all the same.

'Yeah, you'd better,' I jousted back.

'Nah, let's leave him there in the dungeon, with the rats and the leg irons. Like you said, that copper looked berserk, which probably means he's taken a trip down the stairs already. I knew he was lying about what was on those tapes.'

'We could sell him back to the Yanks,' I suggested. 'Biggest entrepreneur since Howard Hughes responsible for biggest murder since Manson.'

'It'll sell shitloads!' Barry roared.

'Seriously, though, I hope Linehan is scaring the fucker the way he scared Neil. I wouldn't like to have to come up against him.'

'I hope he's swinging open the iron maiden right now,' Barry agreed.

'Surveillance on his house, and the murder site, eh?' I reflected. 'So all those conspiracy theorists could be right, it could have been an obsessed fan.'

'Like I said the other day, they always give themselves away in the end,' Barry nodded. 'I've read all the books, you know.'

Indeed he had. His bookshelves were lined with true-crime titles, especially ones about the Manson family. I'd sampled a few, but such books are rarely well written, usually reading like catalogues of carnage, as flatly monotonous as the killers they describe.

'So what do you reckon? They deliberately came back to the scene of the crime to taunt the Old Bill?'

'Could have done,' he nodded. 'If they thought the pigs weren't being clever enough. Remember Ed Kemper? He kept ringing the fuckers up when he couldn't take it no more, and they kept telling him to stop bothering them. It's fucking unbelievable, but it happened.'

'And now the killer gets to have his celebrity fix.' Another thing I remembered from Barry's True Crime Library. They all desperately wanted the world to know their names.

'That's about the size of it,' he nodded grimly. 'The cunt.'

'Well, it all works out neatly for our next issue,' I mused. 'Almost as if Bambridge directed it.'

'You sure you don't want me to ring him?'

'Nah, I'm gonna wait for Monday to torture him about the night I had on Friday. Chatting to Niall Flynn at the Deansgate. You were right about him, Barry, they were all winding me up, because he really is a lovely guy. Not only did he apologise and buy me a drink, but he got rid of some fucking little psycho who was trying to wind me up at the bar. Then he spent all night talking to us.'

'I thought he would be diamond. So what were you up to then, chasing after him? Thought you already had a new fella?'

'Shut up!' I whacked him with one of his red satin cushions. 'For the millionth time I do not fancy Simon Everill. No, I wanted to go back to that club to show Hugh. It's fucking brilliant there. And Bambridge, surprise surprise, wanted me to get an interview with Flynn. He said he never gave them. Not even to girls like me.'

Barry chortled. 'Oh dear, that'll please his nibs. Anyway, next time you go there you can take me, if that's who you're hanging out with.'

'Too right I will. Neil can stuff the Groucho up his arse.'

'Oooooh.' Barry put on his gay voice. 'But he'd love that. It's ever so roomy up there with his split-crotch pants.'

'And all those Americans.'

'Well, speaking of Flynn, I got *The Slaves of Solitude*.' Barry reached under the table for the videotape. 'But they don't reckon they ever had a copy of *Next Door To Danger*. Bloke said Psychotronic's probably the only place that's got it.'

'Oh, don't worry about that,' I said. 'It's brilliant that you got one of them.'

'Let me just give me mam a quick call, make sure they're all right.'

'Will do.'

I settled down on the sofa, replaying the scene from Scotland Yard in my head. It was funny, but Linehan's expression reminded me of Niall Flynn as Marley. Maybe he had the same desire to crack heads. And they both came from Ireland, similar accents, maybe even the same place. Coincidences popped through my mind like the tabloid flashbulbs outside the Yard.

Barry came back. 'They're all right where they are, but there's a right old storm going on there an' all,' he told me, pushing the tape into the video. 'Apparently, me brother's lost half the tiles off his roof. Right.' He plopped down on to the sofa beside me. 'Here we go.'

The screen filled with flickering black-and-white images. London in the Blitz. A steam train travelling up from Paddington and out into the suburbs, viewed from above as the titles filled the screen. No lights on in the carriages, the whole of the capital under the cover of the blackout. Tense, string-led music rode the rhythm of the locomotive, which finally pulled, with a hiss, into a station called Thames Lockden.

The engine seemed to wheeze with relief as it disgorged its load: doors slamming open from each carriage, a stream of commuters coursing down the platform. At first they were just shot en masse; men in suits, bowler hats and the era's trademark thick, round glasses, clutching their briefcases. Women in big coats and smart hats, their hair rolled up away from their faces, secretaries and nurses, home from their day in the beleaguered city. All of them walking towards the camera with tight, hurried expressions, passing through the ticket barrier and going their separate ways.

Then the lens panned in on one face in particular.

An oval face, framed with upward-swept black hair, big dark eyes conveying a resigned, almost bored expression. She was wearing a beret and a long dark coat, nipped in at the waist, flowing out to mid-calf. Her gloved hands clutched a handbag and a newspaper. The camera followed her as she left the station, took the path next to the river. Emily Davey.

'Bloody 'ell, pet, it's you!' Barry dug me in the ribs.

'No way. She's much too pretty.'

All the same, it was disconcerting watching her, walking into the darkness of a 1960s film set, an Ealing back-lot turned into a 1940s suburb, a fake moon rippling across the surface of the black, fake river.

Emily Davey's Miss Roach was about to meet the man who

would turn her world upside down, a man who would disrupt her suburban existence more completely than the doodlebugs and V2s falling like rain on the city. He would come to her with a smile and an outstretched hand. She would be so taken aback by his interest, she would invite him across the threshold of her staid, unremarkable life with a recklessness she didn't know she possessed.

But, for the moment, she walked on, not knowing.

The Sunday red tops didn't tell us much.

Neither did the first editions on Monday.

I was quite disappointed by the lack of tabloid tenacity. Normally, every trashcan in Camden would be crawling with them by now, forcing fivers into the hands of nosy neighbours, digging up relations of the arrested man, whom Scotland Yard stoically refused to name.

Normally something would have broken.

All that was reported was that the man had been charged. With B&E and intent to rob.

'They're just holding him,' Barry reckoned, as we scanned the Monday linens over coffee in the office, 'till he cracks.'

The highlight of the Sundays had been the *News of the Screws'* supershrink proclaiming his own genius:

Kentish Town CID had been on constant surveillance of both the Jackson residence and the murder scene. We know the director returned to his luxury Primrose Hill flat before the killing took place, thanks to the testimony of cab driver Thomas Franks, who went in for voluntary questioning and was released without charge the day after the body was found. Was the killer already waiting for him there? Scotland Yard's top brass say that the investigating officers were sure the killer would come back to gloat over the scene of the crime. And as this paper has pointed out from Day One, this is clearly the work of an obsessive. A mind twisted by the violence witnessed legally, over popcorn and Kiora, in a cinema near you...

Barry had definitely thought that would help him with his anti-censorship piece.

Neil had seemed more agitated than either of us. He'd not been pleased by my failure to get a Flynn interview for a start. Now he was glued to the radio, checking the news every quarter of an hour, desperate for a murder charge. Wouldn't even come out for lunch with us; just brooded over sandwiches which, by the look of the remains, he'd merely picked apart, not eaten.

That afternoon, Barry was off to meet that George Dickinson, to get the criminal expert's opinion.

'See what he makes of it all, Barry,' urged Neil as Hudson tried to leave. 'He must have some insider gen, for Christ's sake, an old hand like him.'

'Or the old Masonic handshake.' Barry waved his arse in Neil's face, shoving his arm between his cheeks like an elephant's trunk.

'Is that how you think they do it?' asked Neil, disgusted.

'Well, you would know. See you all!' He blew kisses from the top of the stairs.

Bambridge looked like someone was holding a kipper under his nose.

The next news from GLR was that Primrose Hill had been sealed off to traffic, as police attempted to keep the tabloids and curious members of the public at bay.

'Have you been up there lately?' Neil asked me.

'No, not since that day...' I didn't want to wind him up any more than he clearly was already.

'When you went to the Hop Poles?' he went on. 'Really, you should have gone back there since. You and Hudson know all those people who won't speak to the tabloids. They'd talk to you. We should really get them involved in this issue. Seeing as you failed to get Flynn, they'd be the ones who'd give us the edge.'

'Well, you'd have to talk to Barry about that one.' I tried to sidestep. 'They're his friends, not mine. Maybe when the cops bring a murder charge, they'll be prepared to speak.'

'Yes.' Neil was twiddling maniacally with a pencil. 'Yes, you're right. Well, let's just hope they get a result, and get it soon.'

The pencil pinged out of his hands and broke in half on the wall opposite.

'What are you worried about?'

'I just want this issue to be perfect,' he snapped. Then tried to about-face. 'Look, don't mind me. I think I need to get out for a minute. Do you want anything from out there?'

'You can get us a Coke,' I said archly. But he wasn't biting.

'OK. Take any calls, Diana. If it's for me, I'll be ten minutes.'

I had my suspicions about Bambridge's agitated demeanour. Most of the people in the music world behaved precisely the way he did, and were equally crap at being furtive.

Here he was, doing his pieces about the murder charge because he wanted to get Woody and Alex in the mag. That was his angle. He just hadn't quite got the nerve to hit Barry with it yet. So he was off to buy some powdered charisma.

What he wouldn't do for those Yanks.

Meanwhile, I had my own mission to contend with. I had finished all my transcribing now. Except for Everill. I picked up the tape, wondered whether I should just go through it now, while the office was empty. Maybe it wouldn't be as embarrassing as I imagined. Maybe it was one of those ones that made you cringe at the time but turned out all right in the end.

I slotted it into my Dictaphone.

And anyway, I had tomorrow night. My final chance, probably, to make sense of Simon Everill.

19

'You,' Jackson's eyes were now burning bright, but his voice remained soft, calm, 'have a real story to tell.'

His aggressor was still teetering between two worlds. Seconds ago, he had felt the fog coming down on his brain, the red, throbbing urge to reach out his hands and lock them around Jackson's throat then squeeze and squeeze until the bastard had no clever words left to say. But now, watching the pleading in the director's eyes, the throbbing was subsiding, he was starting to make out what was being said.

'What do you mean by that?' Mad Jamie Merritt melted back into everyman Andy Smith, tilting his head back, a frown upon his brow.

Jackson swallowed hard and played his hand. 'You have a proper story to tell. Better than all that gangster bollocks. You know, what happened when we were kids.'

It was the other man's turn to feel a needle of fear deep in his stomach. That part of his past was another country. Somewhere he never wanted to return to.

'It's a really important story to tell,' the director carried on, keeping his tone sympathetic. 'Something I think the world should be aware of. That these little rural communities that everyone thinks are so idyllic are capable of covering up crimes as great as the one that happened to you. That, out in the country, we might as well still be living in the 1600s. And Jamie…'

Jackson using his real name now made the man sitting opposite start to feel like he did when they were children, clumsy and stupid and awed.

'Jamie, you wouldn't have to tell it the way it really happened. You can use what they call magic realism, make it almost like a fairytale, then it would have even more impact. I know you like writing, and now I'm in the position where I know people, powerful people, who could get that book in print. No one would ever need to know that I helped you, but we could make you a star, a real star. And you could get your revenge, not just on me, but on the people that did those terrible things to you. Success, I have always thought, is the best form of revenge…'

Clumsy and stupid, he felt, when only moments ago he'd been so powerful and strong.

'Why would anyone want to read a book about me?' he finally asked.

'Because,' Jackson couldn't actually meet his eye, 'I couldn't believe, and I still can't believe, that no one ever did anything to help you. That we lived in a place where all of that could be swept under the carpet. You have the power to tell people that we do live in a world like that.'

'And you think we can make money out of that?'

'Yes,' said Jackson, his voice a whisper now. 'Money to pay back what I owe you, what I took from you.'

He looked searchingly towards the other man, trying to find a sign that his line had worked, that he was off the hook.

Merritt and Smith continued to flicker and fluctuate with each other, caught between hatred and devotion. The man at their centre tried to hold on to hate. 'First you steal my idea.' The words came so quietly they were barely audible. 'Now you think you can steal my life.'

'I'm giving you a new life,' Jackson's brown eyes were pleading now, 'as Britain's best new writer, a man with something really important to say. A man people will have to listen to.'

The other's eyes were fearsome now, like those of a wounded, vicious dog.

'How the fuck do you expect me to believe you?' He leaped to his feet.

Jackson cowered back into his Cadillac chair, his hands, palms outwards, in front of his face.

'Because if I don't do what I say and help you with this, you can go straight to the *News of the Screws* and fuck my life up totally. With my blessing. I know I've done you wrong. Now I want to do my penance.'

A twisted smile played upon the lips of the other. From the jumbling shapes in his mind, Mad Jamie was making himself heard.

'Or I could just kill you now,' he said, as if asking someone to kindly pass the salt. 'You don't doubt that I could kill you, do you, Jonny boy?'

A little boy shredding ducklings, long thumbs gouging into arterial blood, ripping, tearing tiny wings and little legs, eyes far away in another world.

'No,' he whispered, 'I don't doubt it at all.'

'Good.'

And with that, Mad Jamie smiled and fled, leaving Andy Smith's mind pleasantly smooth once more. Yes, here he was again, back in the commanding position, holding Jackson's life in the palm of his hands. Reversing the positions of their childhood, where he was the supplicant, desperate to be accepted. That old tattoo was now a distant hum, a soothing echo fading into perfect clarity.

After all, there was a lot to be said for Jonny's proposal.

This flat, for instance. Wouldn't it be nice to have a place like this, instead of a dilapidated squat in Sodom? Wouldn't it be nice to have good clothes, to be the one that people looked up to? No one would snigger behind his back again when he was famous. They'd have to respect him, grovel to him, even. Starting with Jackson. After all, he would only be taking what was rightly his. His own life story.

To Jackson's eyes, the change ran smoothly over him, like water across stone. 'Good,' he repeated, sitting back down on the sofa, making himself comfortable. 'Because your kind idea has its merits.'

'I'll do it for you, I promise. I owe you, big time.'

'Yes. Another beer please, landlord, to seal the deal. And then you can explain to me more about your great scheme.'

'Fuck that.' Jackson's face cracked into a relieved smile. 'This calls for champagne.' He got to his feet, made for the kitchen. 'Something you'd better get used to.'

Smith licked his lips in anticipation.

'One thing,' the director said as he returned, placing a bottle of Moët carefully down on the coffee table. 'What name are you going to write it under? Have you changed your name officially to Andy Smith?'

The other man glanced up quickly, thinking on his feet. Mad Jamie had to be banished, but Andy Smith, that banal shade, he wasn't the one to take his place. No, if glory was to come it was to be under the name he had chosen for himself, when he had been born again to the world. 'That's just a name I'm, er, trading under.' He forced a laugh. 'You see, Jamie Merritt got swept away under that bridge, even if I didn't.'

Jackson popped the cork soundlessly under a tea-towel. He watched his companion with concerned eyes as he poured out the champagne.

'They give you a different identity when something like that happens to you,' the other man continued, watching the bubbles rise up the glasses. 'They think it'll protect you in later life. Dr Barnardos sent me to a new family, and I took their last name. They let me choose the first name.'

'So what is your name now?' Jackson passed the glass over.

The grey eyes met his.

'Simon. Simon Everill.'

20

By Tuesday morning, the tabloids had him.

Percival Prevezeer was the name of the man who'd been captured in Jon Jackson's house. An only child, but with a large extended family, the *Post* had finally tracked down his brood, and found an uncle voluble enough to speak for the whole clan. He said: 'He liked the film, yeah, and he did dress up like a gangster. But loads of kids are doing that nowadays. Maybe he was a little bit misguided, a little bit out of order. But there's no way my Percy is a killer. We just want the police to stop holding him on trumped-up charges and let him home to his mum.'

There was a picture of Percy in a black suit and white shirt, posing with a Martini glass in his hand, expression on his face like he was the Queen of Sheba. Maybe the family thought he looked sophisticated in this *faux* James Bond pose. Trouble was, it made him look even more of an idiot.

'I don't believe this,' Barry noted. 'This little bum bandit? He don't look capable.'

We were, all three of us, hunched over the papers with our breakfasts, digesting the facts quicker than the toast and croissants still in their paper bags on our desks. Work wasn't going to happen until we had the full SP on what had been going on in the Jackson house over the weekend.

More sinister background details had been unearthed. Percy – or Percival, as he preferred to be known – had worked for the Ministry of Defence for fifteen years. In the Press Office. Obviously no one wanted to breach the Official Secrets Act, but a former colleague, who refused to be named, did say this much: 'Percy was always obsessed with something. Mainly it was James Bond, which is why I think he wanted to work at the MOD. Then that film *Bent* came out. He used to say he'd been to see it over twenty times. You have to look smart for work, but he really pushed it, dressing like one of the Kray Twins.'

Still, he must have picked up some tips from James Bond – he'd managed to break into Jackson's pad while the house was supposedly under surveillance.

'Well, Charlie Manson was a short-arse hippy,' I pointed out.

'Careful.' Barry shot me a mock-angry look. 'You don't want to say nothing out of order about Charlie. His arm is long…'

'I wonder whether it was military intelligence or James Bond films which provided his training.' Bambridge echoed my own thoughts with an arch smile.

He seemed in a much better mood since he'd been out for his little breath of air yesterday. Came back a different bloke – a much livelier one. I wondered if he'd bought up enough confidence to hit Barry with his Woody idea yet.

'Did Dickinson have any theories?' he asked Barry, picking bits off his croissant and pushing them in his mouth.

'He did, actually.' Barry lounged back in his chair, looking serious. 'He said it was highly unlikely that the man they were after would fit the sort of profile that this fucker does. If he gets charged with murder, then we're going to look like we're barking up the wrong tree.'

'Yeah,' I agreed, 'and the *Screws'* supershrink will have been proved right.'

'Nonsense!' Neil chided. 'This is a classic case of obsessive-compulsive disorder. It says it clearly enough in this article alone.' He waved the *Post* in the air, tapping at the James Bond photo with his index finger. 'Lord knows what else he's had his knickers in a twist about before. But he's intelligent enough to hold down a job at the MOD, so he hardly fits the picture of the drooling stalker they're painting.'

'Don't think the gentlemen of the press are going to see it quite that way,' Barry shrugged. 'But we'll see. I'll let you know when I've finished transcribing, you can see what you want me to do with it. And then maybe when I've shown you mine, you can show us yours…?'

'Ah yes.' Bambridge suddenly started rearranging things on his desktop. 'Nearly there, chaps, honestly. I'll have it finished in the next day or two.'

'Hmmm.' Barry raised an eyebrow but said no more.

Little did they know, but I'd been doing some psychological profiling of my own. Going through the Everill tape, in the office, and at home last night. The interview wasn't as embarrassing as I remembered at all. He was defensive all right, but maybe those answers had been leading me down the path of my own intuition all along.

We had things in common.

'Ah, the good old village in the middle of nowhere. Where everyone knows each other's business but never minds their own.'

Small towns and secrets.

'It would be the same in any village in any part of this country.'

Not fitting in.

'If you're ever, ever different from them, they will make your life hell.'

The more I thought about those shared stigmas, the more I thought I could use them to get through to him. This time, I was going to do it properly. No more evasion.

I was home by 6.30. I didn't want to rush anything. I made myself a baked potato and salad, plenty to line the stomach, watched Percy Prevezeer being moved in a white van to protective custody at Brixton while the press and public banged on the doors and chased him down the street, screaming and trying to take flash photographs through the armour plating. I wondered if the little prick still had the same vain expression on his face, but I couldn't tell. He had a blanket over his head.

Once that was over, I rearranged my notes. I'd been thinking of questions to ask all day, but didn't want to write them down fully. Everill didn't need the advantage of seeing something already prepared. I had to come to him as the sympathetic listener. I just jotted down key words on my notepad, words that would remind me of everything I wanted to cover. If he was going to be facetious and evasive again, I needed my guides.

At 7.30, I was ready. Notes in my bag, plenty of tapes, fresh batteries in the machine. Lipstick and eyeliner perfect. Black suit and camel overcoat. I almost looked professional. It would take ten minutes to walk up to the pub. I wanted to be quarter of an hour early, find a good spot.

The street lights were just coming on as I left the house. On Kensington Park Road, the first buds of cherry blossom were appearing on the trees. You could smell a vague perfume on the breeze, of sap rising and things beginning to grow again. I turned left down Westbourne Grove to the big pub on the corner, taking my time, trying to stay calm. There were butterflies in my stomach, and I couldn't quite work out why. It wasn't just the journalistic jousting I knew I was about to initiate. I had put so much time and effort into securing this interview. It went beyond my normal call of duty, as did carefully selecting an outfit to do it in. Everill had intrigued me, drawn me out, in a way that had never happened before. I wanted to brush the obvious question aside, but was Barry right? Had I secretly fallen in love with more than his writing? It seemed inconceivable, because it wasn't a physical attraction. Nothing about his slippery demeanour seemed desirable to me. Everill was kind of misshapen: his head was too big for his sloping, round shoulders, his limbs were too long and awkward and he didn't carry himself well. He flounced, rather than walked, as if he was in a permanent huff. He wasn't ugly, but his distinctive features were not the handsome kind. Those hooded eyes were unnerving; the way he constantly licked his lips added to his general air of arrested adolescence. Everill just didn't have the confidence, the swagger, of a fully grown man.

But he had something most good-looking guys usually didn't need to rely on: a brilliant mind. A mind I might never get to the bottom of. That was the thing that was stirring up those emotions in me, I told myself. That need to know.

In the Earl of Lonsdale, Simon Everill was already seated, in the lounge bar at the back, right where I was thinking of going, pint three-quarters drunk and an *Evening Standard* open on the table before him.

His eyes flicked up from the paper and he smiled.

21

'Over here!' he called, as if I hadn't noticed him.

He stood up as I approached, rummaging in his jeans pocket. 'Can I get you a drink?'

'Yeah, a bottle of their pure brewed lager,' I said.

He went to get it for me. I sat down, noted what he'd been reading. The stars. Superstitious too. I didn't want to rearrange his stuff, so I pulled out my tape recorder instead. Watched him talking to the bar staff, rubbing his goatee and making a joke. He seemed more at home than I did.

The Earl of Lonsdale was a comfortable pub; big, like an old gin-house, decorated in chintzy flocked wallpaper with sturdy, sensible tables and chairs. The jukebox played MOR hits, Queen, Chris Rea and the like, and the drinks were markedly cheaper than anywhere else in the vicinity. It was the least trendy, most homely pub in the area, avoided by both hardcore winos and hipster trust fund babies. Surely, nothing sinister could happen to me here.

'There you go.' He placed the bottle and a glass in front of me.

'Thank you.' I was acutely aware of him watching me pour. He raised up his glass as I finished, clinked it against mine.

'Cheers,' we both said.

He was smiling at me.

'Now let's start again, shall we,' he said. 'From the beginning. What was it that you wanted to know?'

I swallowed. Decided to go in at the deep end. 'In the last interview we did, you said that the story for *Weirdo* was sort of based on personal experience. Would you be able to elaborate on that a bit more now?'

Foam from his brown ale on his top lip. He sucked it in.

'The first time I met you, I didn't realise what sort of a person you were,' he said, eyes shifting up at the wallpaper then down to meet mine. 'It takes me a long time to trust somebody, so forgive my rudeness.' He stretched his long legs out before him, looked down at his pint. 'I didn't tell you the exact truth. The truth was, it was something that happened in my childhood. Something that happened to a friend of mine.' He sucked in his bottom lip again, recrossed his legs. 'A woman went mad in our village. She wasn't the deranged whore I made her out to be in my book. I had to cover my tracks. You know what small towns are like, don't you?'

'Yes,' I nodded, keeping eye contact. 'I've had some experiences of my own.'

He nodded, reached down for a cigarette. 'She was really a quiet little mouse, wouldn't say boo to a goose. Her husband was the local doctor, you know, the pillar of the community. They had three young kids, always turned up at the church fête, you know the sort of thing.' His voice grew sarcastic again, only it wasn't directed at me. He was looking away, beyond the lounge bar, looking back to somewhere else. 'Only the doctor got a bit friendly with one of his patients, if you know what I mean. Left her for a younger woman. A recently divorced younger woman. You can imagine what the WI made of that.' He exhaled a long plume of smoke. 'And all that talking, all that gossiping behind her back, must have got to her.'

'Like you said, the hypocrisy,' I recalled from the last interview. 'Them all going to church and then being holier-than-thou.'

He nodded. 'Exactly. So one night, this old girl gets off her tits on sherry and the contents of the medicine cabinet the good doctor left behind. I don't quite know where she got the strength from, but she somehow managed to smother her three children as they slept. Then she put them in her car and drove down to the river, threw them all off the bridge, one by one.'

'Jesus,' I whispered.

'She was going to chuck herself off as well,' he continued. 'But some old boy out walking his dog saw what she was doing and stopped her. She got carted off to the funny farm. Too late for the kids though.'

He mashed his cigarette out in the ashtray. His eyes were red, filling up. I could feel my own doing the same. I daren't look at him in case he stopped.

The cassette recorder took it all down, the tiny spindles whirring.

'The thing was,' he said, taking a final gulp at his ale and wiping the foam off with the back of his hand, 'I knew one of those kids. The eldest one. He was the same age as me, 9 at the time. We used to feed the ducks together under that same fucking bridge she pushed him off…'

His voice went up octaves. He was trying not to cry. He pushed his hand across his face, turned away from me.

'I'm so sorry,' I said. 'Do you want to stop there a minute? Can I get you another drink?'

'Yes,' he sniffled.

I got up straight away, hurried over to the bar. I figured he would want a few moments alone. It all made sense now. That rage. The passion that came through those pages. You can't fake that kind of stuff. Now all I had to do was keep him talking.

I bought another bottle of brown ale, another bottle of lager and took them back to the table. Everill had composed himself.

'Sorry about that,' he said.

'Don't be.'

By instinct, I put my hand on his shoulder as I sat down. He jumped as if I'd lit a charge under his skin.

'Sorry.' I said it now, feeling a blush rising up my neck. Whatever feelings had been stirring in my brain before I entered the pub were deepening now. I knew I really cared about this man.

'No, no.' He smiled nervously. 'Don't worry, it's talking about this, it makes me jumpy.'

'I can well understand.' I sat myself down again, must have

stared at him as earnestly as any 16-year-old. 'I knew you couldn't have written like that if it wasn't from real life.'

He nodded, looking down at the floor.

'All the crime books I've ever read,' he said, 'were all about how clever the detective was, or how cunning the killer. No one ever writes about what it's like for the victims. I just wanted some justice for Jamie.'

'Was that his name?'

He nodded. His thin smile disappeared and he looked as if he was about to fill up again, his voice high and rasping. 'I'm sorry, I can't tell you his surname, I have to keep that secret. But I couldn't forget what happened to him.' He finally looked at me again. 'I can trust you with this, Diana, can't I? This is just for your magazine – you're not going to run off to one of the tabloids with it?'

'Of course not. I couldn't do a thing like that.'

He stared at me for some time, so long I could feel my face burning.

'Yeah,' he finally said. 'I don't think you could.'

I fumbled a cigarette out of the packet, lit it nervously, avoiding the intensity of his gaze. As if sensing my discomfort, he continued his monologue.

'And after that, it was me who became the weirdo.' He laughed, bitterly. 'I kept having nightmares about him. They never went, and I started drinking when I was about 11, heavily. You know how it is in those places, the older kids can always get you some.'

I knew all about older kids and what they could get for you. But this was no time to start dwelling on that.

'Got into acid when I was about 14,' he continued, as if suddenly the act of unburdening couldn't come fast enough. 'I fucking loved it. It took you into a different world. I used to find it funny. My sister once saw me walking round a lamp-post for an hour. I don't know what the fuck I was doing, but I was obviously enjoying myself. Luckily she found it funny too, so she never told me mum. I carried on like that for a couple of years, until I finally had a bad trip.'

I don't know how but I knew: 'The vision of Jesus?'

'Yep.' He looked startled again. 'That was it. Fucking hell, you have been paying attention. It was Christmas Eve and I was completely fucked. I'd drunk a load of cider and started on the brandy and then I'd done a couple of tabs with the local bikers. We were up in the woods dancing round a fire, pretending we were pagan gods or some such shit. Anyway, I got bored of that and decided I had to walk into the middle of a field, lie down under the stars, and I'd have some kind of mystical vision. I was sure of it. Well, I fucking did, but it wasn't quite what I had in mind. I got to the middle of this one big field, I was spinning about, trying to find the exact centre of it, because I thought, when I did, I would be in the centre of the constellations of the stars too. Then I saw this figure walking towards me. This little ragged figure. I thought it was one of the bikers at first. But then he got closer...'

He shivered like he had the cold chills all over again.

'I swear to God...' he started, then barked out a harsh laugh that made me the one to jump. 'He had the crown of thorns, stuck right into his head, he was bleeding all down his face. Blood on his hands, blood on his feet, blood on his chest. He looked at me with terrible eyes...'

He stared at me with an equally painful expression.

'You couldn't believe the look on his face. And he wouldn't go, he was just there, staring at me and bleeding.'

'What happened?' I heard myself whisper. I felt an urge to put my arms around him, tell him I had seen horror too, in those old familiar places.

But he broke eye contact again, sucked in his bottom lip and regained his composure.

'Luckily for me a couple of the bikers had followed me. If they hadn't, I think I might have lost it for ever out in that field, frozen to death or something. They just found me lying on the ground, crying. And that was it for me. I never touched the stuff again.' He lit another cigarette. 'Or went near the church. I don't know which is worse.'

We both laughed at this, rather too loudly. Breaking the tension.

I drained my glass, said: 'Another?'

'Too fucking right, I need one after that. Let me get them.'

He winked at me as he swooped up the empties, went back up to the bar.

'So what happened after that?' I asked as he returned.

Everill settled himself back in his seat. 'Well, after that, I started writing stories to escape,' he said, stretching his arms out and crossing his legs. 'I'd always been good at English, even when I was fucking up the rest of my schoolwork. Stories and music. Like we were saying the last time we met. You were right about that. I mean, those bikers started me off on Hawkwind and all that, I got really into prog rock and writing. My mum was pleased. I hardly ever left my bedroom for years.'

I laughed again at this, slightly drunk now. Drunk and something else. I was seeing Simon with new eyes. I was seeing him almost as a male version of myself – damaged but defiant. Obviously, he'd come out of his traumas more powerfully than I had but, nonetheless, there was something between us that most people would never understand.

'Which turns me back into the classic adolescent fuckhead,' he continued. 'Which in a way, was a fucking relief.'

'Well, I was the classic adolescent fuckhead as well,' I smiled. 'Here's to it.'

We clinked glasses.

'You're from a shitty small town too, aren't you?'

'Yep. A tatty seaside town. Great place – to get away from.'

'Yep,' he smacked his lips together. 'They all are that. Well, that's a load of my shit for you,' he said lightly. 'Bet you think it's funny that my soul was saved by Hawkwind, don't you? Bet you don't like that kind of music at all.'

'How can you tell?' I laughed.

He pretended to scrutinise me.

'The absence of tie-dye, perhaps? The fact that you don't stink of patchouli oil? Hippy birds,' he snorted a contemptuous laugh, 'look like shit.'

'That's what I keep telling my mental neighbour Jerry,' I told him. 'But he keeps insisting that I look like the *IT* girl.'

'*IT* magazine?' Everill prompted. 'That was based around here, wasn't it? Surprised you like it so much. From what I've heard, this place used to be crawling with hippies.'

'Still is in my house,' I told him. 'It's still a minute before midnight, 1969, in Jerry's world.'

'So is this close to your house?'

The question was casual. But something in the atmosphere was starting to crackle.

'Yeah,' I nodded. 'It's just round the corner. I hope you didn't have to come too far.'

'Not at all,' he smiled. 'Only from cop circus, Camden. My uncle's place, we share the gaff. I really used to like that place until all this happened.'

'No, really? I didn't know you lived there. Jesus. It must be a nightmare at the moment. I used to hang out there all the time. I mean, all my favourite music venues are up there. All the bands I used to write about.'

'You like those rocker bands, do you?' he asked.

'Yeah, I'm not like you in the music department. I like it when it twangs.'

'Well, maybe you could show me the error of my ways,' he considered. 'Take me to a few of these gigs. Seeing as I'm on the doorstep.'

He smiled. Setting out some intention. Vague maybe, but there all the same. Hanging in the air between us.

My face grew hot again, not just from the drink. I found that I had to look away, otherwise he might see what I'd been thinking throughout the night right there in my eyes. He started to laugh.

'Have I said something wrong again?' he asked.

'No, not at all.'

My stomach was lurching now. At the same time, my mind

was shutting down. Like it always does when sex starts to hint at being on the agenda. I still didn't know what it really was that I wanted, or what he wanted, for that matter. I realised I had to buy myself some time, try and compose myself. Otherwise, I could soon start looking like an idiot.

'Look, I've just got to go and powder my nose,' I said quickly. 'Excuse me a minute.'

'Of course.'

I could hardly look myself in the mirror in the ladies. What the fuck was going on?

Tried to think straight. Think in facts like:

He's just given me a great interview.

I think he wants to fuck me.

His book is a work of genius.

But I don't find him physically attractive.

We have things in common.

Does that matter more?

He doesn't look anything like men I fancy.

He's probably just trying to make friends and I'm overreacting.

But what if…

Small towns and secrets.

It would be wrong. I can't date someone I'm writing about. I never dated musicians in all the time I was working in the music press. I knew what they said about girls who did, and how far it got them.

I'd already been damaged goods once.

I heard the bell clang for last orders. Thank fuck. Let's just get out of here.

In my haste, I hadn't brought my bag into the lavs with me, so I couldn't redo my lipstick. Maybe that was better, though. He might have thought I was doing it for him. If I was embarrassed as I rejoined the table, he showed no sign of noticing it.

'Do you think that's enough for one night?' he said, instead.

'Well, I don't want to push things,' I smiled, hoping he would take a double meaning better than Bambridge. 'It must have been pretty harrowing going through what we did tonight…'

'I thought it would be,' he mused. 'But I like talking to you. And look.' He placed his hand over mine. 'Don't think I'm trying to start something else here. I wouldn't do that. Unless I thought you wanted me to.'

He gave my hand a squeeze and then lifted his own. He looked totally sincere. I felt like an idiot.

'Well, let's do this again soon,' I suggested.

'So long as you get the best story, Diana,' he winked.

'Can I walk you home?'

My mind started going blank again.

'It's only round the corner. It's on the way to the tube, though.'

But on the doorstep, he didn't go. He put his arms around me instead and I did nothing to stop him. Bowed his head down and kissed me and I did nothing to stop him. His lips wet, his tongue in my mouth like a thick, burrowing worm, his goatee harsh against my chin.

My mind said no. But my body, that submissive bitch, she wanted it.

I opened my front door and he went in with me.

22

It happened just the way Jackson said it would. First, they worked on the manuscript. Dim memories of dark times filtered back to Everill, at first tentatively, then almost like a tidal wave. Like the little boy who'd been silent so long before his first meeting with Jonny, now history seemed to be repeating the effect they had on each other. Simon found he couldn't get it out fast enough. And if Jackson was uncomfortable having him spend so much time in his home, he was wise enough not to say so.

Everill had taught himself to type before, but he never liked it. The ideas came out much easier just through his arm into a pen, on to the pages of the nice thick notebooks Jon bought him from Rymans. Then Jackson would type it all up for him on his fancy computer, the celebrated director acting as his private personal secretary. Revenge, along with the coffee and Danish Jon thoughtfully left for him to eat while he worked, was starting to taste sweet.

But it was also giving him a purpose he'd never had before. He wrote his story in the language of his childhood, through Jamie's eyes. The tears that had welled as he later told Diana about that poor, bedraggled child fell often as he did so. He could see young Jamie as he once was, hiding shyly under the dropping boughs of the weeping willow, watching Jackson feeding the ducks like a dog watches a table. Jackson with his smart new anorak and his bright red boots, looking clean and loved and confident.

'Here you go,' Jonny shouted loudly to the ducks, throwing the crumbs towards them.

Quack! Quack! Waddle, waddle. The feathered creatures fussed around him.

Everill saw the moment he had turned towards him with a big smile on his face.

'Do you want a go?' he called.

The realisation that he was being talked to had come slowly to little Jamie. It wasn't something he was used to.

Jonny held out the bag of breadcrumbs.

'Come and have a go,' he beckoned. 'There's some ducklings here. Come and have a look.'

He remembered how Jamie had gingerly reached out his hand.

'That's right, get a big handful. Look, they'll all come running.'

He did what he was told and stared in wonder at the impression it created amongst the waterfowl community.

'What's your name?' the duck boy asked. 'I'm Jonny.'

It was the start of a long summer, during which Jamie had at last found someone he could talk to. Someone he could be comfortable with. And Jonny liked his company too, it seemed.

They'd always meet in the mornings, under the bridge. Jonny would come with his pockets full of sweets, biscuits, cake and pop, enough to keep them going all day. They'd roam out of the village, over the farmland, to a little thicket where they'd found a bashed-up old chicken roost that they turned into their hideout, covering it with a camouflage of branches. Once they'd exhausted themselves physically, they'd retreat into the shelter to eat Jonny's bounty and tell stories.

Jamie told Jonny he hated Farmer Barnard, whose land he lived on, and made up plenty of lurid tales to explain why. Jonny, in his turn, was fascinated by the WI ladies who met in his front room with his mother to cast aspersions on the rest of the village. Especially the vicar's wife, with her huge backside swathed in straining floral skirts and her viper's tongue, always going on about heathens and fallen women. Those stories merged as the weeks progressed, the two boys beginning to forge a fantasy narrative, based around the farmer and the vicar's wife's gossip. Their stories became more and more extravagant. Jonny had even got to the stage of bringing a pad to the hideout and writing some of it down. They ended up with the idea that the vicar's wife had secretly fathered Farmer Barnard's eldest son when she was a teenager, and the vicar didn't know.

But then, in that August of so long ago, when the holidays had almost stretched out to their end, Jonny suddenly went missing. He stopped being at the bridge, or the hideout, or anywhere else Jamie looked for him. Maybe, he thought then, he had moved away. He never knew that Jonny had looked over the bridge one evening, as he walked past with his dad, and saw him down there killing ducklings. Never knew, because he'd never realised he'd done it. When the red fog came down on adult Simon it was hard enough to remember the details. Little Jamie couldn't recall a thing.

Jamie had wandered under that bridge every morning for days, calling Jonny's name and getting back only the echo of his own despairing voice. Then he'd sit for hours in the empty hideout, straining to hear the tell-tale crackle of a twig being stood on that would tell him his friend was coming, sit there forlornly until the sun went down on another lonely day. After a few weeks, he stopped even looking. Just wandered up and down the river, staring with red-rimmed eyes. Hurling stones into the water as the wind from the sea bit saltily into his vision. Or sitting alone on the bank, driving a stick into the earth so that part of the turf would come away and fall into the onward swirl of the river.

Simon couldn't make himself put that bit of it into the story. He felt too sorry for Jamie to let all of that be known. But he did use the vision of Jesus appearing on Christmas Eve in Farmer Barnard's sugarbeet field. It hadn't been until he got older and another boy had offered him an acid blotter that he finally twigged what the 'communion wafers' actually were. After that, he'd taken a few trips, but nothing like that had ever happened again. He reckoned that was because Mary wasn't there. Mary, his poor little sister, the only girl he'd ever cared for. This book wasn't just revenge for him. It was for her as well.

Jamie had actually gone to the village school for a while, had even enjoyed it. But that was before his mother had got so lazy she'd demanded he stay at home to look after his siblings; before the truant officer had given up on the Merritts along with everyone else. Reading had been his best subject, and he'd passed his skill on to his sister. They'd been through that Bible together. Those were the only stories they'd known.

The worst bit was living through the end again.

Everyone had tried to keep the details from him, assuming he'd blanked them out of his mind in the years afterwards when he couldn't even bring himself to speak. But after Jamie became Simon, he'd found out how to use the local library to access old newspaper reports of the 'tragedy'. He wanted to see how they told it, how it compared to the scenes that came back to him each night and made him wake up in a cold sweat, silently screaming, his mother's ghost eyes staring at him from the corner of the room.

The river had taken his mother. They'd found her body washed up, days later. Mary had been dead before she hit the water, suffocated in her bunk. But he had been the lucky one and merely passed out. The water brought him round, and as he hit the surface, he began to yell.

The noise alerted a local man, out walking his dog on the green. Jamie had been carried by the tide straight into a reed bed by the river bank and deposited there like Moses. The man, middle-aged but fit from his nightly walks, had been able to pull him out. Those cries he'd made then were the last sounds that came out of his mouth for the next two years.

Jamie was sent to a home in Norwich – far enough away for everyone in East Melsham to forget about it quickly. Dr Barnardos took over from Farmer Barnard. They found him a new family, the Everills, a couple who had plenty of experience with problem children, and could handle his nightly hysteria until it started to recede, and gradually, the power of speech came back to him.

When Simon next saw Jonny, it was a photograph in the *NME*. The face looked familiar, the story underneath filled in the details. The boy had done good. He was at St Martin's School of Art, making pop promos for bands.

A bit different from Simon's own trajectory. There had been more dark times, even after the Everills had taken him in. Simon just couldn't stay settled for long. He didn't like to stay sober, either. Drink and drugs could black out his nightmares better than the kind words of his foster parents, and as he hit his teens, Simon was rarely at home to hear them anyway. Eventually his experiments in taking and then dealing acid had got him in trouble. He'd spent a few of his teenage years in a reform school.

But at least in there he'd been able to study, had even passed some O levels and made it into sixth-form college when he got out of Norwich Young Offenders' Institute. English was by far his best subject, maybe because he had spent so much time reading everything he could lay his hands on while he was incarcerated, including spending his monthly allowance corresponding with record collectors and buying subscriptions for music mags.

When he saw what Jonny was up to now, he'd thought that maybe the two of them could combine their talents again. Whatever had happened to Jackson at the end of that summer? He must remember his old friend, surely?

Simon had told his English lecturer he knew someone famous and was going to send him a filmscript. The kindly Mr Haylett, who'd done his best to encourage the lad, gave him a word of advice.

'It's a good idea, but never send out anything without keeping a copy,' he told him. 'Make a carbon of it, then post a copy to yourself at the same time. When it comes, keep it but don't open it. That way, you can always prove it was your idea.'

Neither Mr Haylett, nor the recipient of the script himself, truly thought that Simon was so serious with his intensions. But that was then. Now as Jackson got to the end of Everill's weirdo manuscript he'd had to admit he had sorely underestimated his childhood friend. He had almost seemed envious of what Simon had managed to write and how well he'd been able to write it. But he kept his promise, delivered both Everill and his manuscript to the top agent he'd found and stood back in silence as *Weirdo* took off and Simon made a name for himself.

But if Simon thought Jackson was about to leave it there, then he was sorely wrong.

23

It was the strangest dance I've ever danced.

Everill and me.

At first he was hungry, like they usually are. Couldn't get my clothes off fast enough. Shedding layers rapidly in the cold of the room, pressing down on my single bed, not waiting for me to turn on the heater or offer him a drink. The harshness of the main light, him wanting to see everything in stark detail. Like he wanted a scenario, a tableau. Not just impromptu sex, but something he could choreograph. Arranging me in positions rather than letting me move. Keeping me still while he craned his neck around every angle, every corner.

Kissing, that urgent thick tongue filling my mouth while his fast hard fingers filled everywhere else. And then stopping, sitting up. Staring. Rearranging. Getting my legs just so and letting himself in. Pumping and then stopping. Staring. Rearranging.

Going on for hours like that, until it felt like some strange piece of performance art, something mechanical. Nothing to do with two people coming together to share some warmth. Yet all the time him trying to offset the abnormality of it by saying things like:

'Fuck, you are beautiful. You know, I have never seen a woman this beautiful before. You are amazing to me. Jesus, you are amazing.'

Me feeling like I'm watching this, I'm not really a part of it. Feelings confused. Feelings switching off. Feeling: can I go to sleep now? Get this over.

Finally, just before dawn, him ramming away like he's going to drill me through the wall, then screaming as he comes. Falling on to me, exhausted, muttering: 'Jesus, you are beautiful.'

Stroking my hair until he falls asleep.

Me sore, uncomfortable. Thinking: I wonder why I did that.

Trying to sleep in the grey light that's pooling in under the curtains. Thinking of the blue light, the sound of the sea. Trying not to feel dirty as cold clammy him trickles out between my legs. And then, the alarm clock.

'Jesus!' he sat bolt upright, practically threw me out of the bed.

'Sorry.' I clapped a hand over it. 'It's only an alarm.'

He ran his hand through his bristly hair, so that it all stood up on end, rubbed his hooded eyes open and smiled.

'Wow,' he said, putting his arms back around me. 'Sorry. Well. That was some night.'

'Mmmm.'

Before I could say anything more, his tongue was in my mouth again. Rolling around in there for a good five minutes before letting me up for air, smiling at me like a cat.

'Suppose that means you've got to go to work now, does it?'

'Yeah,' I said, trying to extricate myself from his grasp. 'Do you want to use the bathroom? Only I've got to.'

'No, you go ahead,' he said, happy as Larry. I could feel his eyes full beam upon me as I struggled into my dressing gown.

'I won't be long,' I murmured.

It was freezing in the bathroom. I stamped my feet as the water poured into the tub, wrapping my arms around myself. Better to be in here in the cold than in there, with him. I was desperately trying not to feel dirty.

Trying not to feel the soreness from where his fingers poked and probed, where his cock was mere hours ago. Trying not to think that somehow I had fucked up by doing this. Pushing that thought away, putting it back in the room, letting my mind hum on static, on nothing. Feeling glad of the water's warm embrace. Glad of the soap. No time to wash my hair now, though, have to do it later. Tonight, when I can be on my own and figure out what this was all about.

I went out via the kitchen. Be polite, I thought. Make some coffee, bring it in on a tray, say to him: 'Sorry, I haven't got anything to eat, but will this be OK?'

Everill was stretched out in my bed, one hand behind his head, the other languorously smoking a cigarette, the ashtray on his stomach, watching cartoons on BBC2 and giggling like a child.

'That's brilliant,' he said, helping himself.

I put on my make-up quickly, botching it as I did, eyeliner all over my top lids, mouth drawn in at a comical angle.

Everill still snickered away. The room was filled with irritating cartoon music and KA-POW! noises coming too loud from the television. By now I was grinding my teeth. Putting my knickers on under my dressing gown. Turning away from him and fumbling my way into the nearest things to hand. Black sweater, black trousers, black boots.

He finally stirred, said: 'S'pose I'd better get a move on, eh?'

'Sorry.' Despising myself for saying that. 'But I'd better not be late for work.'

'Of course not.'

He stepped out of bed, calmly put his clothes back on. I didn't really want to see any more, but still my eyes took it all in. Long skinny body, round shoulders, pigeon chest. Abortionist's fingers doing up his flies.

I felt a twinge like cystitis already coming on.

'Bathroom through here, is it?' He smiled, draining his cup and smacking his lips.

I stared after him, wanting to cry. Thinking, I shouldn't have done this.

I turned off the TV, snatched up the cups. Took them through to the kitchen and washed them all up, slammed the milk back into the fridge, hoped he wouldn't suddenly come in and see the bread and the cereal I really had stashed away in there.

I heard the toilet flush, rushed to get back to my room before him. Get my bag together.

The tapes were still in there from the night before.

'Right!' he said, banging through the door all jolly and smiling.

'I'll come with you to the tube.'

He sat with me on the tube, hand firmly on my leg, grinning and laughing, smacking his lips. All the way to Edgware Road.

'Well, that was a great night, Diana,' he said, far too loudly. 'I'll see you again very soon.'

'Yeah, OK,' I mumbled. 'Give me a call in a day or so.'

'Right you are.' Still grinning and waving at me as the doors close and I hurried up the platform, feeling his eyes on my back. Feeling them all the way down Bell Street.

I was still flustered as I reached the office. I forgot to go and get a coffee first. The lack of sleep was making everything seem surreal.

'Allriiiight darlin',' screeched Barry as I picked my way downstairs. Then, as he saw the state of me: 'Jesus, you look a bit rough.'

'I feel it,' I sighed, slumping down at my desk.

'Well, there's no time for slacking.' Neil was slapping his hands together in glee. 'I need all your copy in by the end of the week. We're going to press this Saturday.'

That was a week early. It jolted me.

'Why?' I said. 'What's happening?'

'It's Neil's big American friends.' Barry filled me in. 'They want their Death Special in early, so they can fly us all over for a big party and we can sell loads of issues in the States. Isn't that right, Mr Bambridge?'

'Indeed it is.' Neil nodded proudly. 'So what have you got to give me? Luther Lang, Jack Hall, that Scottish woman and Simon Everill? Have you finished interviewing him yet?'

'Y-yes...' My blushing face, my bad make-up, my ratty hair must have said it all.

'Oooo, I should say she has,' taunted Barry. 'Up all night over it, were we?'

'Shut up, Barry.' I wanted to cry. 'I got a very good interview with him last night, if you must know, and it's all stuff that no one else will have.'

'Like his inside leg measurement?' Barry continued, remorselessly.

'Like the fact that book was about himself. As I said to you before!' I snapped.

'I'm only teasing you, pet.' He looked concerned. 'Don't take offence.'

'Sorry,' I made myself say. 'Look, this deadline's come as a bit of a shock. Let me just get on with it, otherwise we'll be in trouble.' I tried to think straight. 'Luther Lang's finished, so is Kay McLachlan. I'll have Jack Hall by the end of the day and then you can have Everill tomorrow. Is that OK?'

'Just about.' Neil nodded furiously. 'Now Paul's coming in tomorrow lunchtime to do layouts. I want everything you can by then. We'll work through the night if necessary.'

Paul was our designer. We could only pay him enough to spend a couple of days on each issue. If he was already booked, then I would have to find words from somewhere, words to gloss over last night.

That was just what I needed.

'Barry, how's yours coming?' Bambridge continued.

'Just finishing off me copper. It'll be ready by the end of the day.'

'Excellent, excellent.'

'And how's your major piece, sir? Are we to take it that you've finished transcribing?'

'I'm going to work straight through tonight to get it finished.' Neil sounded pious.

'You still don't want us to see it, do you?'

'Don't be silly, Barry, of course I want you to see it. Now look. We'd all better get on with things so as we don't miss this deadline.'

Barry sniffed. 'If you say so.' He turned back to his headphones.

I tried to turn back to Jack Hall. The transcription was done, but piecing it together was like wading through treacle. My mind kept going in circles, flashbacks to scenes of the night before. I had had so little sleep I was practically hallucinating. By lunchtime I had written one paragraph five times over. My insides were burning and my head was a blur.

'Lunch?' enquired Bambridge, at round about one.

'I can't,' I mumbled. 'I've got to get this finished.'

'You sure?' Barry looked concerned. 'Maybe it'd do you good to get out for a bit.'

'Well, I could do with going to the chemist's,' I said. 'I'll just take a stroll and pick up a sarnie on the way back.'

We left the office together, but as we got to the door of the caff, Barry said: 'Neil, you go in and get a table. Order us sausage and chips if they ask. And a tea. I'll just walk this one up to the chemist's.'

'Oh.' Bambridge looked mildly perplexed. 'If you say so. See you in about ten minutes, then.'

As soon as he'd closed the door behind him, Barry put his arm around me. 'Are you OK, really?' he asked. 'I didn't mean to upset you this morning.'

We'd walked up the road a few steps when I started to cry on his shoulder.

'I'm just tired, Barry,' I snivelled. 'Tired and stupid.'

'Shhhh, shhhh.' He stopped walking, started stroking my hair. 'You're not stupid. We all thought we had another week for this issue.'

'It's not that,' I said. 'It's something else. I did a stupid thing last night.'

'Hey, now.'

'You knew I would. I slept with Simon Everill.'

'Was he that bad?' He said it gently, trying to joke.

'He was, actually.'

Barry propelled me round a corner, off the main street, held me in a bear hug until I could finally stop shaking.

'Did he hurt you?' he asked.

'No, it wasn't that.'

Even though he had, I couldn't tell Barry.

'It's just a stupid thing to do, isn't it? It's not going to look good for me. I'm going to look like a groupie.'

'If you fucking knew what other people get away with, you wouldn't even think like that.' Barry sighed and shook his head. 'Look. You're both adults, you can do what you like. The piece is not going to come out with a by-line saying "Diana Kemp fucks the truth out of Simon Everill", is it?'

'I suppose not.' I almost smiled.

'Is that what you're worried about, really?'

I nodded. I didn't need to tell him the sordid details.

'Well, don't. I'm not going to tell anyone. Neither are you. And from what you've told me about this bloke, he doesn't tell anyone anything. So what have you got to worry about?'

He looked at me as if trying to discern what else it was.

'Nothing,' I whispered. 'I suppose.'

'It happens, this kind of thing,' he said pragmatically. 'To everybody. Don't ever think that you're some kind of groupie. You're far, far better than that. You're far, far better than most people I've ever met.'

I bit my lip so I wouldn't cry any more.

'Now let's get you up to that chemist's before his nibs starts worrying. I'll keep him talking in there for an hour, you sort yourself out, have a bit of peace. Have forty winks if you like.'

'Thanks, Barry.'

He ruffled my hair. 'Daft bird,' he smiled.

I did as he said. Got some Cystemme from the chemist's, a bottle of water to go with it and a cheese sarnie from the newsagent's. Back in the office, I calmed myself down, took a long drink of the potion.

I felt like I was about to fall asleep. So I turned on the radio to keep myself awake. At half past one, the news came on.

'This just in,' said the excitable presenter. 'Scotland Yard has released the man they've been holding since Saturday in connection with the Jon Jackson murder investigation. Percival Prevezeer, of Clapham, South London, was charged with breaking and entering the film director's Primrose Hill flat, and will face magistrates on that charge next month. But Chief Inspector Phil Benson, leading the Yard's enquiry, said his team were satisfied that Prevezeer had nothing to do with the murder investigation itself.'

Benson's soundbite platitude: 'I'm afraid the real killer is still out there. We will be concentrating all our efforts on bringing him to justice as swiftly as possible.'

The announcement continued: 'Prevezeer, who tabloids have claimed this week is a press officer working for the Ministry of Defence, left custody in secret at 10am this morning. Benson would not elaborate on where his search would be heading next.'

Neil seemed oddly disconcerted when I told him this.

'Let him go?' he frowned. 'Whatever for?'

'He's not the killer,' I said.

'You're not in the clear yet, Bambridge,' quipped Barry. 'What's the matter? Will this fuck up our schedule? Just when it was all coming together so nicely.'

'Don't be stupid, Barry.' Neil crashed down into his chair. 'And stop winding me up. I'm getting on with my transcription.'

Barry winked at me.

We all continued typing in silence. I had now gone past the point of tiredness, had reached that self-generated speed moment when suddenly the Jack Hall piece just fell into place. Analogies flooded in from the hidden files in my brain, references to a lineage of writers – Gerald Kersh, Graham Greene, Daniel Farson's *Soho in the Fifties*; snapshots of London past. Jack Hall belonged to that Soho Bermuda Triangle, that was it. All the old queens and sinners had bestowed him their patch, told him to keep up the bad work. I knew exactly where to insert all his best quotes and how to tie it all up. The trip to the French and the Deansgate was a sudden inspiration.

By six o'clock it was finished. I read it through twice, tidied it up, and astonished myself by how good it seemed.

'There you go,' I said to Neil. 'Jack Hall's in the raw copy folder. Take a look at it if you want.'

'Yeah, and you can have mine an' all,' Barry chimed in. 'Censorship – I shit it. It's in the same folder. I'll dig out some visuals for you tonight from me stash.'

'Well, well done you two.' Neil seemed genuinely amazed.

'We'll work late tomorrow if needs be.' Barry pulled on his coat. 'And the rest of the week.'

'Right, yes, if we all pull together we'll make the magazine of the year.' Neil stretched expansively. He looked so pleased with himself, I wondered if he was about to broach the subject of Woody and Alex.

I prayed that he wouldn't.

He opened his mouth.

'Barry?'

'Yes?'

Bambridge frowned, then looked away, as if he'd thought better of it. He probably assessed that he'd done well enough out of him for one day.

'Thanks for all of that.'

It was Barry's turn to frown. 'I'm only doing me job, chief. Don't turn all gay on me now.'

Neil almost blushed, waved us away with what sounded like a cough. 'Well, I'll see you both tomorrow.'

'Cheerio.' Barry propelled me up the steps.

It was the last time any of my prayers would be answered for a long time.

24

When Barry left me, as I insisted he did, after a cup of coffee and more reassurances, I found that old bottle of 90 per cent proof Yugoslavian plum brandy I'd brought back from one of my *Melody Maker* trips and got stuck in. It wasn't that I didn't feel bad enough already. I just wanted to feel worse.

There had to be a soundtrack for this misery. Nick Cave's *From Her To Eternity* would do it. In the film *Wings of Desire*, the angel sees the woman he will turn mortal for, as Cave and the Bad Seeds sing the title track in some suitably decadent Berlin basement. It made me think of the one night I was picked out in a nightclub by a singer, the one night I spent with someone who felt like an angel.

Which of course would make me feel worse still.

'Hello girl,' he had said, touching me on the shoulder lightly.

I had spun around in amazement.

Jon Jackson sitting down on the table next to me.

Dark eyes, big nose, even bigger smile.

'You from round these parts?' Him deliberately stressing a rural burr.

Me laughing back: 'Arrr, that's roight. From yaander Art College, in't I?'

'What you studying?'

'Fashion.'

'I'm doing graphics at Norwich.'

Warm breath, sweet with beer, his arm touching mine. Asking: 'You know what they say about graphics and fashion students?'

'No, what?'

'That they have a special relationship.'

His eyebrows dancing as he laughs, his leg touching mine. His intentions clear. My heart lurching like I've just woken up. Woken from a thousand-year sleep.

Lisa, my so-called friend, noticing with that radar she has so finely tuned even when snogging a punk rocker, that I'm getting more and better attention than she is. Barging her way over, dragging the mohicaned one after her, a look of bemusement on his face. Her expression is superficially friendly, yet daggers lurk behind her eyes.

'What are you two up to?'

An edge of hysteria behind the forced laughter in her voice.

'Hello there.' Him offering his hand, deflecting her. 'I'm Jon.'

Her sounding breathless as she replies: 'Lisa Lamb.' Fixing him with mooning eyes, realising too late she still has Sid Vicious attached to the end of her other arm, and muttering apologetically, 'Er, and this is Lucas.'

Lucas Vicious looking at Jackson almost as enthusiastically as Lisa.

'Great show, mate.' Pumping Jackson's hand. 'I seen you before, one time, at the Jacquard. You were supporting King Kurt.'

'Now that was a night.' Jackson laughing, at the same time putting his hand over mine. Lisa clocking this with the daggers unsheathed.

'All that shit they chuck around on stage.' Lucas enthusing. 'Fucking foam and chicken intestines. And then, my mate Chris, they got him up there and stripped him naked! Threw him back in the crowd with nothing on but his Doctor Marten boots!'

'Nothing like a bit of male bonding.' Lisa darkly sarcastic now, sparking up a cigarette with ill-concealed impatience.

'Jonny!' Another goth girl, all white spiky hair, Siouxsie Sioux leathers and fishnets, tugging at Jon's sleeve from the other direction.

'Jonny.' Her voice a whine, every bit as attention-seeking as

Lisa's. 'Can you come over here? We need to sort out the lifts home.'

'Ask Charlie, love.' Him smiling back at her. 'I'm not coming back to Norwich tonight. I'm staying here.'

His grip on my hand tightening. Her mouth dropping open in shock.

'Wh-what do you mean?' Sounding as if she was about to cry.

'Don't worry, Vanya, Charlie'll get you home all right. There's plenty of room in the van.' Her eyes filling up.

Her mouth opening and then closing again like a goldfish. Then, noticing his hand on mine, she spins around, almost running away.

Lisa, taking it all in and not liking it one little bit. But taking advantage of the intrusion to working on another angle. Leaning on one hip with her cigarette circling in the air, Lucas' hand long since discarded. Making a pouty face and asking Jackson: 'Where are you staying, then?'

Him looking at me and smiling. 'Where do you fancy? The Dorchester or The Ritz?'

Not being able to reply, just staring at him in awe. Him fucking off all these people just to be with me.

'Only,' Lisa blowing her Superking smoke right in my face, 'she's supposed to be staying at mine tonight. She doesn't actually live in town. So why don't we all go back there? There's plenty of beer in the fridge.'

My heart dropping. There were usually two outcomes to this scenario. One: Lisa would shamelessly vamp up to him until it got to the point that she was 'showing him round' her flat and I'd be left with Lucas, twiddling thumbs and wondering what happened to our dates, while laughter and other noises emanated from behind her locked bedroom door. Two: she would proceed to get ostentatiously arseholed, put on her Patti Smith records and start singing and then crying along to them until I had to put her to bed. By which time, both Lucas and Jon would have made their excuses and disappeared into the night.

Either way, Lisa won.

But instead, I heard him say: 'Thanks for the offer, but there's a ton of guesthouses in this place. And I fancy going for a walk.'

Jumping off the table, still holding my hand. Saying: 'You coming?'

Breathless, wanting to laugh out loud. 'Why not? See you later, Lisa.'

Lisa looking at him in utter disbelief. For the first time ever, not being able to muster a crushing put-down by way of reply.

Knowing this would be the end of our friendship. Thanking him inwardly for that blessing.

Pushing our way through a throng of goths and psychobillies, all of them patting him on the back and offering their compliments on the gig; savouring the astonished looks on the faces of the girls; running down the steps of the Brunswick, him saying: 'Is she your mate or your mother?'

Letting rip that laugh that had been building up inside me, laughing long and loud as we cross over King Street, past the waiting minicabs and the swarms of beer boys, staggering pasty-faced and under-dressed, outside Peggotty's and The 151, down past the park, towards the seafront.

Nothing this brilliant has ever happened to me before.

The night clear and warm, the stars shining hard. Us standing on the promenade, staring out to sea and all the lights from the oil platforms scattered blinking across the horizon.

'I love the sea,' he says, as he swings me down on to the sand.

Staring at me, almost whispering: 'I'm sorry. I never even asked your name.'

'Diana.' Staring back into his eyes, his laughing, dark eyes.

Kissing then, under the bright dome of stars and seafront neon, the taste of salt in the air, on his lips, the whoosh and hiss of the waves over pebbles. Fingers entwined, walking down to the water's edge, then along towards the Wellington Pier, where more lights marked the patches taken by night fishermen, sitting out the night with their rods and flasks and windbreaks.

A night of stars and bright lights in the darkness.

Walking all the way up to the pleasure beach, talking excitedly, kissing still more so, until I can hardly bear it and ask: 'How are we going to get a room at this time of night?'

'Don't you worry, girl.' Him smiling down at me. 'I've got a mate here whose mum owns a guesthouse. He was at the gig, he'll still be up.'

It all happening as if by magic. Us climbing back up the sea wall under the shadow of the gigantic rollercoaster; kissing under there too; strolling around the outside of the now empty funfair, the rides throwing up fantastical shapes in the dark. Me telling him stories about my summer job in a guesthouse and all the lardy guests demanding their chips with everything, hiding tubes of KY jelly under their pillows, leaving their peeled-off sunburned skin all over the carpets.

'Well, I can't promise this'll be any classier,' he says, leading me through a maze of streets and squares just off the front, 'but I promise not to peel all over you.'

Lights on at the Kingston Guest House. Just like he promised, a friend opening the door, ushering us into a chintzy front room bar, with a copper counter and comedy tankards hanging from the walls. A huge fishtank full of tropical species in the corner, posters for Cannon and Ball at the Britannia Pier and the Biergarden at the Wellington, the Model Village and the House of Wax all over the wall. Drinking brandy with his friend until two in the morning, his friend being so calm and charming it felt I had known him years, had always been with Jon. Then the keys being handed over.

Forgetting all about the past at the sight of his long, lean, brown body, the taste of his lips, his gentle hands. Rolling over and over like the waves, as easy, as natural. Until the blue light of morning filters through the curtains and he smiles at me while he sleeps.

My most perfect memory.

I lay on my rumpled, cold, single bed, a hundred miles and

nine years away, the crude alcohol burning my throat. I held up that memory like a talisman, against the darkness I felt seeping in all around me. I had that one night, and no one could take it away from me.

Then another vision intruded, one that made me jump up off the bed, tear off all the sheets and pillowcases and stuff them into my laundry bag, pull out fresh ones from the wardrobe and manically change them over.

Simon Everill's smile of triumph as he said goodbye to me on the train this morning.

I tried to shut him away, but he kept popping back up like some jeering Jack in the Box. I thumped the pillows like I was thumping his face, thumped them over and over again, wishing they were his face, wishing his teeth were breaking, smashing into bloodied stumps under my knuckles, so that he could never smile at me that way again.

Wishing I had never read his fucking book, never gone to the ICA, never met him at all.

When I slid inside the clean sheets, they were cold and unwelcoming, as if they too were affronted by last night's intrusion. I curled into a ball and lay there shivering, waiting for a tiny amount of warmth to generate, waiting on the threshold of wakefulness and sleep for my consciousness to shut down and give me an escape.

A hundred miles and nine years. Not a star in the sky tonight for me.

25

I wanted to put it off for as long as possible. Transcribing those tapes. But I only had two and a half days until deadline.

All the way into work I felt the weight of them, in my bag, as if they were heavy rocks instead of flimsy pieces of plastic and electromagnetic tape. Aware of the price they had extracted from me.

Still, when I first got to my desk, Neil proved an unexpected ally.

'Will you do me a favour?' he asked, rubbing bleary eyes, his hair sticking up all over the place and his clothes even more rumpled than usual. 'I've been at it for most of the night, and don't think I'm seeing things straight any more. Would you mind going over all the copy again for me? There's a hell of a lot of pages there and I'm sure I've probably missed a few tricks. Paul's coming in this lunchtime to start designing them, and obviously we need to get as many pages finished as we can today.'

'Not at all.' I welcomed the suggestion. Put off the inevitable for as long as possible. By the looks of things, there'd be enough there to keep me at it all day.

'I'll get Barry to lend a hand when he gets here.' He stood up groggily and stretched. 'Although, first off, I think I'm going to take him out for breakfast.'

'You're going to ask him about Woody and Alex?' I surmised.

'Yes,' he said thoughtfully. 'I thought it best if I didn't drag you into that, you know, if he wants to have a row about it. And Christ knows, I could do with getting out for a bit. There's not much to be said for attempting to catnap under a desk, however noble one's intentions.'

'Well, you've done bloody well,' I remarked, impressed, my eyes scanning down the list of files on the computer desktop. I was searching for one in particular. It still wasn't there.

'Isn't your Jackson transcript done yet?' I tried to make my voice sound casual.

Bambridge gave a huge yawn before answering. 'It is, but I'm still not one hundred per cent satisfied with the writing, so I'm not going to give it to Paul until I am. But don't worry, I'm not asking you to meet a deadline I'm incapable of keeping myself.'

As if on cue, the door opened upstairs.

'Cooeee!' yelled Barry. 'It's me, the cat.'

'Ah, excellent.' Neil clasped his hands together. 'Barry, don't take your coat off,' he called up the stairs. 'I want to take you out to breakfast. Discuss the fine-tuning of the issue.'

Barry appeared at the top of the stairs. 'Oooh, we are honoured,' he teased. Then clocked me sitting at my desk. 'What, not Di?'

'I've already explained to Diana.' Neil was hauling himself into his coat. 'We need her to sub all this morning, so there's plenty ready for Paul when he gets in, but you and I have a few things to go through. I thought it would be more pleasant to give her some peace while we chew things over, so to speak, down the road.'

Barry shrugged, and handed Bambridge a carrier bag full of books and papers. 'All right, chief. But could you do us a favour and just put these on my desk? That's the stuff I pulled out of my stash for visuals. I don't want to lump that all the way down the greasy spoon – it might get contaminated.'

'Very well.' Neil passed the bag over and smiled brightly at me. 'See you in a little while.'

And they disappeared up the steps.

I thought for a moment about going through Neil's hard drive and reading his transcript. But I had so much to do, it would be obvious if I had been snooping. Besides, I wasn't sure how long this breakfast meeting would last once Neil had dropped his big question.

Cunning of him to get the censorship piece out of Barry first. Might as well start with that.

Barry had written his tour de force, it was obvious from the first sentence, the quote from George Orwell that had been banned from *Animal Farm* for thirty years: *'The sinister thing about literary censorship in England is that it is largely voluntary.'*

It was another relief to have something so engrossing to work on, to keep that tap-tap-tapping of Everill's bony fingers out of my mind.

Over an hour had passed before the two of them returned.

God knows what Neil had pulled but it had obviously gone better than I anticipated. They were animated with chatter as they clanked down the stairs, throwing names around for the party in America, most of which sounded like their fantasy league of porno stars to me.

I tried not to look surprised, just remarked: 'Excellent piece, Barry. You really pulled out all the stops this time.'

'You like it?' Barry hung his coat up on the back of the toilet door.

'You've convinced me.'

'Ah, well, you didn't need convincing, pet. It's the great unwashed out there, it's them that needs to get it.'

'No, Diana's right, it's the best piece of work I've ever seen you do,' complimented Neil expansively. Despite his untidy appearance, he exuded the aura of a man who had his hands on absolutely everything he wanted. 'It's a focus point for the whole issue, it proves that what we are doing has real value and meaning. Unlike all our rivals across the print world.'

'Blimey,' noted an equally satisfied-looking Barry. 'Get him.'

They were pleased as punch with each other. I wondered if Neil had slipped something into Barry's tea.

I listened in wonder as Barry picked up the phone, dialled a number he obviously knew off by heart and said: 'Woody. How do, sir. Not too early for you, is it? Good. Now listen, I've got a favour to ask. Would you be free for an hour or so this afternoon? Yeah. I'll meet you up in Camden and I'll take you for a pint, tell you all about it. Yeah, it's a bit schtumm, don't want to say too much about it on the phone, know what I mean?'

He started laughing at a joke cracked on the other end of the line. Neil's eyes were positively gleaming with triumph.

'About three, perfect. You don't know if Al's about, do you? Oooo, is he? Would you do that for me? It concerns the two of you really. Aw thanks, mate, you're a gent. All right. See you then. Cheerie bye.'

He rang off with a decisive *triiiing*, said to Neil: 'Well, I'll give it my best shot, that's all I can promise.'

'That's excellent, Barry.'

I kept silent. Wondered how Neil had done this, and why he needed me out of the way to do it. As if reading my mind, Barry asked: 'All right, pet?'

I nodded, not quite meeting his eye.

'Good. Let's crack on, then. I'll go over the stuff you've written, give you a chance to get on with your other stuff.'

The tapes, waiting in my bag like harmful radioactive matter. I didn't want to touch them, let alone listen to them.

Still, there was enough subbing to keep me occupied throughout the rest of the morning and through a hurried lunch of sandwiches eaten over the keyboard, until Paul got in and started to lay things out. Barry was busy scanning his pictures in for the designer up until two-thirty, when he put his coat back on and started out to meet Woody and Alex.

'Right,' he said, slinging his bag over his shoulder and looking pointedly at Neil. 'I'm going to meet them two now. I'll see you in as long as it takes.'

As soon as he was out of the door, I had to ask: 'How the fuck did you do that?'

Neil cradled his hands behind his head, leaned back in his chair, smiling.

'Barry's been doing a lot of thinking,' he said. 'Since he's been writing that censorship piece. He realises it's the moral focus of the issue now, of our tribute to Jon, so obviously he wants to get the thoughts of those closest to him into print. So that's what he's doing now.'

He looked at me as if challenging me to disagree.

'Well, I'm amazed,' I said, unable to keep the sarcasm out of my voice. 'I thought you might have slipped him a happy pill or something.'

He snorted out a laugh. 'He's perfectly capable of changing his mind, you know. You just had to give him some time.'

'If you say so.'

'Anyway, I thought you agreed with me about it. You said it's what you'd want to read.'

'I know I did. I didn't think Barry would be so easy about it.'

'Well.' Neil stretched his arms wide. 'Everything is possible.'

'You can say that again.'

'How you doing anyway?' He changed tack, became ingratiating. 'Only I don't want to hold you up from your Everill piece for much longer. I know how hard you've worked on it. I can take over now if you like.'

'It's OK.' I brushed him off. 'I think we should crack on with the pages today, like you said. I've got all tomorrow to work on Everill. If you want the issue to go on Saturday, let's get through this lot today.'

'If you're sure?'

'Positive.'

'Right.' He turned his attentions to the designer. 'How do you think you'll do, Paul?'

'If I can have all the outstanding text and pictures by tomorrow lunchtime, we'll be OK. We'll do the cover last, tomorrow night.'

'Right.' I shuddered inwardly, and not at the amount of work that was expected from me. I was used to him piling it all up for the end of an issue, even without interfering Americans and their deadlines.

'I'll get on with it, then.' I turned my eyes back to the computer screen.

'Me too,' chirped Neil.

Towards six o'clock, we reached a lull. Paul had ripped through the features, but now was on the fiddly news pages, which required a lot more picture-scanning and the tricky fitting of short items on to the pages to his artistic satisfaction.

'I'll do the scanning,' Neil had immediately suggested. 'You can get on with your transcription until some more comes through.'

My heart felt like a stone. The tapes were waiting. At least I had transcribed the first one already. I wished I had left it at that, left it at the ICA, written him off as an arrogant wanker and been done with it. Too late for that now. And I couldn't put it off any longer.

I pulled the tape recorder out of my bag, set it to rewind. In the meantime, I opened the file on my hard disk of the previous transcript, scrolled down to the end and wrote: 'Interview 2' as a heading.

As if I needed to remind myself.

The tape clicked itself off. I plugged the earphones into the socket, put the headphones on. Lit a cigarette with fumbling fingers. Inhaled deeply and pressed PLAY. Clenched inside, waiting to hear my first question, hear the not knowing in my voice, the confidence I had had to think I was conducting a major interview. I dreaded what I would sound like.

Before I got chance to find out, the door slammed and Barry came stomping back in.

'Barry! How did it go?' Bambridge shot to his feet.

Glad of the distraction, I clicked the OFF button. Barry looked as if he had come in under a cloud.

'I've not got much,' he frowned at Bambridge, 'because they don't think it's right to try and speak for him.' He put his bag down on his desk with an air of weariness. 'Tell you the truth, they thought I was a cunt for asking.'

'But surely you explained to them...' Bambridge didn't get any further.

'No,' Barry said sharply, 'don't give me no third degree about this, Neil. I went in and done my best for ya, they saw things differently.'

'Well, did they say anything?'

Barry stroked his fingers through his goatee. He looked more gutted than angry. 'They didn't want to go on record,' he sighed. 'And I can't make 'em. It's all I can do, and that's that. You don't know what that might have cost me.'

'Barry...' Neil began.

Paul was more tactful.

'I've laid out your censorship pages, Barry,' he cut across Bambridge, 'and I think I've used all the pictures you wanted. But do you just want to check it's OK, whether you think the pull-quotes work, and everything?'

'Thanks, Paul.' Barry sounded genuinely grateful. He returned to his desk and hunched over his task without a further word to anyone.

I was dying to ask him what had really happened, not just with Woody and Alex but this morning with Neil. But his silence seemed too ominous, his body turned away from the rest of the room inviting no further conversation. And now Paul was back on his news pages, there was nothing to do except go back to the tapes.

Maybe I'd just read through the first transcript again, see what was useable. Then I could maybe write an introduction. The book was in my bag. I thought I could pick out a few paragraphs to use. It was a miserable way of putting it off, but it worked. Though the tape recorder sat opposite me like a small grey box of disapproval, I carried on with my charade, looking thoughtfully through *Weirdo* and marking things off with a pencil every time someone looked my way.

Tomorrow, I kept thinking, I'll be much more able to face it tomorrow.

It only took an hour for more pages to start coming through from Paul, which sent the whole office back into a flurry of activity. By ten, we'd finished off the news pages and Paul was on to the final page, the contents.

Neil stood behind him, clapping him on the back. 'Bloody good show, old boy, at this rate we can catch a last drink.'

'Thought you were working through the night?' Barry almost snapped.

'Well, we've all been at it all day, and we're on schedule. What's the harm in nipping out for a swift one?' He checked his watch. 'We'll only have time for a couple anyway.'

'If you don't mind,' said Paul, 'I'd like to finish up here first, be on time to catch the last train home. I'm on a roll now, so I don't really want to stop. But you all go on.'

'Well, as I say, it's only going to be an hour or so,' thirsty Neil continued, beaming over at Barry and me. 'And you two can knock off after that if you like. You've done brilliantly today. We do the same tomorrow and we can really celebrate.'

Barry looked at me and shrugged.

'All right, Neil.' I was more of a pushover. I would rather have done anything than go back to the tapes. Now they would have to wait until the morning. If it had to be done in a last-minute rush, I wouldn't have so much time to dwell on it.

'Excellent,' beamed Neil, reaching for his coat. He was up the stairs in no time.

The Bricklayers Arms was as full as it ever got, and we managed to get through the lines of resting workmen to the bar pretty easily. Neil handed Barry a tenner and said: 'I'll have a pint of bitter, you get whatever you want. Just nipping to the loo.'

'Hmmmm.' Barry watched him squirm through the throng to the Gents. 'What you havin', pet?'

'Just a pint of shandy. I'll get us a seat.'

I settled down in my favourite corner, feeling a wave of fatigue roll over me. Neil came out of the bogs, looking just the opposite of how I felt – a new brightness in his eyes, a jerkiness to his movements. We were all settling down with our drinks when an unexpected voice called out loud across the bar.

'Aha! Here you are! Mind if I join you?'

It was Everill.

26

He was staring straight at me, coming towards us, smiling that big cat smile he'd been smiling yesterday morning. A cat with half a sparrow stuck out of its mouth.

'Gosh, hello, Simon,' I finally said. 'I didn't expect to see you here.'

'Didn't you?' He seemed amused. 'I thought you said to drop by this evening. Don't you remember? I've been waiting nearly an hour.'

He looked at me quizzically. His tone seemed so reasonable, it sent my mind into a tailspin. When had I said that to him? Not on the train the other morning, I was certain of that much. Jesus, was it that night, in some wiped-out drunken blur, had I invited him here? I couldn't remember.

'Well, you told me how to get here all right,' he continued. 'Now aren't you going to introduce me to your friends?'

'Oh.'

Now I was really confused. Had I really told him where the office was on Tuesday night, or some time before? Maybe at the Coach and Horses? I was too tired to piece it all together. Meanwhile, Barry, Neil and Simon were all looking at me as if I'd beamed in from another planet.

Good old British manners intervened.

'Barry, Neil, this is Simon Everill. Simon, this is Neil Bambridge, my publisher and editor, and Barry Hudson, my co-editor.'

We all stood up, about to shake hands. But first: 'That's it!' Neil snapped his fingers.

'That's where I've heard your name before. Jon Jackson told me about you. Very pleased to meet you.'

He went to take Everill's hand. Everill's face turned to ice. Barry stared from them to me, mouth open. Bambridge looked at Everill's face and realised.

'Oh, good God, I'm so sorry. He must have been a friend of yours. I don't know what I was thinking, please forgive me.'

Everill's expression changed in the flicker of an eye, melted away into a half smile. His eyes glittered. He said, softly: 'What did he tell you about me?'

'That he was buying your book.' Neil eager to make amends, forcibly trying to ingratiate himself. 'Because it was so brilliant. It was going to be his next movie. And Diana here's been telling me about the book all this time, and I never put two and two together, and now I've made a right fool of myself...'

'It's all right.' Everill, utterly composed now, smiled and clapped a hand on Neil's shoulder. 'Look, I didn't know him all that well. I only met him the once. There's no need to worry, you haven't offended me.'

'Well, here.' Neil peeled another tenner out of his wallet. 'Please let me buy you a drink.'

'Thank you very much.' Simon plonked himself down firmly. 'I'll have a pint of Best.'

Barry and I slowly sat back down, Barry looking from Everill to me as if to say: 'What's going on?'

'I didn't know you knew Jon Jackson.' I frowned at Simon.

'I didn't.' He smiled back. 'I told you, that time at the Coach, I'd had people sniffing around trying to buy the film rights.'

'Oh yes.' That much I did recall. 'And you weren't too pleased about it.'

'Why not?' Barry swivelled round to face him. 'Most writers'd die for that.'

'That's what she said,' Everill chuckled, looking at me like a twinkly old uncle indulging a small child. 'And I'll tell you same as I told her. I just can't see it as a movie. It's too complicated.'

'Well, there's not that many that'd turn their nose up at the cash,' said Barry doubtfully.

Fawning Bambridge returned with Everill's drink.

'So you're going to be in our next issue,' he continued, arselicking. 'Diana says she's got the best interview.'

'She has that.' He raised his glass to me. 'I made sure of it.'

I made a feeble attempt to raise my own glass in return. Took a sip of the shandy. The cystitis, which had been hovering in my system since Wednesday morning, kicked back with a twinge so sharp I almost dropped the glass. Barry noticed me wince. Everill turned his attention back to Neil.

'So, you knew the late Mr Jackson well, did you?' he asked.

'Not really. I only met him once too. Did an interview with him, turned out to be his last one. Bloody awful affair.'

'Yes, it was shocking,' Everill agreed. 'He was a great director.'

'He was a great bloke an' all,' Barry said sharply.

'So I gather,' Everill continued smoothly. 'What did you make of him, Neil?'

'Perfect gentleman,' Bambridge nodded. 'Bloody clever bloke.'

I suddenly felt sick.

'Excuse me,' I stood up. 'I've just got to go to the toilet.'

I barely made it down there in time. The sandwiches I'd had for lunch, the packet of crisps and Kit-Kat that had made do for supper and the one sip of shandy came right back up. I hung over the bowl until nothing more would come, then sat back down on top of it, head in my hands.

The room was spinning. I needed to go home. I couldn't work out what was happening here. Couldn't cope with it. What was Everill doing, coming in here like smoothness itself, ingratiating himself with Neil? I racked my brain for a memory of us arranging to meet. I knew we hadn't. Which gave way to another, more sinister thought. Had he been following me?

No, surely that was paranoia. I was in a public place, with friends. All the same, I wasn't going to stick around to see what he had in mind for the rest of his evening's entertainment. I was leaving now, with Barry.

I splashed water on my face, tried to make myself look human. Failed. Staggered back to the bar, towards Barry.

Simon and Neil were locked in earnest conversation. Hudson sat back from it, a deep frown on his face. They weren't paying him any attention. He got up when he saw me.

'You need to go home, don't you?' he said.

I nodded. They noticed this.

'What's wrong, Diana?' Neil frowned. 'You look awful.'

'I don't feel too good,' I murmured, and looked at Simon. 'Look, I'm really sorry, but I'm going to have to go. I haven't had enough sleep and I shouldn't have tried to drink, it's made me sick.'

'Oh dear.' He looked genuinely worried. 'Shall I get you a cab?'

'You're all right, I'll see her home,' Barry said firmly. 'I'm going in the same direction as her, and I need to get back too. I'll make sure she's all right.'

'Well, that's very kind of you.'

'I'm her mate,' Barry snapped, clearly irritated by the tone of the other man's voice.

'Will you be all right for tomorrow, though?' Sympathetic Neil at the top of his form. 'We can't miss this deadline.'

'Fuck off,' said Barry. 'She'll be fine. I'll see to it. You lot carry on.'

'Oh, all right,' said Neil huffily. 'I'll see you tomorrow.'

'See you soon, Diana,' said Everill.

And Barry propelled me out of the door.

In the fresh air I felt less dizzy, but I still had to lean on Barry to stumble down the street. He didn't say anything until we were on Edgware Road.

'Try not to look drunk,' he commanded. 'Otherwise we'll never get one to stop.'

Edgware Road swam before my eyes like a carnival, visions in robes and fezzes and Arabic headscarves wafted past me from the juice bars, hookah emporiums and Moroccan restaurants that

filled the thoroughfare. Barry a black silhouette against the blur
of lights coming down the road, arm out, trying to catch one of
those orange lights and get it to take us home.

He grabbed my hand as a cab pulled over.

'Ladbroke Grove, mate,' he told the driver as he bundled me
inside. 'St Charles Square.'

Then he shut the window between the driver and us and said:
'You never invited him out tonight, did you?'

I shook my head, wanting to cry.

'Then what the fuck is he doing? Stalking you?'

'I don't know. I can't remember if I did say anything to him the
other night or not.'

'Well, you're staying at my house tonight. I don't care if you
throw up all night. I don't like that cunt and I don't like it that
he knows where you live. And I don't care if you think I'm
overreacting. You were perfectly fine until you saw him. And
now he's got you into a right old state.'

'Thank you.' I was so glad to hear him make sense of the
shadowy forms that were stirring in my brain.

'I don't think I'll be sick again,' I said. 'I think I just need to
sleep.'

Barry put his arm around my shoulder. So much bigger and
more comforting than Everill's bony limbs.

I leaned against him and stared out of the window, images
merging in my mind as we passed through Paddington, Bayswater
and Westbourne Grove, right down the Grove to St Charles
Square. The lights in the streets had an almost hallucinogenic
quality and I swam in a slipstream of neon images, blurred
against the darkening sky. I was probably dreaming already. I
don't remember much of getting in, except Barry covering me in
blankets on his sofa, feeling safe in his house, pitching headlong
into sleep.

27

I slept long and deep. The blank somnolism of total exhaustion.

So that when my eyes finally opened, I had no idea where I was, except sunk in the middle of a big leather sofa, with a TV on softly in front of me and the smell of percolating coffee coming from the kitchen. The gentle patter of rain against glass.

Slowly it came back. I was at Barry's.

With wakefulness came pain. My head was clear, but my insides felt like they were being strafed by briars. The cystitis kicking in. Reminding me of everything that had gone on in the past forty-eight hours.

'Oh fucking hell,' I murmured, shifting myself upright.

'Sleep well?' Barry came through from the kitchen, big steaming black mugs in his hands.

'Yes, thank you.' My lips were cracked and it hurt even to smile.

'You went straight out,' he said, setting the mugs down on the glass coffee table that was painted with hands of poker cards and dice. 'I had to carry you in. You've been sparko for over nine hours.'

'I needed it,' I said. 'Do you mind if I have a glass of water?'

'Not at all.'

I fumbled out of the blankets, looked around for my bag. Barry had placed it neatly by the side of the sofa. Found my packet of Cystemme. He watched me slowly tear a sachet open, stare at the dissolving contents in the glass.

'Still not feeling too good?' he hazarded a guess.

'I'll be OK,' I said, taking a slow sip. 'What time is it now?'

'It's half eight. I've run you a bath. Go and have that when you're ready and I'll make us a bit of nosebag.'

'Thanks, that would be great.' I continued to sip at the cloudy water. It tasted of saccharine and artificial lemon. Please God it did its work.

'Anything on the news?' I asked Barry, becoming dimly aware that that was what was on the television.

'Not much,' he grimaced. 'A bit on that Prevezeer ponce. How the police are now following a new line of enquiry. Cunts have got fuck all, you ask me.'

I drained my glass, picked up the coffee. It was strong and good. Barry was putting his diary and notebook into his record bag. My heart sank. It was tomorrow now, and that meant I'd have to transcribe that interview as soon as we got in. Listen to him all over again. The moments leading up to...

'I think I'll have that bath now.' I got shakily to my feet.

'Take your time, pet. Use anything in there. You know, shaving foam, aftershave.'

He winked.

'I'll make breakfast.'

Barry's bathroom was so much warmer than mine, and he had a thick, white shagpile carpet in there too. A heated towel rail and big fluffy black towels. The bison's skull was now resting under the sink, the bath itself was full of bubbles. It was like paradise. I could have stayed in there all day.

Except for that fucking deadline. Except for Everill.

I didn't like getting back into yesterday's clothes, they felt itchy against my skin, like they were soiled with bad memories.

'Barry,' I asked, once back in his front room, 'do you mind if we go back to mine before we go into work? I'd like to get a change of clothes.'

'Course, pet. I'll come with you.'

It was raining outside, the city hung in a miasmic pall. The iron-grey sky closing in on us as we walked up Ladbroke Grove. As we neared Arundel Gardens, a single magpie took off from the trees in the communal gardens, streaking black and white across my eyeline.

One for sorrow.

I looked for a mate. They usually came in pairs. But today, there wasn't one. Bad omen.

Barry's eyes darting everywhere as we walked towards my front door. Like he was expecting someone to jump out at us. The road was empty. I unlocked the front door. The house was still.

Pressed on the hall light, went through the fire door, down the steps to the basement, Barry right behind me.

Jerry's front door slammed open. He stood there in what was once a blue-and-white striped dressing gown, now blue-and-fag-ash-grey, thick black hairs sprouting out from his chest, down his legs. His face was bright red.

'I want a word with you,' he spluttered.

He was never normally up at this time of day. He'd obviously been waiting for this.

'You whore.'

'I beg your pardon?' snapped Barry.

'I'm not talking to you,' the peace and love man ranted. 'I'm talking to this slut here. Listen, missy, I've turned a blind eye to your gentleman callers over the years, but the night before last you made so much fucking noise, all night long, that I couldn't get a wink of sleep. Don't you have any respect? And do I have to remind you that our tenancy agreements specifically prohibit any overnight guests?'

'I-I'm sorry.' I stared wide-eyed at the raging, hirsute inferno Jerry had become. Barry stepped past me, walked right up to him, eyeball-to-eyeball.

'I thought your generation believed in free love,' he said, quietly.

'Look, this is nothing to do with you!' Jerry spluttered. He crooked his head around Barry's shoulder, jabbed a forefinger at my face. 'I'm warning you, next time this happens, I'm going

straight to the landlord and getting you thrown out of here. And
you call off your thug here too or I'll do it straight away.'

'Barry.' I pulled at his sleeve. 'Leave him. Come on, let's go
inside.'

Barry didn't move. His fists were clenched. The shark ring
gleamed evilly in the dull light.

'I'm warning you!' Jerry shrieked, and backed into his room,
slamming the door in Barry's face.

'I know where you live,' Barry whispered after him.

'Come on, Barry.' I had to pull him forcibly away. 'He's not
worth it. Don't get me chucked out of here, please.'

'It's not worth living here,' Barry grimaced, but he followed me
into the bedsit all the same.

'Does he always talk to you like that?' he fumed.

'No, normally he's far more lecherous and drunk,' I told him,
pulling fresh clothes out of the wardrobe. 'Look, you just stay
here while I go to the bathroom and change. Don't do anything.'

'And what,' Barry caught my arm as I tried to walk past him,
stared at me with wild, violent eyes, 'did that fucker do to you in
here? Was he raping you?'

'No, he wasn't.' I pulled my arm free, recoiling from the
mention of that word like he'd just dropped scalding water on me.
'Look, I don't want to talk about it, let me get changed, please. I
want to get out of here.'

My voice was getting higher and higher – even to my own ears
it sounded unnaturally loud. Jerry would be loving this. Loving
it.

Barry dropped his arm and his eyes. 'Sorry,' he muttered.

As I crashed into the hallway, the hippy was halfway up the
stairs.

'I warned you,' he said. 'I'm calling the landlord now.'

'Do it, Jerry,' I spat back at him. 'Do it if it makes you feel like a
man. And while you're at it, let me talk to him about the amount
of times you've kept me up all night with your shit music and

your boring reminiscences. Go on, you swinging motherfucker, do it.'

I slammed into the bathroom with him still standing there, ratty address book in his hand.

I could still hear him, though, in that echo chamber of a room. He didn't go on up to the phone. Instead he slunk back down the stairs to his lair. I heard his door shut and lock.

Three years of pent-up bile and resentment all out in one heady rush. I almost felt good. I gathered up my clothes, marched back into my room.

'Come on, Barry, we're leaving.'

'That was classy,' he said. 'Swinging motherfucker. I like that.'

'You're right,' I told him. 'It's not worth living here. I'm gonna look for somewhere else just as soon as I can.'

We set back off down the Grove, as great, grey hunchbacked clouds swept across the sky, heavy with rain. Down by the tube station, a lonely pilgrim was making his way in the opposite direction: a man I had seen on many occasions but couldn't explain his purpose. He was a sorrowful-looking black man, carrying a white-painted cross on his shoulder. He hauled his large burden up Ladbroke Grove at the same time every day, his sad dark eyes fixed upon the pavement. Today, more than ever, he looked like the bringer of storms, the collar of his black overcoat turned up against the wind.

Bad omen.

When we got on to the platform, the downpour began.

28

Still sheeting it down as we came out of the tube.

It was 10.30 by the clock in the tube station. My fracas with Jerry had made us late. No doubt the weather was sent by Bambridge as a judgement on the tardiness of our arrival, the impending doom of deadline reflected in the sky. We hurried down the underpass, under the roar of the dual carriageway, juggernauts sleeking rain as they thundered towards the A3.

Both of us ran up Bell Street, towards the office, Barry getting to the door first, turning the handle and putting his weight behind it. Bouncing off.

'Fucker's locked!' he exclaimed.

I caught up with him as he pulled out his own keychain, rattled the iron into the hole.

'Hello!' he yelled as he pushed the door open.

Silence.

'Neil?'

The place was deserted.

'Can you fucking believe it?' The words were hardly out of his mouth before the phones began to ring.

'Hello?' He snatched one up, dripping all over the tabletop.

'Neil? No, he's not in yet. Can I take a message or can anyone else help you?'

I looked around. It looked messier than usual. Messier than when we'd left it last night. Something about it didn't look quite right.

'Well, I am his business partner, yes, and can I ask who you are?'

I moved over to Neil's desk. A heap of papers slid on to the floor.

'Shit.' I bent down to pick them up.

'From D. C. Arnold? The Americans?' Barry was asking.

Neil's briefcase was on the floor, beside his desk. It was open.

'And he told you to come in when?'

Neil never went anywhere without that briefcase.

'Well, that should be fine, if that's what he told you. I tell you what, as soon as he comes in, or if he phones in before that, I'll get him to call you. Can I take your number?'

I stood up slowly. There was a bottle of malt whisky on the shelf by his desk. Two glasses. Beside them, a CD case with tell-tale powdery smudges on it.

'Thank you. Yeah, speak to you later.'

Barry put the phone down.

'Stroppy cunt,' he said.

'Who was that?' I asked, still staring at the evidence of Neil's night's work.

'That was David Goodman from D. C. Arnold,' Barry mocked up a New Yoik accent. 'The fuckin' Yanks. Bambridge was supposed to be calling him this morning to confirm a meeting in here tomorrow – suppose he's going to show them the finished dummy. But, would you believe, Mr Goodman is unaware that Mr Bambridge has any other business partners. He can't discuss issues with me or you. He can only speak to the top dog.' Barry's eyes were blazing, his cheeks had gone bright red.

'Well, come and have a look at this,' I said. 'This is what he meant by working through the night.'

'He was gonna do all that and then finish the magazine?' Barry looked at the glasses and the CD case in disbelief. 'And why are there two glasses? I thought Paul wanted to knock off in time to catch the last tube?'

'That's what he said,' I nodded. 'And there's something else, Barry. Why is his briefcase still here?'

'You what?'

I pointed at it. I didn't want to touch it.

'It's open,' Barry noted. 'What the fuck is going on? Do you think he's fallen asleep in the bogs?'

'Well, he said he went to sleep under his desk the other night, so I suppose it's possible. Go and check.'

Barry clattered across the room.

'No, he's not in here.'

'Then where the fuck is he?'

I felt dread pouring into me like poisoned wine, down through my heart to the pit of my stomach. *Black rain and single magpies. A downpour of sorrow.* Bad omens.

'Barry, he never goes anywhere without his briefcase.'

'Well.' Barry scratched his head. 'Maybe he's just nipped out to get some breakfast or something. After all, he took his keys, he's locked up.'

'That's true.' I nodded. 'Do you think you should go up to the caff and check? I mean, if that bloke was desperate about speaking to him, we'd better tell him he's late.'

'OK.' Barry looked about him, as if scanning the disorderly room for clues. 'I'll run up there. I'll be five minutes.'

Still dripping, he went back up the catwalk.

I didn't like being in there alone. The dread had draped its shroud around me. Like the weight of the cross on the old black man's back. I didn't like the fact there were two glasses. I didn't like the fact that the last time we'd seen Neil, he'd been with Everill. Everill, all charming and nonchalant. Everill who knew Jon Jackson and had never said before.

I nudged the mouse on Neil's desk. His computer sprang back to life. It hadn't been switched off, only sleeping. Nothing was open on the desktop. I went through everything that was on there. All the layouts Paul had done yesterday.

The contents page had a time beside it: 23.08. Maybe I was just panicking. Maybe Neil had come back down and talked Paul into a snifter for the road. After all, he'd been desperate enough for us to join him for one drink, and after a line or two of that stuff, one drink wouldn't be enough.

I looked on his hard disk. Surely, he'd have been working on that. Nothing had been copied over. He should at least have looked at those contents or been working on his Jackson piece. But nothing on there was labelled. What had he been doing?

The front door banged. 'He's not there,' Barry shouted, running back down the stairs.

'His computer's still on,' I told him. 'Only I can't see anything here he could have been working on.'

The phone shrilled out again, making me jump. Barry snatched it up.

'*Lux*, can I help you? Oh hello again, Mr Goodman. No, I'm afraid he still hasn't turned up here. No, he hasn't called either.'

I could hear the angry voice of the American ranting down the phone.

'Well, are you sure there's nothing I can help you with? OK then. Yes, I'll pass that on. Yeah, thank you. Bye.'

'Fuckin' arrogant arsehole!' Barry slammed the receiver down.

'He's still not called?' I asked.

'No, and Goodman says he's not happy about that. He was told everything would be signed, sealed and delivered by Saturday morning and Neil had better remember that and call him at his hotel before he books on to an earlier flight.'

'What's going on, Barry? Neil would never fuck up with the Yanks. Never in a million years. It's what he's been waiting for.'

Dread, still silence, creeping over the office. Thoughts forming twisting shapes. *A single magpie flying out of the communal gardens, flying right across my line of vision.*

'Ring Paul,' I urged Barry, too frightened to put in the call myself. 'It looks like Bambridge coerced him into some after-hours drinking. The timer on the Mac says he finished designing the last pages just after eleven.'

'Good idea.' Barry delved into his bag for his address book, riffled quickly through the pages.

I watched him dial the numbers, sat on the side of his desk. It seemed like an eternity before he got a response.

'Ooo, hello, mate, did I get you out of bed?' Barry doing his best to sound jocular. 'Sorry about that, but we're missing Neil and I've got some American on the phone says he's supposed to be arranging a meeting with him. Yeah, now. No, he isn't. I was just wondering what time you left last night?'

The frown deepened across Barry's forehead as he took in the reply.

'You never saw him? But he came back here, he's left his briefcase.'

Two people. Neither of them Paul.

'I guess you must have just missed him. Yeah, so do I. It's a bit puzzling, to say the least. Look, sorry I got you up. I guess so, yeah. See you at one. I will, yeah. Cheers, mate.'

He put down the receiver, looked at me grimly.

'Paul says he never saw him come back. He presumed he'd gone home after the pub. He finished up and left here about quarter past eleven. Neil had given him a spare key, so he locked up.'

'Quarter past eleven? How did they miss each other?'

'I dunno, pet, but this ain't looking good.'

We stared at each other in tense silence, suddenly broken by the sharp ring of the doorbell.

'This'd better be him,' Barry practically flew up the stairs.

As he opened the door, I heard a voice say: 'You in some sort of trouble?'

Barry coming back down the stairs, face white.

Behind him, padding on soft-soled feet: Detective Sergeant Linehan.

Things were starting to come loose in his mind now. Whereas, only a few days ago, he had felt supremely in control, now he had the terrible feeling that he had made a mistake.

One that would bring everything crashing down.

There were too many loose ends.

He sat in his room, sweating. There was a storm raging outside and the wind had always spooked him, even as a child. Now it made him doubt his sanity. Had he taken it that one step too far? Had that last act, which he had thought of at the time as a risk worth taking, had it really been the start of his undoing?

He held a cassette in his hands, twining the reels around his long fingers. The others lay scattered across his bed. What was on them, quite possibly, could have sunk him stone dead in the water. But at what price their retrieval?

He had done this thing recklessly, and that was out of order. But, maddened by the thought that this snobby little man had some knowledge he was about to use, Jackson talking behind his back, he had acted without thinking it through. Had let the red tattoo, throbbing in his head, direct him.

The wind howled outside, turning dustbins over, sending their metal lids spinning down the streets, spilling decomposing foodstuff, papers, tin cans, all over the pavement. Car horns blared. Somebody was shouting, a maniac monologue of incoherent abuse, while the windows rattled in their frames; insanity spilling into his quiet room, reverberating around the walls, stirring up evil spirits.

The panic was taking him over. He hadn't had it like this for years. He could feel the contents of his mind slowly downloading like a computer with a virus in it, methodically deleting file after file, eating the programs that made the mainframe function. Then the stabbing pains in his arms and across his chest. That screaming pain that preceded the sudden, merciful black-out.

He fell from his bed to the floor.

'Is Mr Bambridge about?' asked the detective, his voice almost as quiet as his footsteps.

'No,' I said before Barry could open his mouth. 'We don't know where he is.'

'Well, maybe you can help me. Diana, isn't it?'

'Yes.' He was looking at me strangely, a half smile on his lips.

His tone was mild but, behind his piercing blue eyes, he looked as if he was piecing something together in his mind.

'That interview he did with Jon Jackson,' Linehan continued. 'Was he thinking of running with it any time soon?'

Barry and I exchanged glances.

'Yes,' I replied slowly. 'Yes, he was. We're supposed to be going to press with it on Saturday.'

'Oh.' Linehan's eyebrows raised. 'Did he happen to show it to you first?'

'No.' Barry's voice was harsh and flat. 'We were actually looking for it now. Only it seems to have gone missing. Along with Neil himself.'

Linehan's expression changed. His eyes sparked like a sudden flare had gone off behind them.

'What do you mean, missing?'

Barry sighed deeply. 'We came in late to find the office empty. We thought we were in trouble because he's pushed our deadline forward a week. But he's not here. And we've just had a bunch of calls from an angry American publisher who's in town specifically to see him. The guy got in this morning and Neil was supposed to be calling him to set up a meeting. He's heard squat, and I'm telling you, it ain't like Bambridge.'

'But,' I looked from Barry to the copper, 'his briefcase is still here. He never goes anywhere without it.'

'When did you last see him?' Linehan was pulling a notepad out of his pocket.

'Last night.' Barry shifted uncomfortably from one foot to the other. 'He said he was gonna be working here through the night.'

Linehan was writing in his notepad.

'Only, we know he came back here,' I added. 'Because there's this half-empty bottle of whisky that wasn't here before. And two glasses.'

'Two?' Linehan's pen poised in mid-air.

'Yeah.'

Magpies, black rain, crosses. Cursing hippies. Stupid whores.

'We left him with someone in the pub.' Barry picked up the thread. 'So we presume he invited him back here for a drink. Our designer had already left, I've just been on the blower to him.'

Linehan looked like a hound on a scent.

'What time was this?'

'Quarter past eleven, he reckons. He wanted to catch the last tube home.'

'So do you know the fella he was with last night?'

Barry and I exchanged fearful glances.

'I do,' I finally said. 'It was a writer I'd just been interviewing. Simon Everill is his name.'

Flashes behind Linehan's eyes again. Hound with his tail up. Taking a handkerchief from his pocket, using it to cover the phone, picking up the receiver and saying: 'You mind if I use this?'

My heart was hammering, louder than the rain.

'OK,' Linehan was saying. 'Send a patrol car round right away. I'm just getting you the address…'

Barry reeling it from memory: 'Top-floor flat, 29 England's Lane, Belsize Park.'

Linehan repeating it, saying: 'Right away. Call me when you get there. This number…'

'0171 262 2600,' Barry barking.

'Thank you, David.' Linehan replacing the receiver, turning back to us.

'Now I don't want to alarm you, but it just so happens I want to speak with this Everill. And I think you media types know which enquiry it's in relation to.'

As I looked at him, the world suddenly turned black and white. The world turned widescreen. Stretching out into infinity like a rubber band, with the lines of blackness between it, just like a cinema screen gone mad. Then, just as suddenly, it all pinged back into one little white spot.

Barry shouting: 'Catch her.'

A tiny white spot, then blackness.

As I fainted into the arms of a policeman.

29

I came round with a wet flannel against my forehead. I was still in Bell Street, my temples pounding, arms weak and trembling at my side. Barry's arms were around me; he was saying: 'It's all right, she's back.'

'Diana, are you OK?' Linehan's pair of blue eyes stared down at me.

I tried to stand upright, still leaning heavily against Barry.

'I'm sorry,' I said, wincing at the light. 'I've never done that before.'

'It's perfectly OK.' The policeman's voice was calm. 'Only I've got to ask you some questions, and it's important, really important, that you answer them now.'

'OK.' I disentangled myself from Barry, tried to stand up straight on wobbling legs.

'I'll get you some water.' Barry pushed over his swivel chair. 'Sit down here.'

I was facing the detective.

'How well do you know Simon Everill?' he asked.

'Not very well.' My voice sounded tiny. 'I met him at a crime festival at the ICA a few weeks back. He was there making a bit of a show of himself, which was why I found him interesting. I'd read his book, and the way he behaved seemed so different from what he had written.'

Linehan nodded. 'So did you interview him at the time?'

'I did, but I didn't make a very good job of it. He wouldn't tell me anything, and I didn't want to come back here empty-handed. So I went back the next day and asked him if I could do it again.'

Sipping at the cold water. Stars still dancing in my vision.

'And how was he then?'

Everill standing at the water's edge. Throwing stones across the lake.

'Very different.' I frowned, trying to make words of the pictures in my head. 'He didn't have his punk rocker's head on at all. He seemed more human than the day before, more vulnerable, almost. I was sure there was something in there I could get to. I thought I'd got him to open up a bit. Anyway, he said he'd consider it, and he called me up a few days later, set up a meeting.'

'He called you here? Did you give him the number?'

'No, he said he'd got it from his press officer.'

'Hmmm. So when did you meet him?'

My head was hurting too much to retrieve the facts.

'Barry, can you get me my Filofax? It's in my bag. I can't remember offhand.'

Scrabbling through the pages until I came to the one I had scrawled it down on. 'It was the 29th of March,' I told the detective. 'At the Coach and Horses in Soho.'

Linehan writing this down too, saying: 'Which one?'

'Which what?'

'Coach and Horses. There's two in the West End. One on Poland Street…'

'Not that one. The one by Cambridge Circus.'

'Ah, Romilly Street. Your Jeffrey Bernard one.' He winked at me. 'So what happened then?'

'Well, nothing, really. We just ended up talking. About music and books. I never got an interview that night.'

'He was stringing her along.' Barry butting in. 'I told her at the time.'

'And I told him that I thought Everill was testing me out. To see if I was OK.'

'That's an interesting thought.' Linehan studied me. 'Do you meet many people in your job who give you that impression?'

'I've met a few.' I nod. 'Mainly musicians. They're quite

precious about what they do. Sometimes it takes a few meetings
to get them on side.'

Linehan nodded. 'I understand. So did he call you again?'

'Yes. The very next day.'

'Here, at the office?'

'Yes. He wanted to meet up again that night. But I couldn't.
We were celebrating the deal with the same Americans that Neil's
supposed to be talking to today...'

Neil. And Everill. My fault. My fault.

Hot tears shot up behind my eyeballs.

Linehan's voice was calm, reassuring. 'Come on, Diana, don't
stop now. When did you meet him again?'

'Two days ago.' I looked down at my diary to try and hide the
smudges of water trickling out of the corners of my eye. 'April 4th.
And that's when I fucked up...'

I couldn't hide anything now. Couldn't stop crying. I'd let him
in. Let him over the threshold. And now look what he's done. It
was all my stupid fault. Always wanting too much information,
always wanting to find out things I'd be much better off not
knowing at all.

Linehan put a hand on my shoulder, made me look at him.
His eyes were burning like blue flame. 'Diana, you've got to tell
me everything. What happened that night?'

Barry's hand was on my other shoulder, his voice was urging
me: 'Keep it together, Di, tell him. It's not your fault, for fuck's
sake.'

But already, he was thinking what I was thinking.

I snivelled my way through it: 'I met him in a pub near my
house. The Earl of Lonsdale, Portobello Road. He gave me an
interview this time. A proper one. Told me all about his book,
and how it was about his childhood. How his friend got killed by
his mad mother and he started drinking and taking acid 'cos he
was so cut up about it. Had a vision of Christ on Christmas Eve.
All this mad stuff that he wrote the book from. It's all there, on my
desk, if you want it, all the tapes. Only...'

Snotty great globs of tears were falling now. I could scarcely breathe, let alone speak. So Barry did it for me: 'Only she got a bit pissed and she let him come home with her. She won't tell me what happened, but I don't think she enjoyed it much.'

'All right.' Linehan stood up. 'That's enough for now. So, Barry, maybe you can answer this better. What was he doing in the pub with your colleague last night?'

'The fucker said Di had invited him, was bold as brass about it. Only she didn't. I think he was hoping to confuse her, just like he did before. But he knew where we were all right. He must have been stalking her. I knew there was something fucked about him, but I didn't know it was gonna be this bad...'

Barry covered his eyes with his hands.

'Right, well, we don't know how bad anything's got yet.' Linehan moved in the direction of the door. 'Only I want you, Diana, to come to the station, and I want those tapes you have of your interview.'

I nodded, stood up and went over to my desk, mechanically picked up my tape recorder and the boxes that had the Everill tapes in them, and swept them all into my bag. Linehan gave a final glance over Neil's desk. He asked: 'Have you touched that briefcase?'

'No.' I shook my head.

'Good. Anything else?'

'His computer,' I admitted.

'Those glasses, did you touch those?'

'No.'

Barry: 'No.'

'Right, I'm gonna have forensics come in here. When they get here, Barry, you're going to have to leave the office and stay away until further notice.'

It really was happening. Had I killed Neil?

'And I don't want you,' Linehan was saying to me, 'to go back to your house until we've had Mr Everill in for questioning. Have you somewhere else you can stay?'

'I can take care of her.' Barry nodded. 'When you've finished at the station, come straight round to my house. I should be back by then. I'd better just call Paul and the Americans, tell them not to come in.'

'Good.' Linehan examined his watch.

Barry came straight out with it: 'You want Everill for Jackson?'

But the phone rang, as if preordained. Linehan picked it straight up, not dropping Barry's gaze. 'All right? No sign of life? Well, go in, David. We'll worry about the paperwork later. I'll worry about it. I want you to go in there. I'm on my radio, going back to the station.'

He put the receiver down, saying: 'That's all for now, Barry. Thanks for all your help.'

And with that, he propelled me through the door.

It was the kind of place where the secrets spill.

All the killings, the rapings, the hold-ups, the muggings, the petty thievery, those acts of desperation.

In a dull, flat room, painted a dull, flat green, the sort of end-of-line colour only used in institutions 'cos no one would want it anywhere near where they lived. Scratched walls, scuffed skirting boards. How many lives had split open in this dull little room, under this unblinking light? How many sad-eyed shoplifters, red-eyed junkies, pin-eyed muggers with their stories unravelling before those old police posters tacked to the walls:

WATCH OUT! THERE'S A THIEF ABOUT!

I sat facing Detective Sergeant Linehan and W. P. C. Furrows under the bright light in the dark room. Talking about Simon Everill.

While Simon Everill was out and about in London. And my boss, Neil, was nowhere to be found.

His flat, entered by the police, was empty, the answerphone flashing incessantly. On it were lots of angry messages from the

Americans. Messages from the day before, telling them he had not come home last night.

I talked into a tape recorder, going through it all again. Telling them what Everill told me about his small towns and secrets. Linehan nodded like he already knew the story, occasionally making a note in his pad.

'Right, so shall we take a listen to those tapes?' he said.

I pulled everything out of my bag as the policewoman intoned, '11.43am, Diana Kemp removes cassette recorder and two cassette boxes from her handbag.'

But as I put the things down on the table, I realised something was wrong.

'Hang on,' I said, pressing EJECT on the recorder.

It was empty.

'What the…?'

Picked up the two boxes that had had the Everill tapes inside them.

Empty too.

'Oh my God.' I looked up into Linehan's saucer eyes. 'They've gone.'

'What do you mean?' He frowned. 'Between here and the office, they've disappeared?'

'No.' My voice was a whisper. 'They were never there. He took them. That's what he came back for.'

'You sure you've brought the right ones? You were a bit shaky back there.' Linehan stared at me.

'Yes, these were what I was about to start working on. I left it all out on my desk because it was the first thing I was supposed to do today.' I felt a scream welling inside me. 'Don't you see? It means it *was* him. He came to the pub last night to get my tapes back. Neil let him into the office and now…'

'All right, Diana, that's all conjecture, so I think we're going to have to leave it there.' Linehan sprang to his feet. 'I may have to ask you for another statement later, but right now, without these tapes, we're wasting our time. As of 11.58am, Thursday 6th April, 1992, this statement is concluded.'

He turned off the tape.

'I-I'm sorry,' I started to say, my voice sounding hysterical.

Linehan shook his head but his voice was soft, reassuring.

'Let's just find a patrol car and see you home safely, eh?' he suggested, propelling me back out of that interview room with as much haste as he'd got me out of the office.

At the front desk, Linehan sorted out a man to drop me back to Barry's house. Taking my number, he shook my hand with that same firm, dry palm.

'We'll be in touch.' He handed me his own card before disappearing back into the dull bowels of the factory. I shuddered, not quite believing it was still daytime. Stepped out into an unmarked car, a cheery young constable asking the way.

'St Charles Square, off Ladbroke Grove,' I told him, tears forming in my eyes.

30

When the panic attack had subsided, he was lying on the dirty carpet of his bedroom. At first, he didn't know how he got there. It was the wrong shape and he couldn't see the shutters. Somebody had changed the van around. And where was Mary?

The sounds of the traffic brought him around. His first reality dissolved into the present. No, he was far from there now. He had come to the city, remember. Come to take back what was his.

Head thumping like piledrivers were inside his brain, he lifted himself up on to the bed. Felt himself drain. It had all gone wrong now. Like it always did.

He looked around the room. Motes floated on the lugubrious air. As his vision cleared, the stars stopped dancing in front of his eyes, and he also remembered he was no longer alone. There was a visitor in the corner of his room. Not that he was saying much. Which went to show, it was finally over for London. He'd never brought anyone back here before, and was never likely to again. No, the visitor could have the room. Shame really. It wasn't half as nice as what he was probably used to.

Still feeling wobbly, he managed to get to his feet, to move into the corner and inspect his handiwork. A broken neck. Tongue lolling stupidly out of the mouth, eyes filmed over. He had shown a kind of mercy by making it quick, almost felt some kind of empathy for the guy. He'd been a man of wealth, yes, and taste too. But while he could appreciate the company of a fellow con man – and a good one too – there simply wasn't enough room in this story for both of them. And wealth and taste aside, the fatal flaw of this one had been lack of attention to detail and an over-eagerness to beat his competitors to what he saw as the grand prize. To reveal to him that he had one vital piece of information that linked him to Jackson.

But how he'd wanted to talk and boast about it first. Once Everill had made up for his 'indiscretion' and once Diana and her thug boy were out of the way, he'd had the toff singing like a canary. A few more jars, a wrapper of something passed under the table with a sly wink.

Cocaine, he guessed, and by the expression on his companion's face, he was now expected to run along to the Gents and partake of it, too. Like it was some sort of treat. Well, he'd had his share of drugs experiences, didn't fancy any more. Not that coke was harmful, really, well, it wouldn't bring on visions. He just made a show of going to the Gents, playing along, coming back touching the side of his nose like that time Jackson did in the Hop Poles, like they were all mates together.

Then it had been, 'fancy coming back to the office, want to look around, take a look at the new issue?' For a while he had almost let it take him over; the desire to lay one on this show-off little prick had been fierce. But that would never do. Before that time could come, he'd have to ease the evidence out from him. Besides the fact that Diana's tapes were probably in the office. Let's not forget, that was what he had originally come for, and a good job he had now that this new information was all being laid out for him. He'd better calm himself down, gather together everything he needed.

'Go on,' he'd wheedled, as they opened a bottle of Scotch the toff just happened to have in his drawers. 'Let's just have a listen to what Jon Jackson said. After all, you're going to press Saturday, there's fuck all I can do about it. I just want to hear the scoop with my own ears. Listen to what might have been.'

Bambridge had obviously felt sorry for him at that point because he got out a cassette and flicked through it to the point in which Jackson had mentioned his name. He pretended to listen in solemn silence, out of respect for the dead.

What he had heard could not have been more damning.

By the sound of it, Jackson had taken Bambridge to one of his drinking clubs. There was a murmur of chat in the background, the sound of wine being poured and the click of a Zippo as cigars were lit.

The dead man's voice sounded jocular on the tape. 'What I eventually want to achieve,' he was saying, 'what I'm going to be working on next, is a film that is more concerned with the truth.'

'This is it,' Bambridge had pointed out unnecessarily.

'Yeah, yeah,' the director's voice went on. 'We can certainly talk about my next movie, and I'd like your magazine to have an exclusive on that. I think far more of *Lux* than any of the rest of the media.'

The toff had smiled smugly as he played that back.

'There is a lot of shit that goes on in this country that gets swept underneath the carpet,' Jackson was saying. 'I know, because I come from the country, from the Fens, and they do things very differently there. I was always conscious, in that society, of not being what they would call normal. I'm half-Spanish, or in Norfolk parlance, a "chocolate drop". There are some tightly knit covens of people there, who look after their own, don't welcome strangers and bury their own secrets. I hope each and every one of them watched my last film, 'cos they're exactly the people I want to take money off in order to make the next one – the people who are gonna hate it the most. I've been sent a book by an agent that says everything I want to say in a film.' Jackson dropped the bombshell. 'It addresses all these issues, so look out for it. It's called *Weirdo* and it's by a guy called Simon Everill. No one knows who he is now, but they will.'

'What's it all about then?' On tape, Neil could hardly keep the excitement out of his voice. In reality, he had just signed his own death warrant.

'It's set in an unspecified village, that could easily have been the one I grew up in,' Jackson breezed on. 'It's about a family of freaks, all born to a drunken mother and fathers that range from local bikers to gypsies. They live in a caravan on some wasteland by a farm. All the kids have got something wrong with them, either mentally, or physically, or both. But one of them, the Weirdo of the title, is desperate to have some kind of connection with reality, because he alone realises the insanity of his situation.

'As all the other kids drop off one by one – accidents with farm machinery, fratricide, leaving to join the gypsies – he makes friends with a normal little boy who goes down to feed the ducks by the river. In his head he becomes this little boy. Then, in the end, when there's only him and one sister left, the sister he actually likes, the farmer comes round to evict them from his land. Of course, the drunken mother can't handle this. So she smothers both her children, drops them in the river and throws herself in after them.'

'My God, that sounds even more far-fetched than *Bent*, if you don't mind me saying.' Neil sounded doubtful.

'Ah, but you see, it's not. I've met the author of this book. Again, this is off the record, 'cos I don't want anyone to know this, not yet. But he says that everything in the book is true. It went on in the village where he was born, and the locals hushed the whole thing up. As I said to you, I've come from a place like that, I can quite believe it. Only the author doesn't want that information generally known. I actually think he's afraid. So don't, whatever you do, print it. I want him to get all the credit he deserves for the book, before I bring my vision of it to the screen.'

'Well, I can see the Francis Bacon imagery in that.' Fatuous Bambridge hardly containing the joy of what he had here on tape.

'Too right.' Jackson, sounding smugger still. 'It's going to be like Thomas Hardy meets *The Texas Chainsaw Massacre*.'

After that, the toff turned off his tape and went for another toot on his nose candy. His guest declined, so he did the other line as well. By now, Bambridge was obviously reeling drunk.

It had been all too easy to remove the tape from his Dictaphone, while his host was taking a piss, replace it with another one that was lying handily nearby. All too easy to erase the files from the computer while Bambridge blundered around in the little boy's room, trying inconspicuously to take another line of coke. Another little trick he had picked up from Jackson, from when they'd worked on that manuscript together, how to bin a computer file.

He recognised Diana's tape recorder, lying on her desk, and the boxes of tapes she'd used from the other night. Almost blithely he removed them too, not even bothering to find replacements. Let her realise, from him she had no protection. He could do what he wanted when he wanted.

Then, as Bambridge noisily blundered back into the room, it had been a simple matter of diversion. He'd asked the public schoolboy a couple of questions about the art books he had piled upon his shelves. He didn't half love to jaw on about that shit. And then, another toot and a couple more glasses of that fine Scotch. Rounded off the evening nicely with an invitation to see his work in progress. After all, Sodom wasn't too far away, on his way home, and what was a couple of quid's cab fare to a toff like that? By then, the guy was too arseholed to object to anything.

And now he was too dead to object to anything. The tape he'd kept all to himself, his great exclusive, had brought him here, to a foetid corner of an anonymous room. Just like Jonny, he'd made one move too far.

What I really want to get to, is the heart of darkness.

'Well, I showed you, didn't I, Jonny boy?' he laughed bitterly to himself. The funny thing was, Jackson could probably have got away with it if he hadn't had to try and make *Weirdo* his as well. He had quite enjoyed being famous, thought he could probably go on enjoying it too. But no. Nothing was ever enough for Jon Jackson, was it?

So he had to be shown what it means to open the door on

absolute horror and have no way back to the other side. It was better than a film, wasn't it?

The truth.

And yet...

The one thing that still got to him, the one thing he could now never work out. Why had Jackson really wanted him to write that book? He'd already told him the stories about Mong and Fists, the way they had finished up when they were kids, and he'd stuck to the same lines again, even though it wasn't exactly the truth. Same with Jake; he had run away with the gypsies, but that was because he had, by then, realised that he was likely to be the next person to have an 'accident' with the farm machinery. But Jackson had continued to press him on all the details, just like he had when they were little. Like he was getting a thrill out of it.

And then there was the way he had twisted his own story around Jackson's childhood when he was talking to Diana in the pub. Why had he wanted to weave the things together like that? Why was he grateful still now for some of the little tricks his old adversary had shown him?

He shook away the nagging, awful suspicion that Jon Jackson had somehow got inside his head and, having done so, would always be there. There was no time to dwell on that now. His time was coming to an end now, he could feel it.

For a while, it would be hard for anyone to find him here, because no one knew where here was, apart from his houseguest, who was now free to take up full-time residency. That tape, he wouldn't be needing it now. It could stay here, with the person who helped create it. Diana's would come with him. He didn't want to let go of her yet. But he wouldn't need to take much more with him.

There was a wedge of cash he'd been saving. As soon as the cheque for his advance had cleared, he'd drawn it all out of his account, never trusting in money houses when you could just have hard cash. It was a fair old bundle, and he was sure it would be more than enough to take him where he wanted to go. He only really needed to take his tools, and they all fitted neatly into his little sports bag.

And Glasgae Boab's St Christopher to guide the way home. Just one call to make on the way.

31

Jon Jackson's last night on earth began in fine style.

The National Film Theatre was packed for his sell-out lecture. Most of the cast of *Bent* reassembled along the front row, Niall Flynn right at the centre, his white hair a beacon in the dim lights before the curtain came up. Alongside him, the great and good of the movie world traded gossip and slapped each other on the back – producers, fellow directors, journalists and money men. Behind the rows of illustrious company, stretching to the back of the hall, Kray Klones in their shiny suits sat on the edge of their seats, trying to pick out the celebrities from the wanabees. The air was alive with excited chatter.

Only one man at the back didn't share their enthusiasm.

Not that he wasn't looking forward to the events that were about to unfurl that night, oh, indeed he was. It was just that his interest took a different form. The people here tonight, even the famous ones, well, they were just paying punters. They didn't know there was going to be a private show later, for an audience of one. For the man in the black crombie coat, slumped down in his seat, turned away from his nearest neighbour, this was just the hors d'oeuvre.

He'd been planning it all now for about four weeks, ever since the last time he'd spoken to his agent.

He called her each Friday on his mobile, to catch up on business. He didn't give out his own number to anyone, not even her. Alison Varley, slick old money matron that she was, didn't bat an eyelid at such eccentricity. She privately thought of him as her little J. D. Salinger, the wilful recluse.

Only that day she hadn't projected her normal aura of calm. That day she had sounded practically girlish.

'You'll never guess who I just had on the line,' she had gushed. '*Jon Jackson!* He's read the book and he loves it, darling! And he only wants to option it for a movie...'

It had taken a few seconds for that to sink in, and when it did, he had quietly pressed the button on his phone to cut off the call. Then, he had thrown the stupid thing against the wall and screamed in a manner that would have stripped the honey-blonde highlights out of his agent's Harrods' helmet hairdo, had she had the misfortune to hear it.

Luckily for her, he was far away in Sodom, where noises like that are par for the course.

It had taken a while to calm down from that. His room had taken a bit of a beating. Bed overturned, chair smashed in half, he'd even made holes in the wall.

But when he did come to his senses and realise, a strange sense of calm flooded over him. Of course, this was it now. The time had come. Maybe he had deluded himself that there wouldn't be a need for it once, but now he could see that he couldn't escape it. It was fate, guiding him, all along.

The first thing he had done was buy a ticket for this lecture. One right at the back, next to an exit, so that he could slip away unnoticed. Then he had got his kit ready, and his waiting room all furnished.

He had known all along where it would take place, that's why, he realised now, he'd kept the copies of Big Tony's keys safe in his drawer with the St Christopher and the date-stamped envelope.

When the book thing had taken off, he'd decided to stop working for Big Tony. Told him regretfully that he was going to have to leave the stall, because he couldn't afford to keep on living in London. Tony still believed the lad to be the shy kid he'd helped out of the gutter, so wished his friend well, told him to keep in touch and thanked him for all his hard work. The big man never was a one for books, nor for the sort of arty magazines that carried pictures of Simon Everill while proclaiming his genius. It wouldn't be until it reached the front pages of the tabloids that poor Tony would realise just what his kindness had bought him.

But as far as Everill was concerned, now that Andy Smith had served his purpose, it was best that he dissolved away completely. Which meant staying away from Camden. And the good thing about London was that this could be so easily done: no one really moved out of their patch and their routine, so even though Everill continued to live a mere mile from his old job and haunts, Big Tony would never see him again.

He'd done a few recces to see how the land lay in the early morning hours around those arches. Isolated as they were from the High Street, the area was empty and desolate. Letting himself in, a little exploration had led him through a hole in the brickwork to a derelict arch. The only things that had been hanging around the whole time he was there were a few mangy alleycats and a whole lot of rats.

So much the better.

The night before the *Guardian* lecture, he had brought his kit and his change of clothes, laid them out neat and ready. Then he went home and had a long sleep to build up his strength. Set the alarm so that he had plenty of time the next day to wash and get changed, get himself down to the South Bank and his seat right at the back of the hall, while everyone else was milling about at the bar. It was the perfect position to watch, but not be seen.

Jackson appeared on the stage to rapturous applause, kitted out in his best Savile Row suit, hair oiled and gleaming. His subject, obviously, was his favourite British gangster movies and he had selected movie clips from the BFI library to illustrate his points. It started with *Brighton Rock*, Dickie Attenborough's skin-prickling portrayal of the teenage psychopath Pinkie. The chosen scenes illustrated the favoured settings of British noir – the races, the seafront, the artificial paradises of the working classes and the twitching curtains over the cheery façades, the dank treachery that lurked there. Everill yawned through it all, and the clips that followed: *Hangover Square*, *10 Rillington Place*, *Get Carter*, *Ganglord*, *Performance*, *The Offence* and *Villain*. The audience seemed to be lapping it up though, hanging on to Jackson's every word, his every little in-joke and knowing smile. If only they knew what a faker he was. That this was the real façade. But still, they'd find it all out soon enough.

After the lecture had concluded, there was an intermission for drinks, before *Bent* would be shown in its entirety.

Well, Everill had seen that once and he didn't need to put himself through it again. He slipped away as everyone went back to the bar in a chattering babble, but not before leaving a little token with the guard by the backstage door. Some flowers and a card of congratulations to pass on to the director.

The same card he'd sent with his manuscript. Arnie in *The Terminator*. Jonny, he knew, would realise who it was from as soon as he saw it. He wondered if the director would enjoy the rest of his evening so much after that.

Which was enough to keep a spring in his step as he crossed back over Waterloo Bridge. The lights glittered on the surface of the Thames, pretty patterns skimming across the black currents beneath. London all lit up for a night on the town.

He caught the tube at Embankment, came out at Chalk Farm just after nine. After that it would be a bit of a wait, but what were a few hours between friends?

And anyway, it was all worth it when he finally heard the keys scrabbling in the lock, heard a faint curse as the door swung open.

Then there was a snap at the lightswitch and all was revealed.

'All right there, Jonny boy?'

Jon Jackson dropped the keys he'd been about to unlock his flat door with.

Everill was standing casually beside it.

'How the…' Jackson began.

He supposed he'd better explain it to him. 'A lock's not a hard thing to go through, really.' Simon smiled. 'Especially when you've been to special school, like I have. They teach you everything there. Well, the kids do, not the teachers.'

He enjoyed the way Jackson's pupils dilated, the way for once he could not hide how he was really feeling.

'What do you want?' Jackson stuttered, his voice rising to an unnatural pitch.

'Had a good evening, did you, Jonny boy?'

He was still smiling, lounging against the doorframe like he had all the time in the world.

'I stayed for the first half, but really, Jonny, you do go on. I was getting a bit bored of the sound of your voice. And I don't think I could sit through that terrible film you made a second time, not if you paid me. But I hope you got the flowers and the card. I chose them especially. To celebrate the news my agent's been telling me about you trying to buy my book.'

He let the words hang in the air, seeing that he'd pitched it exactly right. Jackson looked like the proverbial rabbit, trapped in the headlights of his gaze.

'So then.' He strode forwards, hand outstretched. 'Congratulations, Jonny boy. You made a right good film out of my idea, and wormed out of me a right good book about my life. Thought you'd get it all back, didn't you?'

Jonny flinched away, tried to avoid physical contact, said: 'Look, Simon, you've got it all wrong. I'm not trying to rob you of anything, I'm trying to make you a star...'

Still trying that old line.

Everill's fist caught him on the side of his head so hard he dropped straight down to the floor.

'Did you see any stars then, Jonny?' he asked. 'You're so very fond of them. Don't give me all that crap again, will you? I've heard it all before.'

In all his life, no one had ever so much as raised a finger to Jackson. He was stunned more than registering pain. He tried to struggle to his feet, tried desperately to think of a way out of this situation. But Everill stood over him, stood on the corners of his coat so that he had to look up at him, had to see the maniac gleam in his eyes, the flecks of foam forming at the side of his mouth.

'What's the matter, Jonny?' he taunted, cocking his head to one side for a better look. 'Are you scared?'

Jackson was, and it showed. He realised exactly what he was looking at, but the blow to his head had robbed him of not only action but also coherent thought. He could only open and close his mouth like a landed fish.

'Up you get, Jonny.'

A hand encased in a black leather glove came down and grabbed the prone superstar around the scruff of his neck. With a strength that barely seemed human, Everill pulled him to his feet, kept him standing upright, pinned against the front door, even though his legs were ready to buckle at the knee.

Then, the pièce de résistance. The starting pistol he had kept from the old place. Dug into Jackson's back, it felt just the same as a real, loaded gun.

'You got something wrong in that film of yours,' Simon continued smoothly, 'and just so you don't make the same mistake again, I want to show you how it's done, properly. If you don't mind. Open the door, Jonny.'

But Jonny just shook his head, cowed.

'Oh dear, Jonny, looks like I'll have to do it myself, then.'

He kept the pistol pressed into the film director's kidneys, while his other hand scooped up the keys from where they had fallen on the floor, neatly pocketed them in a black overcoat.

'Come on, Jonny.' He pulled him roughly away from the doorframe.

'Aw, little Jonny, all scared now, like a lickle girl. Does it give you the motivation for another film, does it? Or another book, perhaps? Can you feel my pain now, Jonny? Can you feel my sister's?'

'Noooooooo.' Jackson was blinded by sudden, scalding tears.

'If you won't come to me like a big boy, I'll have to treat you like a baby.'

He smacked him again, on the back of his head. Jackson swayed in his arms as he pushed the door open.

They looked like two staggering drunks as they rolled down the backstreets of Camden. People would rather cross the road than take any notice of what was going on there. It was hard work, but he got him there all right, to the corner of the railway arches. He suspected that the constant reminder of cold steel on Jackson's back was helping matters no end.

The hardest part now was getting Jackson through the hole in the arches to the pre-arranged place. He was flopping about and moaning like a sleepwalker trapped inside some terrible dream. It was better to cosh him out again and pull him through. Easier to arrange him properly too. Let him have one last dream. A dream that would be a mercy compared to what Jon Jackson woke up and found himself faced with. Hanging from the ceiling by his heels, in a dank, dark railway arch, alive with the scratching and squealing of rats, two torches fixed upon his face, giving enough illumination for him to see how and with whom it was going to end.

'Ah, the master awakes.' Everill's gloating voice slid like an evil yellow mist into Jackson's ears, filling up a head already rushing with blood, piledrivers pounding in his temples and no way of moving to protest. His arms had been fastened, securely, behind his back, with a roll of black gaffer tape and a length of wire. Tape was around his mouth too, and the blood that bubbled and burst out of his nose made it almost impossible to breathe. In terror, he began to spin uselessly around, which only served to disorientate him further. The words, the creeping mist, continued to wind their tendrils around his brain.

'Yes, as I was saying, there was one scene you got wrong in there, old boy.'

Footsteps stalked around him, the voice swirling about the room, swimming in the redness of his head and his gaze. 'The scene with Marley's brother. It was probably artistic licence to you. But I didn't want him crucified upside down. Mary wouldn't have liked that, you see.' A grey eyeball was now level with Jackson's brown one, boring its hatred into his skull. Jackson screwed his eyes shut, choking on the blood, feeling nausea rise in his gut and, at the same time, a sudden warmth flooding down his abdomen, running down his torso, into his face, as he began to piss himself.

The voice moved away, the footsteps circled, the torchlight altered so that it was more directly in his line of vision.

'No, I thought the bloke was a pig. So he should be slaughtered like one. And the funny thing is,' the voice, right in his ear now, turning from mist into freezing fog, 'when people die, they make the same noises as pigs.'

Jackson didn't want to open his eyes, but he did. They came to rest on a long, silver blade nestling right under his nose, curving away into infinity.

His bowels went then, thick, sticky, sliding down on to him.

'Yes, they do that too,' Everill continued. 'You find these things out when you live on a farm. Like I did.'

The blade flashed in the torchlight.

Jackson could do nothing but watch, his every flight instinct drained, only now the hypnotic eternity of waiting for what surely was to come.

'I would say it's been a pleasure knowing you,' the voice went on. 'But that wouldn't quite be true.'

The blade coming up through the air, into the soft part of Jackson's belly.

The scream partially contained by the gaffer tape, guttural, unearthly clamouring in the dread air.

Spinning as the knife continued its work, splitting his insides. Opening up a gaping, steaming tract from which spilt all manner of organs; long and stinking, slivering out of the parted flesh.

The rattling sound of blade against bone.

The force which possessed Everill crescendoed like a symphony. Jackson was disembowelled almost instantly. All life poured out of him as he spun from his ankles, spraying blood, shit and entrails around him like a demented carousel.

The laughter welled up from deep inside Everill, like sparks shooting out of his throat, just as mighty orgasm shot through his loins, the sweetest, most delirious pleasure he had ever known. High-pitched, hysterical, the sound echoed around the brick walls like all the clamouring of Bedlam condensed into one minute of the most deranged noise you'd never wish to hear. Laughed and laughed until he was forced to sink down on his knees to contain his wheezing breath, and watch in wonder the masterwork he had created there, the abstract bloody carnage that had once been a body. A work of art no film director could ever have conceived.

Laughed and laughed until he had to finally lie, exhausted, stomach cramped up with strain.

'Write this up, you fucker!' He gargled on the foam washed around his mouth, flecking his goatee beard.

He hooted at his own lightning wit. 'Get a wide angle on that, you fucking cunt.'

The sweet smell of revenge enveloped him. It was the performance of a lifetime. 'And they said he never had it in him,' he chuckled to himself, as if there was a rapt and attentive audience around him, *ooh*ing and *ahh*ing with pride at the fine floorshow they had just witnessed. As if he was in the middle of his very own *Guardian* lecture, floodlights illuminating his smiling features as he made to take a bow.

And then he realised. The show was over.

His nemesis hung limp from the ceiling, a gutted, glittering mess. Not even Picasso could have constructed the shapes Jon Jackson now made, the streaks and shadows of nightmare.

The smell of hell.

Awkwardly, Everill picked himself up from the floor, dusted himself down and went over to inspect what he had made.

The eyes, glazed for eternity in a mask of horror, staring into the final abyss. The face stretched and contorted, so slick with blood as to be virtually unrecognisable. Blood ran from the tips of his dark hair down into a pool on the concrete floor.

His eyes travelled upwards to the hanging gardens of Jackson's insides.

'He had a lot of guts,' he snickered to himself, remembering the line from an old James Bond movie.

He walked around it, inspecting it from all angles, savouring the fine details, committing them to memory.

The perfect tableau.

And now he must leave this masterpiece for others to find. And feel the sense of awe.

Even as he congratulated himself on his achievement, he could somehow feel the audience leaving the stalls. The sense of magic dissipated as he became aware that he'd made a mess of his trousers again.

He must change.

Neatly, he stepped out of his clothes, folding the soiled ones into a pile, and putting on the clean set he had stashed there earlier. Now, he took the mirror in his sports bag, checked whether his face had been badly splattered. He removed the gore with cheap women's make-up remover.

Cleaning his hands on a rag, he grew sensitive to the fact that he might mess up the inside of his coat pockets. He noticed there were carrier bags lying around the place. He picked a couple up.

They were from the local butcher's.

After he'd thrown the detergent around the place, he wrapped his hands with them, plunging them deep into his pockets, his left hand still curled around the knife.

When he had finished up, he took one last lingering look at the spoils of victory.

Then slipped like a shade back into the night.

32

Barry was waiting at his window as the car drew up. He was at the front door before I had even got to the top of the steps. He ushered me past him while he craned his neck outside, scanning the street and the departing police car in one long swoop before shutting the front door.

We stood in the hallway, staring at each other with hollow eyes.

'You all right?' he asked. He looked ghostly pale.

'I don't know.'

'C'mon, let's go upstairs. I've brewed some strong coffee. You look like you need it.'

I followed him up to his flat. The television was on, tuned to the ITV lunchtime news, and the heady aroma of coffee hung comfortingly in the air.

'What happened?' he asked me.

I gingerly sat down on the sofa.

'Those tapes,' I told him, 'the interview with Everill. They were all gone.'

'You what?' His face appeared around the kitchen doorway. Steam rose around him, lending him an even more satanic air than usual.

'Gone. All of them,' I repeated. 'That's what he came to the pub for that evening, Barry. He told me too much, so he wanted the tapes back. God almighty, why was I so stupid? What have I done?'

'Will you stop saying that.' Barry came over with two heavy mugs, placed them down on the table. 'It's not just you that cunt has conned. It seems to me like he's got away with fooling the whole publishing world as well. And if they didn't know there was something wrong with him, how were you supposed to? You were just doing your job.'

I picked up the black enamel mug, sipped slowly at the hot, bitter liquid. All of a sudden I felt desperately tired. I guessed it was shock.

'I suppose so,' I reluctantly agreed, still aware that it was more than professional curiosity that had caused all of this.

'So what did you tell them?'

'I just went through everything. Everything I could remember about my meetings with him, all the weird things he said and the way he played around with me. I don't think I forgot anything. But that copper, that Linehan, he knows something. Which means that Everill is probably the killer. And that Neil obviously got in his way so he was next…'

'Don't start on that,' Barry admonished sharply. 'We don't know what's happened to his Lordship yet. And there's no point getting into a state about anything until we do.'

I put my cup down, fished in my bag for a cigarette. The cathode ray tube blinked on in the foreground, calm newsreader voices discussing the issues of the day. Whatever they were, I couldn't take any of it in.

'What time did the police get to the office?' I asked Barry instead.

'About ten minutes after you left. I know what you mean about Linehan,' he was forced to admit. 'He's not fucking around.'

'Did they ask you anything?'

'No, but they took my number here in case they have to.'

'What did you tell Paul?'

'Just what we know. He was really fucking upset about it, obviously.' Barry shook his head. 'He said he was gonna ring around all of Neil's clubs, see if he showed up any place. It's a pretty good idea, well, at least it gives him something to do. Then I had to speak to the Yanks.'

'How was that?'

He rolled his eyes, put his own cup down. 'Well, eventually I got them to take me seriously. I'm sorry, but I'm gonna have to nip out later this afternoon to see them.' He looked at me with sad eyes. 'I didn't want to leave you on your own,' he stressed, 'but I can't see another way out of it. Neil had all these plans and they've come all the way over here; someone's gonna have to try and sort it all out if he doesn't turn up.'

I didn't envy him that task.

'Don't worry about that,' I told him. 'Have you explained to them about everything? About the police and all that?'

He shook his head, eyes grazing the carpet.

'Not all of it, no. I didn't know if it would be wise, in case the silly bugger is pulling some stunt and turns up right as rain right in the middle of me telling them he's the subject of a murder investigation. I need to try and find out what the future is going to be for us. Besides,' he added darkly, 'I want to know what kind of deal he's actually made.'

'What time are you going to see them?'

'Three o'clock, at their hotel in Mayfair. I left it as late as possible to make sure you got back here all right first. But I'll need to leave in about an hour. The police have got this number, in case anything happens or they need us to make any more statements. Paul'll probably ring in as well. You be all right to answer it?'

'Of course. I'm glad I'm here, Barry.' I felt tears suddenly prick behind my eyelids. Like a little girl, I didn't want to be left alone. 'I don't ever want to go back to my flat again.'

He put an arm around my shoulder, gave it a squeeze. 'Don't worry, you won't have to. Well, not alone, any road. You can stay here as long as you want.'

'Barry?'

'Yes.'

'I hope it is all a mistake. I hope Neil did go to one of his clubs and fell asleep there.'

'So do I, pet. So do I.'

No one had rung by the time Barry left. We had pretended to watch the telly, each of us lost in our own separate thoughts, forms too dark to articulate. I still didn't want him to go, but I didn't think it was right to say anything. He had a job to do, and it was probably my fault he was in this position. Instead, I watched him haul himself into his thick black overcoat with a wan, unconvincing smile plastered to my face.

'I shouldn't be too long,' he said, doubtfully. 'And if it looks like taking longer than I think, I'll call you.'

'It's OK.' I nodded. 'Take as long as you need.'

He opened the flat door as if to leave, then suddenly turned around and hurried back over to the sofa. He bent down and kissed my forehead.

'I'll bring us back some pizza,' he promised, 'and a bottle of wine. Or two.'

'Thanks, Barry.'

'Oh – and there's spare keys on the mantelpiece if you need to go out for anything. They're inside Satan.'

He gestured to a ceramic mug shaped like a leering devil's head. It formed part of a display of similar knick-knacks – model hot rods, ceramic va-va-voom girls. Barry's collection of objets d'art.

He waved again from the doorway, then he was gone, footsteps hurrying away down the stairs and out of the front door.

I got up and went over to the window, pulled back the net curtain, watched him disappearing up the street. He walked quickly, bent slightly against the wind, which was tossing the branches of the trees in the little park opposite, swirling cherry blossom away into the grey skies. An ugly storm, hurling the delicate beauty of the flowers away in its rage, to pile up sad and grey, ruined in the gutter.

When Barry had disappeared from view, I dropped the curtain, went back over to the sofa. The TV was still blithering away, some game show with Bob Monkhouse. I didn't feel like any more coffee, had already smoked too many cigarettes. All that I felt like doing now was sleeping. Barry's sofa was easy to squish into. I put some of his cushions under my head, curled my feet up, let my eyelids droop. Before Bob could drop another pearly one-liner, I was fast asleep.

The phone woke me at five to four. It was Paul, straining to sound calm.

'Have you heard anything?' he demanded, once he had established who he was talking to, and the whereabouts of Barry.

'Nothing yet. Did you have any luck with the clubs?'

The room was dark and I felt disorientated. A kind of pressure was filling up in my head.

'No.' His voice was high-pitched and raw. 'I've tried everywhere I can think of. Why the fuck didn't I just stay in the office ten minutes longer? Or go to the pub with you lot? None of this would have happened.'

I found myself repeating Barry's advice. 'You can't think like that, Paul. We don't know what's happened. He may yet turn up with the Americans.'

But I knew my voice sounded insincere.

'Well, I suppose it could have been a bird,' he considered, equally as doubtful. Barry's words again, from that evening in the Bricklayers, a month, or was it a thousand years ago?

'I tell you what,' Paul went on, a tiny spark of hope growing in his voice. 'I'll try a few of his usual suspects. Will you still be at this number in an hour?'

'Yeah, and maybe Barry'll be back by then. Maybe he'll have some news.'

'OK, Di. Well. Let me know if you hear anything before then.'

'I will.'

'See you later.'

'Bye, Paul. Good luck.'

I put the receiver down, hunted for the lightswitch. As the room flooded with colour, I realised why I felt so strange. Little lights at the side of my vision told me a migraine was on its way.

I went through my bag looking for headache tablets. Trouble

was, all the traumas of the past few days had caused me to go through my entire portable stock. I had a packet, and it was empty. Shit, I hoped Barry had some in his bathroom.

I riffled through his cabinet. Plenty of shaving foam and Black'n'White hair wax. Even some condoms, rainbow-coloured ones. No painkillers, though.

The lights formed an arc in my left field of vision. I could hardly read the labels on anything in there, but none of the boxes looked promising. Maybe he kept them in the kitchen, like I did.

No luck there, either. By now I was half-blind, and the throbbing at my temples told me the mother of all headaches would soon kick in. Shit. I'd have to go to the shop now. I couldn't sit here and wait for it to pass, or I'd be banging my head against the wall in half an hour's time.

'Fucking hell,' I cursed out loud, making for the horned key holder. Turning Satan upside down, I rattled out the keys. At least there was a chemist's on the corner of the street. I snatched my purse out of my bag, took my coat down from the pegs in the hallway. I'd leave everything on, I thought. I'd only be a minute. I stood at the doorway, looking back into the room. I hadn't forgotten anything, I only needed a quid or so for the tablets. Still, something inside nagged at me to stay. I hesitated, and sure enough, the phone rang.

'Di.' Barry's voice was flat, hard. As if he was having to suppress a violent rage. 'You OK?'

'Y-es,' I said doubtfully.

'Well, listen, I'm really sorry but this is gonna take longer than I thought.'

'Has Neil shown up?'

'No, he hasn't.' His voice then dropped to a whisper. 'And if he does, I'll kill him myself...'

'What's happened?'

'I can't talk now.' He resumed his brusque manner. 'But we'll be needing more than a couple of bottles of wine by the time I get back, I'll tell you that much.'

'Shit.'

'I'll probably be home about eight,' he continued. 'You be OK till then?'

'Yeah, sure.' No point in worrying him about my migraine. Just when you thought it couldn't get any worse, it obviously had.

'All right then, I'll see you later.'

'OK, Barry.'

'See you.'

He cut the connection. What was going on now? I felt even more loath to go out, but then, I couldn't wait long enough to ask him to pick some pills up on the way home.

'Don't be stupid,' I told myself. 'Get them now, or you'll be sorry. You'll be back in five minutes.'

I had to hold on to the banisters as I walked down the stairs. I could hardly see a thing. It was like the two halves of my vision had merged into one, and walking straight ahead was no longer that easy. Similarly, the front steps were murder to navigate. The wind rushed up to meet me in an icy blast, and I had to steady myself on the stone pillars at the bottom before carrying on, clutching keys in one fist and purse in the other, head down against the wind.

I was halfway to the corner where the chemist's shop was before I realised that someone was running up fast behind me.

Thank God I didn't bring my bag, I thought, it's probably a passing mugger.

I started to turn.

But before I could, something hit me hard on the back of the head.

I began to fall, but arms were around me, stopping me.

My vision exploded into a million stars. And then, blackness.

33

The night is coming down now, the light is fading.

When I was 14 years old, there was a mystery in my village that I wanted to get to the bottom of.

An old man called Ernie, who lived in a shabby old house all by himself and planted plastic flowers on sticks in the garden. I'd never so much as seen him, but all the boys in Bardeswell spent the long nights of the summer holidays there.

Everyone, it seemed, except my brother and I.

Day after day, we'd cycle past, hoping for a glimpse of him. In my mind, he would be some kind of hunchback, maybe with one eye, shuffling around in rags and chains. But we never caught so much as a shadow against the windowpane, a dusty curtain moving.

No one would tell us what went on there, not at first. I had my suspicions. I reckoned the old man let them drink booze there and watch videos. Horror films and electric blues, most likely. After all, I had a brother of my own, I wasn't stupid.

But I had to know for sure.

After some weeks hanging out at the bus shelter, the other social magnet for the village's teens, I managed to befriend one of the younger boys. He was called George, but that wasn't his real name, I soon found out. He was called that after the character in the kids' TV show, *Rainbow*, who was an albino. So was this George. Because the other kids mocked him like they ignored me, we formed a kind of alliance. In return for bottles of my dad's home-made wine, he promised to smuggle me inside Ernie's house, to see for myself what these nightly nocturnes were really all about.

I can see it all now.

Bats are swooping out of the sky, making arcs across the pink sky.

I can hear loud laughter from Ernie's house and I wonder, should I just go? I've been waiting an hour already, behind an old compost heap, smoking contraband John Player Red that George knows how to steal out of the machine in the local pub. I know if I'm not home before dark, I'll have to face the wrath of Dad and shudder at the thought. I stub the John Player Red out on the dry earth, so that the paper splits and the tobacco spills out, mashing it into the compost heap, thinking: a compost heap. For plastic flowers. Ernie is mental.

Suddenly the back door opens. I can see George, framed against the light, his white hair all sticking out on end. He's gesticulating wildly.

'Come on!' he hisses. 'Quickly, in here…'

I waver for one moment. Half an hour and it'll be dark. And then I'll be in for it.

'Come on!' he hisses.

If there's one thing I'm more afraid of than getting in trouble with my parents, it's looking a fool in front of my peers. I scramble to my feet and run to the back door, ducking low as I do so. At the back door steps, George has a finger to his lips. I nod. I'm inside. He closes the door softly behind us.

Ernie's house has that sweet, sickly smell that seems to surround old people. A smell like broken biscuits, crushed up and gone stale, mingled in with a subtle aroma of something else, something fouler.

We are standing in a hallway by the stairs. A load of coats are piled up on pegs to my left, bulky shapes in the unlit gloom. Ahead, the front door, and to the right of that, what must be the lounge. There's a lot of noise coming from that room, a film with the volume turned right up, probably a horror movie by the sound of the music and the screams. Still with his finger to his lips, George jerks his thumb at the stairs, beckons me to follow.

A thick patterned carpet lines the steps, muffling the sound of our feet, but still I am tense, wary of making the slightest creak. Despite the noise coming from below, I am aware I am on enemy territory and wonder what would happen if I am caught.

On top of the stairs, George whispers: 'They're watching *The Exorcist*. I told them I was going home and they all laughed at me, as usual. They know I don't like them horror filums. Ernie's half deaf, that's why it's on so loud. But we don't want the others to find us. We have to be very, very quiet now…'

He opens the door to the room on the left, the one that's directly above the lounge.

The room is more or less empty, the walls have been whitewashed. A dartboard hangs on one of them. This must be the games room. There's a pale carpet that's obviously seen better days, visibly stained and tatty even in this light. An old coat-stand by the side of the door, a pile of electrical junk beside it. A few boxes and a mattress in front of a marble 1930s fireplace.

George grabs my hand and propels me towards the mattress. He's never touched me before, and I shrink away from it. But he doesn't seem to notice.

'This is what I've worked out,' he says, flopping himself down, facing the fireplace. 'There's a loose floorboard under the carpet here, where it's coming away…'

He's so intent on what he's doing I forget that touch, concentrate on George, like a cat burglar, lifting the carpet away from the front of the fireplace, rolling it back enough to get to the loose floorboard.

'I cut it in half when no one was about,' he tells me, 'so I could get it up easier. Brought my dad's saw. No one noticed.'

He's lifting up the piece of floorboard now, it's about a foot long. He places it carefully on to the mattress.

'Now look,' he says, 'this is the good bit.'

I look, but all I can see is ceiling plaster and dust.

'I don't get it.'

'Here.' George fishes a pen torch out of his pocket. The tiny point of light dances across the dark hole, picking up a few little spots where the plaster has come away. By focusing on these spots, you can just about see into the room below.

I concentrate and gradually it comes into focus.

The room below.

Almost exactly as I had envisioned it. There's a colour TV in one corner; it looks pretty new, and a bulky VCR underneath it. The old man must have a bit of cash flying around from somewhere, probably from what he saves on gardening and home furnishings.

I expect to see the village kids sprawled around the room, but it appears to be empty. We're lying above a dilapidated sofa, one of those nylon seventies ones with horrendous orange, yellow and brown swirls all over it. It's bathed with light from the TV screen, but no one appears to be home.

'Where's Ernie?' I hiss.

'You'll have to move over this way.'

George climbs over the top of me, so that I can move to the spot where he was lying. He is lying right against me now, and he presses his hand down on my arm as his torch picks out another little hole.

'Look down there.'

I fidget slightly, hoping he'll take his hand away, but again he doesn't seem to notice. So I try to ignore it, follow the torch beam, squinting to make out the apparition that was Ernie, expecting to see some Norfolk version of the Hunchback of Notre Dame at the very least.

He's sitting in an armchair, on the other side of the TV. I can see the top of his head now, a balding, flaky head with a few strands of silver-grey hair plastered across it. He's wearing a vest and grey trousers, old-fashioned ones with turn-ups, probably from a suit he'd had since his youth, with braces. Bright yellow towelling socks peeking out of his slippers are the only things about him that are really out of the ordinary. Ernie just looks like an average old man. An old man with a hearing aid obviously turned off, asleep in front of the TV.

'Is that it?' I can't help but say.

'I did tell you.'

George smiles at me in the fading light.

'Where's everyone else?' I ask, worriedly.

'Gavin Baxter's having a party tonight.' George smiles. 'They've all gone there, but I weren't invited. That's how I knew it would be safe to bring you here tonight...'

He keeps smiling, but something in his eyes changes. They start to mist over. The moment goes on too long. 'Now then,' he says, and the pressure on my arm starts to grow. 'I've shown you mine...'

In an instant he has flipped up over me, so that he's sitting across my belly. Both his arms are on mine, pressing them into the mattress.

'What are you doing?'

You would think that when something like this happens, you would struggle. You would fight back or start screaming. But I am in a strange house and I can't comprehend what George is trying to do. Not yet. And instead of doing any of those things, any of those things that might have saved me, instead I feel the power draining out of me through my stomach. Like it's not just George but a weight of dread that's keeping me there, pinned to the dirty old mattress in the games room. I open my mouth again, but nothing comes out.

I feel his eyes boring into me. I don't want to look, but I can't exactly move. Not with his arms on top of mine, pinning me into the mattress, making bruises flower forth from my skin.

George's eyes have a faraway look, sickly with need. I am terrified of what I see there. Ernie is asleep downstairs. Even if he wakes up, he'll think the noise is part of the film. No one else is here. Worse still, no one knows I'm here. Meanwhile, the adolescent boy on top of me has turned into some kind of animal.

I sense that to even try to fly from these eyes now would be to run into fists that could mash me across the white walls, create a different shade there. One that would last longer than I am prepared to hang around.

The only thing to do now is show a white flag. Go limp. Take it. So as when he pulls my knickers down, letting loose those unearthly, animal sounds from his lips, he feels that it is his right to be there. He's proved he is dominant. What girl could not give in at this point?

So, when I'm skewered against the mattress, feeling black shafts of rage pinning me back and forth, back and forth, I have left my body. Let him do what he likes. The body can take a lot. A lot more than the mind. Let him screw me into the mattress, I am no longer here.

And when I finally open my eyes I am looking into the shocked face of a shabby old man, standing in the doorway, watching the scene with his mouth gaping open.

It's not a memory that you ever return to. Unless you have to. Unless you can take from it that which got you through the last time, make it feel even less this time.

You can't move physically, only mentally. God, don't let this swallow me up. Let me rise out of it.

The jolt of the brakes wakes me from this screw-eyed reverie, into one even worse. Into a world of pain in my head, then the slow realisation that my limbs are trapped too, pinned where they lie with a brand of fire like barbed wire entwining every muscle, every exposed part.

I can't sit up. My feet are tied together.

I can't open my mouth. Something sticky and hard is holding it closed.

I'm in the back seat of a car, travelling fast.

It is night.

The driver turns his head, knowing even before I do what my next move will be.

It is Simon Everill.

Welcome to hell.

'Diana,' he says, turning back to the wheel, his eyes still fixing me from the mirror in front of him. 'Sorry I had to take you this way. But I knew you'd never come quietly.'

I am blanking out anything that could show up as fear. I am only waiting, with the true stillness that comes over such prey as I am now. Screaming won't help me. I can't run.

I would like to be sick.

But obviously, that is impossible, unless I want to choke on it and die right now.

'I did stop by your office this morning,' he goes on, as if he were telling me that the forecast for today's weather is light and yet variable. 'Only you went and called the police. Really, Diana.' The voice turns at once to cold steel, then retreats, just as quickly, to its previous chummy tone. 'So I had to follow your friend to find out where you'd end up. I knew you wouldn't go back to your flat now. Bet you thought you'd be safe there...'

The vomit, hot and acrid, shoots up my throat right then. Only it can't come out of my mouth. It sprays out of my nose, like branding irons up the back of my throat and down my nostrils. I can't breathe, only suck in hot liquid death, and blind panic propels me off my precarious ledge, my head crashing into the back of the passenger seat. I desperately try and breathe some air back in, my throat choking up with bile, at odds with what my brain is telling it to do. Tears as hot as lead are running out of my eyes. I know too much, for fuck's sake.

The car swerves.

'Fucking stupid bitch!' he screams, his voice so high-pitched he sounds like a woman.

My head against the seat, neck at right angles. My side rammed into the divider between the back seats, bound feet still up in the air. I am snorting diced carrots out of my nose, hyperventilating, panicking, desperate for some air.

The brakes squeal and the car comes to a sudden stop. He gets out of his seat, slamming the door. Cold wind blows in and then he opens the door nearest to me.

'If you scream, I'll kill you,' he says simply.

The last time this happened, this thought was not exchanged through words, only by an implication far too heavy to ignore.

I know what to do.

He rips the tape away from my mouth and I can't even scream, just bring up the rest of the bile, hear a shrill, gasping whine ringing from my nose into my mouth. Is that me?

I feel him pull me back up on to the seat, push my head back, feel his grey eyes surveying the mess. Not that I can speak. I can only pant, gasp, snort, stare at him. What the fuck have I done for this to happen again? You think it happens once; lightning can't strike twice, can it? That would be unlucky. I should have known better, but I didn't want to feel all this again.

His irises change, they suddenly fill out and soften.

'Oh dear, oh dear. We have made a mess, haven't we?'

He reaches for his back pocket.

This is it. He's going to kill me.

He takes out a hankie instead. Begins to wipe my face gently, making soothing little noises as he does so.

'No, no, Diana. I'm not going to hurt you. Not yet. But you already knew I'd have to bring you with me.'

I show you mine, you show me yours.

I wanted to know too much.

He is stroking my hair, thick with sweat, back from my forehead.

'Shhhh, shhhhh now,' he murmurs as if soothing a child. His grey eyes lock into mine, calm on the surface of the lake now, hypnotising me like a cobra does a mouse. He takes his hand away.

Not another car has passed us by. We must be in the middle of nowhere. Worse than that.

That big sky, that flat land, it's familiar. It looks like Norfolk.

'Now listen,' he says. 'I'm going to start driving again in a minute, but I don't want any more noise from you, else I'll leave you where I drop you. You wanted to know my story, didn't you, Diana? Well, now I'm going to show you. Do you understand?'

I nod my head frantically. I make my eyes into those of the understanding mother he never had, the eyes he most wants to see at the end of the night. I can understand this intuitively from the last time.

When they rape you, they are raping their mother. All the emptiness, the cold. George's mother was a drunk too. The local kids mocked him, and he thought I was the same as they were. Only now I was the one with the stigma to bear.

Some other, deeper part of myself, the part I have only connected with before in moments of crisis like this, says to me: 'That's right, go along with him. Humour him now. You can't fight this. Otherwise you die.'

He ruffles my hair again. Then steps back, on to the road.

'Good girl,' he's saying. 'We'll get going again now.'

It has worked.

The shock and nausea make me suddenly limp. As soon as he pulls back on to the road, as soon as the earth is moving underneath me, I fall back into sleep.

34

Hands shake me awake now, I don't know how much later. I feel like I am coming up from deep water, dull and disorientated. Only the moment I hit the surface, the pain hits me back and with it everything becomes real.

I feel his hands, long, bony, unrelenting hands, forcing me upright. But I can't actually focus on anything.

'Do you hear me?' His voice comes through a tunnel of fog.

Some water, cold as ice, splashes into my open mouth. I gulp and cough violently into full consciousness.

The car is parked. Through the windscreen I can see a faint, flat horizon, broken up by a couple of twisted trees. And the moon, full and bloated, hanging low in the sky. Harvest moon.

'There now.' The voice is clear now, along with the realisation.

I am far from home. Hog-tied, in the back of a car, in the middle of nowhere. With a murderous psychopath for company.

But the calm, inner voice is here with me too. She tells me what to do as if my mother is speaking the words beside me, speaking out loud. 'Humour him.'

I try and turn my head, but my neck clicks violently, shooting white stars into my eyes.

'Whoa there.' He begins stroking and smoothing my hair away. His dirty killer's fingers raking against my head, turning my stomach. I want to recoil, but that voice, that clear pool of inner calm, it keeps me together. Keeps me doing what I should be doing. Breathing deeply, trying to relax into my surroundings, making myself numb.

'Diana.' He says my name gently. 'I'm going to untie you now, and that means I'm going to trust you. There are some things here I need to show you, so that you fully understand. Do you hear me?'

'Yes.' A small voice, like that of a broken 14-year-old, responds from what sounds like far away. I try to clear my burning throat and say it again: 'Yes, yes, I do.'

'Good. Now don't be alarmed. I'm going to use a knife.'

I am too limp and numb now to be alarmed. I slump forward as he cuts the tape he has bound my wrists with.

'Shake it out,' he suggests, as if he were an aerobics instructor.

I try to do as he says, but my arms are, in turn, wrenched with pain and completely frozen. Tendrils of fire rush up to my head, so that my vision goes red and then black. I have to fall backwards against the seat and wait for the tide to subside and vision to clear, for pins-and-needles to tingle into my arms and bring them back to life.

'OK, now the feet. Turn sideways.'

Gingerly, I obey, scared of the pain that's going to come this time. The fire shoots up my left arm when I try to put weight on it, and for a moment I think I am going to black out again. He catches the wobble, moves me around himself into the position he wants, lifts my feet out of the car and cuts me free.

'You just sit there a minute,' he says, as if I could do anything else. He returns the knife to a sheath he must have at the back of his jeans. I try to circle my ankles, bring the feeling back.

'You see, you're stronger than you think. Now just try and stand up.'

Leaning on my right arm this time, I propel myself upwards, feeling my knees weaken as the blood rushes gratefully down.

Again he catches me, puts his arm around me. The tender maniac. I can only lean back into him as I struggle to stay vertical. Eventually, whatever adrenalin has been unleashed by all of this lessens the pain in my head. I begin to drink in the backdrop to this surreal scenario.

The sky is a huge dome, studded with stars that shine with a brightness I had all but forgotten in so many nights of London haze. Its still beauty calms me. The air smells of soil and fertilizer, but a gentle breeze brings me grass and spring flowers. A distant aroma of water. The land that I fled from in terror.

'We're in Norfolk,' I say to him. 'We're in your book.'

'That's right,' he replies. 'You're much cleverer than the others. You ran away from this place too.'

'Yes, yes, I did.'

From someone just like you.

'It looks so peaceful like this, doesn't it? Asleep under the stars. You don't see the stars in London.' His eyes are tracking across the broad horizon. 'No one would ever think it. Unless they'd lived here too.'

I follow his gaze. We are in farmland. Vast fields stretch into the horizon, testament to EU produce-quotas and modern farm machinery.

'You don't have a Norfolk accent,' I hear myself saying, as steadily as a normal conversation.

'No,' he agrees. 'I've never had one. I don't know why. Most people think I'm from Yorkshire. You do, though, even though you try to hide it.'

'When I first moved to London,' I tell him, 'no one could understand a word I said.' We are talking as if we are mates, sharing insights over a pint.

'Well, this is it,' he reveals. 'This is the farm where I grew up.'

'It was all true, then. It was your story. Not the story of a friend? Not the doctor's wife who went mad?'

'Sort of.' He sucks in his bottom lip, chews on it, keeps scanning the loom of the land. 'It was sort of right. But I couldn't let you keep those tapes, Diana. What I told you that night was wrong.'

He looks down at the ground, then kicks at a clod of earth for a time. When his head comes back up, his eyes are full of tears. 'I didn't write that book on my own, see.'

'What?' My voice is loud with shock.

Didn't write the book on his own? The book that got me to here? Then who...?

'I'll tell you all about it.' His voice is high, like wind through reeds. 'But first I'm going to show you around. Can you walk now?'

'I think so.' I blink hard, trying to pull together all the secrets he has scattered into the night.

'OK.' He has managed to pull himself together now; his tone has gone down a few octaves and levelled out.

'I brought you here first because this is the field where I saw Jesus.'

'OK.' I nod, wondering *how, what, why*?

'Now follow me.' He takes hold of my hand. His fingers are long and bony, like the handles of knives, his palm clammy. My body takes over from the jumble in my mind and begins to trudge across the field after him.

The field is full of Brussels sprouts, weird, twisted shapes that look like the kind of mutant beings that evolve into flesh-eating creatures from outer space in old fifties sci-fi movies. We walk around the edge of the field, so large it must have spanned about twenty acres, the only sound our feet on the soil. The further we walk, the more clearly I can make out the low shapes of outbuildings, sheds and barns, and, like a stream curving its way around the perimeter, a ribbon of pale grey that must be a driveway.

And a smell on the breeze, the most pungent one the countryside has to offer. Pigs.

As we near the track, we come up to a shed, full of machinery. Beside it is a septic tank. We stop.

'That's where my brother went, in there,' he tells me, pointing to the watery coffin. 'Best place for him an' all. Shit goes to shit.'

Those stories in that book, that now he is saying he didn't write on his own, they are his biography, but I know now that it wasn't quite right.

He stands for a moment, staring with satisfaction at the

tank. A trail of grass leads away from it, up the side of the neighbouring field, to what looks like a compost heap. Beside us now is a field of wheat, about three feet high and still green, undulating in the gentle breeze, the luminous pull of the moon.

'And that's where my stupid sister fell into the combine harvester,' he goes on, following my gaze.

'It's all really true?' I ask again, my voice incredulous.

'That bit of it, sure. I don't know how she got herself up there, or how nobody saw her but, yes, my little sister got herself turned into a haybale.' A high chuckle escapes his lips and spills into the breeze. 'Accidents with farm machinery are quite a common rural hazard.'

Now I know what's wrong.

Dead children, murdered siblings, their ghosts are here with me, clamouring in my head, telling me to listen to their story instead. I have somehow segued into a dark chamber of his mind; he has given himself away to me, his little conquests are not sleeping in the safe burrows of the dead, their restless shades instead are punching him with invisible fists. They say to me: He pushed her in there. He drowned his brother and put the lid back on the tank. He got a taste for it when he was really young and he hasn't stopped since. Angry shades, vengeful wraiths. I can see them, feel them here.

Why is it only his name on the dust-jacket? Who helped him chronicle the story he wants everyone to believe? Who was the last person he invited over the threshold of his mind? He doesn't notice the angry little ghosts. He is more than oblivious, he is looking quite smug. Satisfied, he sniffs the air like it is the bouquet of a fine wine.

He drags me down the driveway, which is pitted and stony, pockmarked with ruts caused by tractor wheels and heavy machinery. The driveway curves around the arc of the wheat field, towards a cluster of buildings that must be the farmhouse, some more barns, a garage. There are no lights on. Early to bed and early to rise out here in the country.

'That's where old Farmer Bastard and his pig-thick sons live,' he spits. 'And obviously, he didn't want us too near the nice family home. I'll show you where we lived.'

'You are Farmer Bastard's son, Bastard's son, Bastard's son,' sing the little ghosts.

Before it reaches the house, the pathway forks to the right, becomes a grass trackway, flattened by constant traffic. It leads past rows and rows of greenhouses and chicken coops, and beyond all this, a barren patch of earth that is the dumping ground for all the agricultural waste. Mangled machinery making hunched, menacing shapes in the darkness. Broken cold frames, tin buckets with holes in them, fertilizer sacks full of rubble. A corner for unwanted trash.

'Our playground,' he smiles. 'And here's where the van used to be.'

It isn't there any more. All that remains is a patch of lighter stubble, streaked with oil stains, marking out the old battle lines.

'I don't think he wanted any unpleasant reminders,' he considers.

Bastard's son, Bastard's son.

'This is incredible,' I flatter him. 'This is why you wouldn't say where you come from.'

'Well done, my little Sherlock.'

From such blighted patches of earth, only insanity could bloom. I can see it now, the dirty caravan rocking and grunting on its awnings, the snot-faced kids playing war in the bombsite of detritus and danger so casually strewn around them.

He watches me taking all this in.

'Now behind here,' he points to a gap in the hedge, 'is the road to the village. Easy access for all of mother's admirers.'

He leads me to it, and indeed there is a road.

'This way.'

It is a long, snaking road, banked by a scrappy hedge on old Farmer Bastard's side, and a thicker, taller, more healthy one on the other, as if the land of the next estate itself is mocking the poverty and disease its neighbour has created. We walk for what seems like miles. My footsteps are heavy and my legs ache almost as much as my head. Eventually, we come to a road sign. A sign that says: EAST MELSHAM.

'Does that ring any bells?' He stops in front of it.

It does, vaguely. It thrums a warning in the recesses of my brain.

'East Melsham,' I say. 'East Melsham.'

A car sweeps past, briefly illuminating us. We obviously don't merit any closer inspection.

'Shit.' I look at him. 'It's where Jon Jackson comes from.'

'Got it in one.' He seems pleased. He pulls me away from the sign, his pace increasing. The fields give way to a village green, a picture-perfect one it must be in daylight, with tall horse-chestnut trees. Small houses clustered around it, the usual Norfolk mixture of really old, flint ones, 1940s utility and bungalows, that even in the dark I know are painted pink and surrounded by boxes of geraniums.

Two little boys.

Simon and Jonny.

Here, in this place.

'All sleeping soundly,' he says, his voice acid. 'Like usual.'

Through the little streets we go, past the lace curtains all pulled shut, threading our way under the orange streetlamps past the windowboxes and the gnomes and the Alpine signs on the door saying things like 'Casa Fina' and 'Tulip Cottage', all nice little names offering up the image of a tidy, tranquil rural idyll.

Under these lights I can see his face clearly now, and he looks determined rather than demented. His grip on my hand doesn't waver.

I can hear the sound of water, louder now, as we climb up a bank behind the end of a cul-de-sac and the view pans out before us with quite disconcerting beauty. It's a lush water meadow, the sort where the grass is always greener and wild flowers wind their stems through the blades where cotton-tail rabbits gambol. The river rushes through it, spanned by an old flint bridge, and on the other side are the tall Edwardian houses from when this place was moneyed, houses now occupied by people who teach in Cambridge and want their children to have this to play in.

'I always used to like coming here,' he says.

'To feed the ducks.'

'To feed the ducks with my friend Jonny.'

Oh, sweet Jesus, here it comes.

'My friend Jonny,' he repeats. 'I used to tell him everything, you know. He was the only person who wanted to speak to me, even though he lived in one of them big houses over there and I come from where I just showed you.'

He said he never had a Norfolk accent, but it's coming through now.

The little ghosts pull at me again, shaking their heads and waving their fists. And now there is another one. He wears a deep blue anorak and bright red boots. His face is a study in incomprehension, his hands are struggling to keep something closed inside his jacket. He is trying to close the hole someone's made in his stomach, trying to stop the entrails from spilling out on to the lush grass and wild flowers. He doesn't speak to me but his brown eyes form one terrible question: Why?

Simon doesn't see him either. He has never been able to see the things he's done. He lives in a separate world from the rest of us, a parallel dimension, like he's always been a ghost.

A ghost, or a monster.

He starts to scramble down the bank, to a path forged through the green by other walkers, to the water's edge. He jerks me after him and I stumble behind with my three hallucinatory playmates in hot pursuit.

'This is where we fed the ducks,' he says. 'This was the only normal thing I had. I told him everything and he stole the lot.' His eyes stare at the water, black under the moon, running at a fair old current, deep and unrelenting.

'I knew Jon Jackson too,' I hear myself tell him. 'He betrayed me once, you know.'

He turns and looks at me, his eyes burning with that same vulnerability I saw in St James's Park, on that hot day a million years ago.

It all comes back to me in a rush, the stuff I hadn't wanted to remember before in my canonisation of St Jon. The breezy way he'd left me the next day to get the bus home, not waiting with me the half an hour you had to wait on a Sunday, just blithely disappearing round the corner without looking back. The way he promised to phone and never did, the nights I spent sitting on the stairs in the dark, waiting for the call that never came.

'Yeah, he picked me up, played around and dumped me,' I say. 'A beautiful user, eh?'

'Well then, you know.' Everill looks me up and down. 'You know better than anyone else. So write this for me, Diana. You wanted the story. Tell them that two little boys from the most miserable patch of soil on the face of the earth first met here. One of them told the other all the personal details of his fucked-up life. Jonny boy remembered the details well. Later on, after my mother went mad and threw me and my sister in the river, I got taken to foster parents, while he was a good boy at school, went to art college and went to London, where he started getting famous. One day, I saw a feature about his pop videos in some magazine, and I thought, oh, Jonny's doing well for himself, maybe he can help me out. So I sent him the idea for a film that I had. I never fucking heard from him again until I saw the fucking film in the cinema with his fucking name all over it!'

Bits of foam are starting to appear at the corner of his mouth. His eyes continue to bore right into me.

'So I thought, right, you cunt, I'm coming to get you. And it took me a while, but, as you must realise by now, I'm pretty good at finding things out that I want to know. So I found him up on Camden market, with his greasy mates. He was as happy as Larry until he realised who I was. He upped and left his friends then, I can tell you. I don't think he wanted them to find out that their golden boy was a fake and a thief.

'I was going to kill him there and then in his posh designer flat that he really didn't want me to come into, right over his fucking leather sofa. But instead he had this idea. It was to save his arse, of course, but at the time, the way he told it, it sounded good. He was always good at talking, Jonny was, right up until the end, when he realised nothing he could say was going to get him off the hook this time. But he convinced me then that I could write my story, the story of my life, and he would help me. He reckoned he could fix things up with this posh agent, get me a publisher. Good old Jonny would make me famous.'

'Jesus,' I say. I don't want to look at him, but I'm scared not to. He looks totally insane. But how could he be making all of this up?

'And it worked, didn't it, for a while? I was quite enjoying it. I was good at being famous, I thought, didn't you? You get to say what you want, any old bullshit that comes into your head, really. You get to piss people off and everyone thinks you're really daring. Fucking marvellous job for an arsehole, no wonder Jonny was so good at it. But it wasn't really a job for me. There's only one thing I'm really good at. And Jonny went too far again, like he always does, trying to get my story back and turn it into another film with his name all over it. You've had your five minutes, Simon, now give it back to me. So I had to show him what I was really good at. I wish you could have seen it, Diana, I really do.' Another of his shrill chuckles blurts out at this. 'It was much better than any of his fucking movie crap.

'You tell them this, Diana,' he continues. 'And you tell them good. I'm fucked off with all of this now. I've had enough. There's too much crap in this world and I've seen it all. I don't even want to kill you now. I just want to finish off what my whore of a mother started.'

He lets go of my hand. His eyes let go of mine.

'You can have these back now,' he says, reaching into his

pockets, thrusting three cassette tapes into my hands. 'I trust you with them. Finally, I do.' And with that, he turns and scrambles back up the bank, vaults nimbly over the side of the bridge.

You're safe, you're OK, says the inner voice. I want to collapse where I stand, but my eyes are still drawn to this tall, lanky figure who has now climbed on to the top of the bridge.

'You see, Diana,' he screams, 'they get into your head and then you can't get them out. Jonny's still in here, the cunt!' He gestures wildly at the side of his head. A dog starts barking at the noise. A door slams open.

'Now you can have him! He's all yours! Look at this, Diana!' he screams.

The knife flashes white under the dark jewelled sky.

'You tell them! Tell them all! I'm back, you fuckers, look at me now!'

The knife sweeps under his chin, into his neck, carving the final smile Simon Everill will ever make.

His lanky body twists sideways as he falls, making abstract shapes in the final seconds before he hits the water. With a loud splash, it sucks him down; carrying him away, every eddy in its current laughing, as the little ghosts laugh before they leave me and vanish back into the Norfolk night, leaving me alone, staring on the bank.

And the only word in my head is: good.

35

I don't know how long I just stayed there, watching the black river take the mangled wreckage of Simon Everill far, far away from me. But someone must have heard the noise he had made, and footsteps came running over the bridge.

'What's going on here?' a man's voice shouted.

He didn't notice me at first. I was just sitting there, staring down the river. But when he did, the man came running down to me. He was middle-aged, quite portly, probably the local busybody. Or maybe the man with the dog that had found an abandoned, half-drowned child in the reedbed here, all those years ago.

His eyes changed when he saw me. He looked shocked and concerned.

'You all right?' he said. 'What happened?'

I opened my mouth to tell him. Nothing came out.

The portly man put his arm around me and led me back to his house. I was swaying, swimming in and out of consciousness as if I, too, was swirling down a black river into the unknown depths of the night.

He phoned for an ambulance and the police while his nervous-looking, bird-like wife wrapped me in a pale blue blanket and sat me on her sofa. I still couldn't make any words come out of my mouth. I remember being lifted into an ambulance with her tiny little hand holding mine.

The kindness of strangers.

Somebody said: 'She's going into shock,' and they put an oxygen mask over my face. Shock or sleep, I don't remember much else, until I was woken up in a hospital ward, because the police needed to speak to me.

They put me in a private room in a private hospital so they could keep the press away from me. Niall Flynn paid for it all. He kept me away from the hounds of the press. What he couldn't do for Emily Davey, he had tried to do for me.

So I told my story to Linehan with the kind eyes, who had been searching for me since Barry came home and found me gone, and with him it stayed. There was nothing I could say to anyone else. I wasn't going to do what Everill wanted. I was just glad he was dead. Let his sick, twisted lie of a life die with him. I wasn't going to glorify him with any more attention. I don't want to be famous because of him. He wasn't going to get what he wanted from me.

Of course, it's never quite that easy. There are too many unavenged ghosts hovering around. Neil for one.

Neil who had sold us out.

It had all come out when Barry went to see the Americans. All Neil's little deceptions, that furtiveness about the Jackson transcript. The tape that he hadn't told anyone about, including the police, that had the 'off-the-record' details on it no one else had got; even Jackson hadn't realised he was being recorded on it. When Neil had sent the final pages off, he had planned on signing a new deal with D. C. Arnold, a deal that made them the publishers of *Lux*. And got him an office in New York.

Over breakfast that Thursday morning, he had let Barry in on some of the deal. He'd already promised to deliver interviews with Jackson's closest friends, so in order to get Barry on side, he'd dangled him the carrot of Barry's greatest dream – that he, too, would be moving to New York.

Which was why he'd gone to interview Woody and Alex so easily.

Apparently I was to have been left in London as the editor in chief of the British side of the operation. Barry had thought it would be the making of me.

Only Neil was lying to get what he wanted. He would have continued lying, right down to the wire, right down until we'd sent the last pages and he had the magazine that would spectacularly have launched his American career. The Jackson feature was supposed to be kept from us. The Yanks didn't want anyone else to see it, in case Barry or I leaked it elsewhere. In case we were as trustworthy as our boss, who had even stitched up Jackson in the interview by pretending to turn the tape off when he hadn't. Only, Neil never got the chance to make his most audacious move. Instead, he himself provided a news story more sensational than he could ever have imagined. And his precious tape provided the motive.

His parents didn't want us to go to his funeral, blaming me in particular for introducing him to his killer. So Barry and I had to stand at the back of the churchyard, by that monstrous cathedral on top of a windswept hill over Guildford, until the cortège had passed. We put white roses on top of his grave.

I couldn't go back to work for quite some time. After I left the hospital, Niall Flynn shipped me off to Galway with my parents for a few months, so I could recover in peace. He came out with us, gave us free rein of his beautiful stone house looking over the sea, stayed somewhere else nearby in case we needed him.

It was like going to a different world. The light there, the dawn spreading over the mountains, the sun setting in the Atlantic Ocean, the very peace and difference of it all probably did more to help me than anything else. It seemed like a little piece of heaven there, after I had been in hell. It was where Flynn was supposed to have lived with Emily Davey after they had married. Well, she might not have seen that paradise, but at least I got to.

Months later, when I was finally ready to go back to London, Barry looked after me, let me move into his flat, so I never had to return to the breached bedsit on Arundel Gardens. My parents and my brother still came often to help out, because the blow to the back of my head had left me what was politely referred to as unstable. It seemed to have opened a portal into another dimension, so that ghosts and monsters drifted in and out of my sight, shadows formed into the shape of a lanky young man. I could hear snatches of tuneless whistling.

I had to scream, to keep myself from hearing it.

Only when I forced myself to go back to writing did these ghosts diminish. Only by re-creating the memories a madman somehow left inside my consciousness did I finally ban him to that coffin at the back of my mind and nail down the lid.

I think I am safe now.

They never found his body.

Other Serpent's Tail books of interest

Antwerp

Nicholas Royle

What connects the brutal murders of prostitutes in the seedy Antwerp underworld? Cult film director Johnny Vos is making a low-budget bio pic about the Belgian surrealist artist Paul Delvaux. He hires women from Antwerp's red light district and from an Internet voyeur house as extras in order to recreate the poses of Delvaux's famous sleepwalking nudes.

When two prostitutes end up murdered, English film critic Frank Warner, in town to interview Vos, turns investigative journalist and becomes personally involved when his own girlfriend goes missing.

Simultaneously macabre and erotic, *Antwerp* is a literary thriller which will not release you until its final page has turned.

Praise for Nicholas Royle's novels

'Enormously accomplished and ambitious' Jonathan Coe, *Guardian*

'A tense intelligent thriller' *Esquire*

'A stylish, mordantly witty, schizophrenic mystery' *Times Literary Supplement*

'Memorable, ingenious and elaborately constructed, the novel impressively occupies a liminal space between literary novel and crime fiction' *Sunday Times*

'A high velocity read opening veins of radiant darkness' Iain Sinclair

A State of Denmark

Derek Raymond

England is ruled by Jobling, a dictator with an efficient secret police and a long memory.

Richard Watt used all his journalistic talents to expose Jobling before he came to power. Now, in exile in Italy, Watt cultivates his vineyards. His rural idyll is shattered by the arrival of an emissary from London.

Derek Raymond's deft skill is to make all too plausible the transition to dictatorship in an England obsessed with 'looking after number one'. First published in 1970, *A State of Denmark* is a classic.

Praise for Derek Raymond's novel

'Raymond's novel is rooted firmly in the dystopian vision of Orwell and Huxley, sharing their air of horrifying hopelessness' *Sunday Times*

'*A State of Denmark* is carried out with surgical precision...a fascinating and important novel by one of our best writers in or outside of any genre' *Time Out*

'Alternative science fiction on the scale of Orwell's *1984* or Zamyatin's *We*' *Q*

Derek Raymond was born Robin Cook in 1931. His novels include *A State of Denmark*, *The Crust on Its Uppers* (also published by Serpent's Tail), *I was Dora Suarez* and *How the Dead Live*, which was made into a film. The son of a textile magnate, he dropped out of Eton aged sixteen and spent much of his early career among criminals and was employed at various times as a pornographer, organiser of illegal gambling, money launderer, pig-slaughterer and mini-cab driver. He died in London in 1994.

Billie Morgan

Joolz Denby

'My name is Billie Morgan. And I am a murderer.'

Billie is in her forties, running a little jewellery shop in Bradford, watching over her godson Natty, trying to live a quiet life, trying to forget the past. Because Billie has a lot of past to forget. She was a biker chick, one of the Devil's Own, real hardcore seventies Angels, speed and acid-fuelled road demons. She lived a life that was hurtling out of control and it ended in murder. Now, years later, she has to face the consequences.

Beautifully written, dark but never despairing, *Billie Morgan* is a perfect fusion between social realism and classic noir; a powerful, passionate novel about an inability to wipe evil from the slate of our lives. Taut like a Greek tragedy, the book is a moving, empathetic account of a woman's heroic attempt to escape her destiny.

'There are speed-freaks, severed heads, midnight burials and extreme sexual deviance in this book, but its eventually apocalyptic tone doesn't disguise how recognisable its suffering is if you've ever stumbled under Britain's civilised veneer…With her brawling, brave, wildly flawed character, Denby joins the like of Helen Walsh in finally putting vivid female rebels on the page' *Uncut*

'A riveting and illuminating, yet searing, tale. Although the subject is grim, a dark humour infuses the story' *Good Book Guide*

'Powerful slice of Yorkshire neo-realism by noted poet and performer' *Bookseller*

'Haunting and lyrical, with a quietly devastating conclusion, *Billie Morgan* is that rare beast: a novel that speaks profoundly of loss, of sacrifice, and of pain, yet never loses sight of the one immutable truth that, without love, we are nothing. It confirms Joolz Denby as one of the most talented and humane novelists that we have' John Connolly

'Different from her previous novels, *Stone Baby* and *Corazon*, in both manner and tone, this wise and gruelling book, chockful of social observation and humour, whisked me back immediately to the seventies and the growing up in Bradford of our eponymous heroine…Denby, always an enchantress, with unstoppable prose, acute and brilliant observation, and sheer intelligence, is becoming more and more interesting as a writer…In Billie, strong, abused and apparently unbreakable, she has created someone who is completely real and yet at the same time part of the mythology of the city of her birth. You may have walked past her in the street' James Nash

'…an acute, funny, tough-talking look at our dreams of who we'd like to be, our fears about who we really are, the way others see us and the way we see ourselves. It's brilliant, nothing less' *plan b magazine*

'Like her earlier novels it'll probably be filed under "crime" on the bookshelves, but it's not some police-procedural-by-numbers' *Telegraph & Argus*

'For me this is the best book, so far, of 2004. It works on all levels, containing strong writing and good plotting, believable characters, a good mix of light and shade, and delivers an acceptable conclusion… Highly recommended' *The Barcelona Review*

'Denby manages to combine blunt pragmatism and the flat shovelhard Bradford accent with a clear-eyed compassion for the inhabitants of this, her third novel. Its language switches neatly between the sensitive and colour-drawn descriptiveness of the author's other job as poet and the hard unromantic pace of real, northern life to compelling effect. It's a tough love story' *Blowback*

'Brilliantly executed, with the right amount of pathos and pain, *Billie Morgan* is a great page-turner about secrets and lies, revenge and eventual redemption. It's also a remarkable meditation on the dark side of the flower-power hippie generation' *Diva*